ALL MOMENTS
ARE
ONE MOMENT

THE ULTIMATE NARRATIVE

Cally Phillips

HoAm Press

Hillhead of Ardmiddle
Publishing

First published in this paperback edition by HoAm Presst Publishing 2020.

HoAmPresst Publishing is an imprint of
Ayton Publishing Limited
www.aytonpublishing.co.uk

ISBN: 9781-9-10601-63-1

For Pat, Claudia and Amanda
Inspiration, motivation and
fearless friendship
In all our moments.

我们舞蹈无翼 无耻

32 FORMS
Open Circle
开圆圈

1. Essential Elements
2. Water Feeds Wood
3. Beyond Language
4. The Cave of Infinity
5. Wood Builds Fire
6. How to Escape
7. A Particular Cave
8. Fire Burns Earth
9. Debts and Promises
10. When Particles Collide
11. Earth Generates Metal
12. Paradox and Meaning
13. A Tsilhqot'in Bear Cave
14. Metal Enriches Water
15. Mind the Gap
16. A Quantum Cave
17. Water Puts out Fire
18. Space and Time
19. More False Premises
20. Fire Softens Metal
21. Not Waiting but Being
22. Possible Caves
23. Metal Chops Wood
24. Butterfly Dreaming
25. The Best of All Possible Caves
26. Wood Stabilises Earth
27. Personal Identity
28. Caves of Enlightenment
29. Earth Blocks Water's Flow
30. Endings
31. Moments
32 .Intertextualities.

24 FORMS
Creative Balance

WUXING
无形

33. Helen feeds Torquil
34. Torquil builds Nick
35. Nick burns Callum
36. Callum generates Pryce
37. Pryce enriches Helen
38. Debts and Promises/PossibleCaves/When Particles Collide
39. Helen puts out Nick
40. Nick softens Pryce
41. Pryce chops Torquil
42. Torquil stabilises Callum
43. Callum blocks Helen's flow

WUJI
无极

44. Mind the Gap
45. The Cave of Infinity
46. How to Escape
47. More False Premises
48. Not Waiting but Being
49. Personal Identity
50. The Best of all Possible Caves
51 A Quantum Cave
52. Paradox and Meaning
53. Space and Time
54. Butterfly Dreaming
55. Beyond Language
56. Quantum caves of enlightenment

32 FORMS
Open Circle

开圆圈

And if we sit in the cave long enough…
The ancients used to say that if you stared at the wall for three
years, the writing would appear.
But what is three years?
What is time in relation to space?
And where am I?
Do you need to ask?
Yes.
When you don't need to ask, then you will have found yourself.

FORM 1

Essential Elements

Stories don't start   There are many points of entry
They are infinite   Birth and death are the ones
You simply come into   We recognise most easily
Them at a particular point   But there are many more

There are five Wuxing elements and they are relational.
But for Qi we also need to explore the Random elements.
They are infinite.
But patterns emerge.
They are points of entry and exit.
They are matters of choice and being.
They are where you and I connect.
Pronoun and particle
Definite and indefinite
Paradoxically

We might observe that life is all about transformation. About being and identity, about becoming who we are and being many versions of ourselves throughout a multiplicity of dimensions. We might observe that our observation itself is part of the creative process and part of the creative being.

FORM 2

WATER feeds WOOD

Galloway 1991

'I don't want to.'
'I don't care.'

It was a battle they played out every day. It was winter. Cold out. Helen wouldn't let three year old Torquil go outside to 'work' with the sheep until he was properly dressed. That meant wearing a hat and gloves. He didn't mind the hat, he took pride in that. Dad wore a hat. But he drew the line at the gloves.

The battle had been played out so many times. So many times Helen faced the challenge that she could not outsmart a three year old.

Defeated by a three year old. It's a situation familiar to all parents. Helen felt it keenly. It was not that she wanted to outsmart him but she felt uneasy about the fact that, somehow, in all their interactions, Torquil always triumphed. It suggested an imbalance.

Her excuse, then, was that she was restoring balance - not the balance of power, just relational balance. She resorted to the master strategy her own mother had employed on her. We learn from the ancestors. Sadly, she'd forgotten how much she had resisted that same strategy in her own youth. Now, the boot was on the other foot – or to be more precise the glove was not on the other hand. And the battle lines were drawn.

We might observe that a strategy is only a good strategy if it stands a chance of working, not just because it resolves a problem. And some problems resist resolution. The intractable problems are always with us. Parent and child. Solve that puzzle if you can.

And if you're wondering about the strategy, as well you might, she had put the mittens onto a string that ran through the back of Torquil's jacket. They dangled there, emerging from the sleeves like dead woollen mice.

Torquil hated it. As much as she remembered hating it. And still he refused to put his hands into them. The gloves were off, and not just metaphorically, even before he'd left the front door open in his hurry to get out to the yard and 'help' dad.

'Don't like gubbs' he said.

'What about if I get you some 'big boy' gloves?' she said. 'Work gloves.

A pause.

He remained unconvinced.

'Like dad wears when he's doing something important?'

It was her best shot. An appeal to his desire to be like dad.

Torquil shook his head.

'No gubbs.'

Helen now faced a choice. She could force his hands into the hated 'gubbs' or let him go off with them dangling free, which would leave his hands exposed to the biting winter cold.

If the dilemma was comfort or safety, Helen knew she would choose safety every time.

She didn't really have a choice. Not now, not ever. He was her heart's reflection. The facts were simple; Torquil would always win.

This problem *was* intractable. The relationship was not defined by power but by love. That most complex of emotional attachments.

Helen brought herself down to her son's level. She squatted down and kissed him on the nose. Looked him in the eyes. With love.

'Why do you hate gubbs so much?' she asked, her tone palpably more loving than she remembered her own mother's had been.

The moment was marked by an understanding that 'you can't fight City Hall.' Instead, Helen tried to get into the head of a three year old. Perhaps if she could simply see things from his perspective.

Sometimes you only have to ask.

'They make my hands like sweating pigs,' he said, voice firm and clear.

A roar of laughter came from Callum who had been standing outside the door, waiting for the power struggle to be over. Like father, like son.

He held the door open, letting the chill inside.

She wondered, did none of them understand that an open door let in the cold? Did none of them feel the cold?

And while she was distracted with wondering, Torquil won.

Who could not laugh at the inevitability of the particular?

Torquil won because Callum intervened. A dad has rabbits a mother cannot pull out of the hat, after all.

'Well we can't have that now, can we son,' Callum said.

'No dad, we can't,' Torquil affirmed.

For that moment, in his mind, they were men, together. Torquil felt respected. Ten years later he would have added, 'see, dad gets it.'

All moments are one moment.

'Are you ganging up on me?' Helen said.

She knew when she had lost. As always, in reality, Callum was the cavalry and she thanked him for it.

If only he would shut the door...

'Tell you what, Torquil,' Callum added. 'Bring the dead mice along with you in your pockets,' he quickly tucked them in, 'and if your hands get cold we'll both put on our gloves, right?'

'No sweating pigs?'

'No sweating pigs. Just toastie hands if we need them. We don't want to clap the sheep and kye wi' cauld hands now do we?'

'No dad.'

Torquil was pacified. For a moment. Until another thought struck him as they left Helen at the doorstep.

'Does Catriona have to wear gubbs?'

'If she comes into my yard she does,' Callum said, 'But she's at school just now. So don't worry about Cat eh?'

'Okay dad.'

And with the matter cleared up in his three year old mind, Torquil proudly followed his father into the yard.

It was perishingly cold.

They went, man and boy, into the 'cow palace.' It had been recently built to overwinter the hundred strong herd - thirty Belties and seventy Charolais cross-Limosins. These were 'the princesses'. Their name stemmed from another family moment.

'Don't be a princess,' Callum had told Catriona one day. She was complaining about a leak in her wellies as she waded through the muddy sludge of the yard. She had been given the responsibility of helping direct the cows back to their new home after a regular session being checked over in the crush. And yet, she was complaining.

She had thought he was suggesting she was a cow - not in that bad, adult way - but in the way that meant her attitude was bovine. The problem was, that for Catriona, bovine was good. Cows were her friends.

A joke can only work when there is shared linguistic awareness. Similarly an insult. Perspective is everything.

So when Helen later asked a muddy Catriona, sitting on the chair by the kitchen range as she pulled off her socks, where she had been to get into such a state, the girl replied; 'taking the princesses back to the cow palace.'

'The princesses?' Helen asked?

'Yes, and daddy told me not to be one,' Catriona said. 'But I want to be.'

'A princess?' Helen was surprised and not a little bit fearful that her muddy six year old was about to turn 'pink'.

'A cow,' Catriona laughed. 'Moo-ve over Torq,' she added, pushing him away from the range where he was warming his hands.

'I love cows,' she said.

'Me too,' Torquil added.

'Who is your favourite cow?'

There followed a long conversation between the children on the various merits of the various cows⋯ until it was agreed that while Teeny and Tiny were great, and Amber was 'precious', the best of them all was Infinitely Small.

Listening to them chatter gave Helen pause for thought about the interactions between parents and children.

Who teaches who? There's so much to learn. Not just right and wrong, good and bad, but how to see things. How to understand them and how to explain. Making meaning through creativity with words. As a family.

Was this what set them apart from other families? Was this their uniqueness? Were they all part, a contributing, essential part, of something bigger than any one of them? Were they family trees even then? Even before.

There was a moment in 1991 when Callum and Torquil stood in the cow palace, warming their hands in the deep, rich fur of Torquil's favourite calf. It was one of 'those' moments. We all recognise them. We all have them. And if we are lucky, we remember them for the rest of our lives. They place us in spacetime. They are part of us and represent when our moment is in harmony with something bigger. All moments.

The family agreed that of all the cows in the cow palace, the Belties were the real princesses. A hardy breed, they could easily have spent the winter outside. But when the weather turned really poor, everyone agreed they deserved to be indoors if they wished. So Callum gave them the choice and usually, as he turned for home, several of them followed along into the byre. He didn't even need a feed bucket. They took little to no persuasion.

And in the moment Callum and Torquil shared in 1991, a particular little Beltie calf was special. He had a name. A back story. And he was loved. He was Infinitely Small.

'He'd like it if you put on your gloves and stroked him that way,' Callum said.

Unlike Helen, he was confident that he was smarter than a three year old boy. At least his three year old boy. Fathers and sons have a bond that is mostly secretive, but strong and secure.

'Would he?'

Callum nodded.

'Did he tell you that?' Torquil asked.

'Sure did. He'll tell you if you listen very carefully.'

Torquil put his ear close up to the calf's mouth. He felt warm breath. He felt slobber. He heard the in and out and the snuffle and nuzzle of living breath. The calf nibbled at his ear, looking for the bottle which served as a teat - his mother having died in the process of a difficult labour some days before.

At that, Torquil jumped back, amazed.

Wide eyed he told his father, 'He did tell me,' with a seriousness reserved for the under fives.

'Then put them on,' Callum said.

'Help me please, dad.'

Father and son worked together to get the dangling woollen mittens onto the small, freezing hands so that a boy might give solace to another boy - a boy who had lost his mother. Because for Torquil, species wasn't important.

There was one thing the family agreed on. Animals were people too. Humans didn't have the exclusive right to be called people.

'Does he miss his mummy?' Torquil asked.

'Who, Infinitely Small?'

Torquil nodded.

'Aye, he probably does, but if you are very kind to him, he'll forget.'

'Forget his mummy?'

'No, forget his sorrow.'

Torquil blinked.

'I won't ever forget my mummy,' he said.

These days don't last. They grow up so fast. Everything is change. But the memories are as permanent as they are fleeting. They exist in more than one place at more than one time. They are always

15

infinite. They are pain and pleasure combined.

On that particular, particularly cold February day in 1991, it wasn't long before the familiar cry came out;

'My hands are sweating pigs. Get the gubbs off, dad.'

And the shadow of a memory yet to come, played over the cow palace.

A birthday cake. Forty candles. A birthday present. A grandchild. And a message from another dimension for a seventy year old woman who had given up all hope.

All moments are one moment. It all depends where you stand.

FORM 3

Beyond Language

All verbs are one verb
That verb is 'be'
For 'beings' (human or otherwise) this holds to be the case.

All words are one word.
Word is a symbol
Word is a concept/idea
Word is particle and wave

Written words can only take you so far
They can only reach in so far
And sometimes it is not far enough

You need to get beyond the marks and the symbols
and reach into the mind of the word
Dance with them.
And in the dance you find yourself.

You find who you are
But you cannot write this down
It defies written language

You cannot tell who you are
It defies spoken language
You can define ways but not something beyond 'the' way.
Each word becomes a particle in the wave.

The wave is.
This is Qi

FORM 4

The Cave of Infinity

Breaking free from the constraints of the novel as narrative par excellence, I remember that I was born a philosopher.

'What is beyond infinity?' I asked when I was being taught to count.

'Infinity is the largest thing there is.'

And other voices said, 'The universe is the largest thing there is.'

I used to lie in bed wondering what was outside the universe. I suspect this metaphysical stance is not common in a three year old. It may, of course, be exactly the nature of a three year old. Only the mind of a three year old knows the mind of the three year old, after all.

However long I followed the yellow brick road in childhood, however many mountains I climbed in search of my dreams, I choked on metaphysics when I came back to it in my teens.

I was not the only one.

I first met J.M. Barrie when I was seven, not through *Peter Pan*, but through a back stage pass to the adult world of drama; which hooked me into the sensuality of plush velvet seats and the dangerous comfort they provide, and even more significantly took me to the parts the audience rarely reaches - the dressing room and the stage door. These places held a fascination for me over and far beyond the stage, the bright lights and the applause.

I broke out of the proscenium arch into the empty space possibilities of black boxes and then out of the black boxes towards infinity, and I learned that there is much more in heaven and earth than are dreamed of in a philosophy, either west or east. *The Admirable Crichton* taught me 'what's natural is right' while *Dear Brutus* revealed that 'the fault lies not in the stars but in ourselves', as Shakespeare had noted much earlier. Creative originality is a river without a source.

Barrie was so much more than a dramatist and a novelist, and he shared my youthful reaction to metaphysics. I know because he told us so. Though with Barrie, nothing is ever fixed. He knew the mutability of the human condition more than most and he played with depth in structure in a way that holds me in awe now, even as I was in awe on that first day in that first theatre. Sometimes I wonder if he was a cognitive scientist before it was invented as a concept, never mind a discipline. He was certainly way ahead of his time. We still haven't caught up with him. I believe we still misinterpret just about everything he said.

Which is perhaps how he wanted it.

Whereas I had a burning need to communicate. To share identity through words and beyond the words.

Barrie wrote pencil sketches of his professors. I reflect on mine. The philosophers who shaped my philosophy. Then.

When I was seventeen
I ran from metaphysics.
Into the arms of fiction.

I told myself it was
Too difficult.
It was not too difficult.
My situation was too difficult.

I recognise now that I was overwhelmed.

Not by metaphysics but by education.
By the chance to inhabit my own identity
To be myself, if only I could find who I was.

I went to the beach.
I found myself.
I went to the pub.
I lost myself.

I talked. I listened. I thought. I read.

And when I wasn't talking or listening or thinking or reading,

I became myself.
A human being not a human doing.
Being and not being.
Life as drama. Not narrative.

Somewhere in Beckett, while waiting for Godot, in the absurdity of Stoppard and the rhythm of T.S. Eliot, there was a murder in a cathedral. I moved beyond Tennyson and Ulysses. I believed in the Gods. I became Athene in some small part of my being. Without knowing it.

I left literature behind. Lost words in my pursuit of thoughts. Then the thoughts turned into dramatic actions. Because I was not the first to think that philosophers have only interpreted the world, while the point was to change it.

I would change the world.

I believed it.

Drama takes words and gives them a multidimensional existence. A meaning beyond the private word read off the page. Actors inhabit the worlds and live the meanings. But that was not enough for me.

I thought I wanted to make meaning.

Still a philosopher, I wanted to think meaning into existence. I was trained the western way. The writing on the wall was there. I was not, nor would I ever be, an analytic philosopher. But that was the training manual I was given. The answers and the questions I was allowed. These were not me. I did not recognise myself. I was lost in the wrong cave.

> I wanted to create meaning.
> I was wrong.
> Being is not creating.
> I am part of the creation not the creator.
> Did I not learn that on the beach?
> Looking up at the stars.
> Somehow it got lost in the translations.
> Of the stories in the songs and the songs in the stories.

But now I return to metaphysics, like Odysseus to Ithaca. To a place I lost somewhere on the journey away from myself [west] selfso/ziran [east] along a path less travelled which nevertheless was not my path. I return to the book of metaphysics called 'The Big Questions', in search of Heraclitus, a philosopher I never knew. A philosopher no one ever knew. A man as elusive as Homer and Lao Tzu [West] Laozi [East].

> They were all brothers in the journey.

The journey goes beyond the blue book and the brown book and that elusive third book of philosophical investigations. Past all the philosophers who talked about 'The best of all possible worlds' and yet none of whom seem to have found what they were looking for, or talking about. They said the path was through logic. The gatekeeper was Wittgenstein. And I was not allowed to meet him. I did not have the right password. My credentials were not measurable in number theory. I was not welcome to play an active part in their best of all possible worlds. I was simply there to make up the numbers. And my numbers just did not add up. I scored 11, repeatedly. In that world this was failure. In my world it was honesty. To be allowed into the inner sanctum I needed a higher score. I had my chance. I sat next to a 96. I could have copied his numbers. But that would have been like stealing someone else's thoughts. Re-writing a story out of cowardice, not honesty. So I threw my dice. I held my 11 fast and firm. And I failed. And in that failing was my success. It simply put me on another path. A path which led through caves of darkness for more than three times eleven. I never accepted the validity of numbers. I never believed in them. I still don't.

Somehow in all the caves I explored I never came across Heraclitus. His fragments were written on a wall, waiting, while I found my way back to the big book of metaphysics. I did not follow as the crow flies. Or even as the rat runs. I was always the random particle. My philosophical spirit was lost in the translation from East to West. A ghost masquerading as a monkey. On a Journey to the West. And my direction of travel was out of the gilded western cage which is still a box by any other name. There are more things in heaven and earth than are dreamed of in any philosophy and any language east or west.

The road less travelled was a shadow on my wall.

The world beyond philosophy, laughingly called the 'real' world, taught me to throw mud at walls, not to sit and look at them. Certainly never to think about the writing that would appear on them if I sat long enough in the right cave.

I was lost in the movie screen wondering if there was *Life on Mars*.

Unlike me, Heraclitus resisted.
Like the Daoist masters he tailored his own cloth.
He did not become part of the cloth.

And so the world turned
The drum beats yin
The drum beats yang.
Heraclitus privileged fire.
Analytic philosophy privileges logic.

But in the world of quantum infinity you can't privilege any element.

Metaphysics is bigger and yet, it's just a word. A word with no bigger meaning than many others.

Beyond the word, it is something that is learned in the fifty six forms which were first imagined by a three year old self. At least for me it is and has been.

In this text and beyond, I am in a place where metaphysics is no longer something to run from. You can run but you can't hide and I am no longer hiding from my natures. I am indistinguishable from the elements which make me. Mind, body and soul admit of no duality or holy trinity.

Nothing is but what is not.
I have discovered.

Paradoxes should be embraced not resisted. Truth lies in paradox. The ancients knew this. The adepts learn this. Do you understand this?

What you make of this is your part of the truth.

Not our truth, not your truth, not my truth. Not Heraclitus' personal truth, not the anti-realists rejection of truth. Just Qi[M] which is a symbol that represents that which cannot ever be understood through representation.

When you understand that the concept of equation is a problem on a fundamental level, you are free to find

$$Reality \approx *Qi[M]$$

Equivalency is a flawed concept. Like Metaphor. Metaphor is representational. Things are described 'in terms' of other things. Some say that metaphor is mapping difficult, partly understood concepts onto easier ones. A theory of target and source. I'm not so sure. It seems like the west skirting round yinyang to me.

The symbol = is a symbol for metaphor in a different language.

I don't like looking at my feet and footnotes are not for me, so this is not a footnote, but since I know you wonder: $\approx *$ represents the perspective that nothing is actually equal. Witness the death of the equation.

If you accept that there is no true equivalency, you come to see that metaphors and equations do not exist $\approx$ in a meaningful way. They are particles (albeit complex particles) in a quantum spacetime.

Things ARE what they are
and all are part of Qi[M]

Feel free to disagree. You have probably been trained in the Western way. You have bought the box labelled 'freedom' which nevertheless constrains.

And so, if you must ask what is on the left hand side of this quantum non-equation, I can give you an answer.

That's you. That's the way. That's what you have to find in order to be.

Let's go mind dancing.

Newton's laws of motion would hold that equations have to resolve to 0
There are so many problems with 0
Can 0 exist?
Is 0 equivalent to nothing in any meaningful way?

Ask Bishop Berkeley. Ask King Lear. Ask yourself.
Trust no one and nothing.
Trust nothing?

And we are in the world of paradoxes again.

That's a good thing.

When a question easily resolves to a paradox, you are in a good place in your being.

In Eastern terms 0 is not a number. It is a concept. It is called Wu Chi. If you use Wade-Giles. If you use Pinyin it is Wuji. Either and both ways, it is an open circle to infinity.

Even simplified as characters, the word as concept has many meanings:

At the click of a button I find three:

舞池 (dance floor)

无耻 (Without any sense of shame)

无持 (wingless)

All depending on your tone.

I was always told I spoke in the wrong tone of voice.

Now I understand.

But finally, it becomes the void, the emptiness, the infinite.

25

Nothing is ever fixed.

A question you ask me and I ask myself is:
How do you place the void in infinity?
The way that is named is not the way.
Find the answer in the question.

Here in the west, we are lost in a world of words and numbers.
Classification and dividing and sortal references.

Words as rules
Words as symbols
Thoughts and ideas.

And if Socratic dialogue was good enough for Socrates (but was it?) and the Greeks, then why is it not good enough for you and I. Or you and me?

Question and answer is just one part of how people arrive by their paradoxes and/or resist the metaphysical world, which is a world of paradox.

Only when you are lost will you be found.

I have read that Socrates may simply have been Plato playing a joke. Reality is what you choose to believe. I believe that. And I don't believe it. Fundamentally what I believe is unimportant and irrelevant to any of the cases.

When I stopped looking for answers, I found that in the space between Heraclitus and Wittgenstein is a dancer. His Wade-Giles name is Lao Tzu. His pinyin name is Laozi. Name is the thief of identity. Also he may never have existed.

This man who perhaps never and always existed says that the western metaphysical tradition (as I understand it, which is not very clearly) seems to be like Western ideas of a garden. Or so I read him. When a garden is something you must create and control, this is not the way. This is not nurturing. Nothing grows honestly unless it is free to roam. Weeds do not exist except in the mind.

One man's weed is another man's medicine.

One man's terrorist is another man's freedom fighter.

And the Ultimate world is not the only possible one. We just got stuck there for a while.

Any way you come to it, it is all part of Qi (because everything is part of Qi)

$$\text{My path is} \approx *Qi[M]$$

Let us dance wingless without shame.

If I were to offer a definition of creativity, I could do no better - in any language.

FORM 5

WOOD builds FIRE

The Cabrach Bunker

'How can you possibly imagine a utopia?'

'What can you do but imagine a utopia. I mean, a Utopia, by definition, isn't real. Is it?'

Torquil looked his son square in the eye and realised that this was the moment he had been waiting for all his life.

Since that last moment.

The moment of his son's birth.

It was a time when both their names were different.

A moment when everything changed.

With one loud, lusty cry, his world had transformed for ever. A birth-day.

And now, twenty years on, contextuality had been achieved. If you followed the pattern of linear time. He understood that it was a pattern they had to break to stay alive.

∞ ∞ ∞

'Let me ask you a question Nick.'

'What?'

'When did you last see your father?'

Nike was trying to work out whether it was when he was six or seven and shut his eyes momentarily to concentrate. While they were shut Troy's voice invaded his thoughts.

'Use emotion Nick, not reason. Think outside the ULTIMATE® box.'

Nike opened his eyes, and found himself enfolded in an embrace from his father.

'Welcome home, son.' Nike could see the tears in Troy's eyes, blurred through the tears in his own.

∞ ∞ ∞

'My childhood wasn't idyllic,' Torquil said. 'But it was real. It was what I wanted for you. To be part of something.'

'Of family?'

'More than that. Family in nature.'

He continued, 'I wanted you to have memories. Then Ultimate came and stole everyone's memories.'

'I have memories,' Nick said. 'And we can make new ones, now, can't we?'

'But they won't be the same memories.'

It was a shared thought. Spoken or unspoken. Sometimes these things matter.

And what is a story? A shared memory. A construction giving life to meaning. An act of creation in which we make and find our own meaning.

And share it if we dare. Or if we can.

'I wanted you to be a real boy.'

'I am a real boy. Now.'

Torquil shook his head. 'No. Now you're a real man.'

Nick felt pride for the first time in his life.

'So what are we talking about here?' Nick pressed him.

'We're talking about what happens in the quantum gaps when you enter the Qi[ ] space.'

'Huh?' Nick was way out of his depth.

Author, character, narrator, reader. All are broken the moment we move beyond comfort and safety. Definitions as names and words as explanations are not fixed. Not any more. Or less.

'Let me tell you about Quantum Infinity,' Torquil said. 'It is the places you long to be. They are there. They are particles in the wave of life. The points we have lost contact with. The points we forget how to find. You need a map of a different dimension to find them.'

'And you're going to show me that map?'

A point of connection was made, and felt.

Torquil took his time.

Troy had shown Nike.

But Torquil could not show Nick.

Not in a true paradox.

'You'll find it for yourself. You have to.'

'Or?'

'Or you die.'

The choice was stark. Nick turned round. He was alone in a dark bunker far below a place that he barely recognised as home.

'Remember that everything is connected.'

Word as thought and feeling.

He took a breath. Deep. In and out. In and out. Open and close. Proving to himself he was still alive in some world, even if it was a world he didn't know. A world that didn't feel real. In which his status was not fixed. Who was he?

And what is reality? Away from the Ultimate world, he struggled to remember. He had lost his place, if not his life.

Grasping for something more important than air, he sensed there was another moment. Was it futile to say earlier? It was just another moment. Another memory. Another part of the story. When and where he was negotiating ways of being.

Beyond thought.

Nick remembered feeling the connection.

As she blew out the candles.

Was he back?

He opened his eyes. It was dark. He opened his ears. He heard nothing. He opened his mouth. It was the last resort.

'Is utopia just another version of the virtual world?' Nick asked.

There was no response.

Either Torquil wanted him to think for himself or he was alone, with only breath and memory to tell him he existed.

'Can we reach it through productive work?'

He asked another question of the silence. Questions were his path. His fundamental nature.

He opened all his senses
and he was back.

'No. Only through 'unproductive' work.'

His father had not abandoned him.
His breath came more easily.

In the dark, unseen, there was the hint of a smile as Nick asked, 'What's that?'

'When you go beyond.'
'Beyond what?'
'Beyond the Ultimate lifestyle experience.'
'And so, I···?'

Nick still couldn't bring himself to ask the question. To face the reality. That this was the world beyond The Project House and Ultimate and··· all this. It could not be real.

Troy was Torquil. The leader of the Immortal Horses was none other than his own father.

Nike was Nick. Alone or not alone in a cave.   And he

wondered, as we all wonder: All this. It could not be real. How could it be?

No one had taught him how to have an existential crisis. Certainly not how to resolve it. In the Ultimate world such things were unimportant. Life itself was unimportant.

An explanation came. From father to son.

'As far as the world is concerned, you are dead. You have been killed by the 100 men. It is time to move into another dimension. Live in a totally different way.'

The father was calm in the delivery of this most incredible of statements. The son was grasping beyond breath.

'Utopia?'

'Have you heard of Hilbert Space?'

Nick shook his head.

"The virtual life is easy to sell", Torquil said, quoting another part of the moment. Another memory. Another mind making meaning.

'It was a version of reality. You did not buy it, you were sold into it. But that's not our reality. I'm offering you reality. In another dimension.'

'Cool.'

If only it were that simple.

'You'll have to make a choice. A real choice. The kind of choice that has been eliminated by Ultimate.'

'How?'

'Ah, now that would be telling.'

'So tell me.'

Nick couldn't stop himself. He turned to face his father. But it was dark. He felt alone. All that was left was breath.

'The Birthday cake. That's the moment.'

It was impossible to know whether this was a thought inside his head or a voice putting the thought into his head.

'The moment?'

He felt saved by a memory. Something to hold onto. Beyond his father's voice.

'The moment we have to get to.'

Torquil gave Nick time to process this information.

'What do you mean?'

'You have to understand context,' Torquil said.

He was patient in the face of questions.

'The question is: Is it possible that, independently of which is the quantum state, the quantum observables each possess definite single value, regardless of whether they are measured or not?'

'That's really a question?'

'It really is.'

'And the answer?'

Nick was impulsive. Like all young people.

Torquil remembered it well. The fact and the feeling.

'Never mind the answer, work on accepting the meaning,' he replied.

'Which is?'

'That Quantum theory exhibits contextuality'

'Which means?'

Even as he was asking the question, Nick knew this was how they were together. How they were meant to be together. How they lived. They were question and answer to each other. It was like looking in a mirror. It was what he saw beyond the mirror.

More than questions and answers. More than words. Mind dancing. The perfect challenge. Father and son together as one. Part of something bigger than both of them.

We all live in caves. Sometimes we make the caves. Sometimes we find ourselves in them. Sometimes we lose ourselves in them. Sometimes we are the cave.

Birth and death are just the most recognisable entry and exit points. They are the easiest and the hardest way to tap into memory.

'A context is a set of mutually compatible quantum observables.' Father.

'And?'Son.

'From Birthday cakes to Plato's cave, even things that appear to be, no, even things that are state-independent, are contextualisable.'

Go beyond the words.
Dance with me.

Think with me.
Be with me.
The world of words is only one world.

'There are thirteen observables realizable on a three-level quantum system and this is the smallest quantum system allowing for contextuality. According to the Yu-OH set.'
    'If you say so.'
Nick was in danger of letting go.
    'It's just a question of where to start.'
Torquil didn't want to lose him.

In the world of probabilities there is always scope for the unthinkable. The story has many endings, even before the beginning.

    'So where should I start?' Nick asked.
    'Where do you want to start?'

The way that can be named is not the way. Each person has to follow his own way. Every path is individual, though not independent.

    'The birthday cake?' Nick said.
    'Question or answer.'
It was hard to define.
Nick felt himself slip-sliding away.
Would Torquil let him off the hook?
Would Torquil let him fall?
Of course he wouldn't.
They were Father and Son.

In all possible worlds.

'Does it have to be one or the other?'

Nick reached out.

Help me. Catch me. Don't lose me. Don't let me go.

Torquil smiled. His son had a natural instinct for this.

'What do you think?'

The door was open. The shadows began to emerge on the walls of the cave.

'Surely, according to what you say, they must be joined··· contextually? And so it doesn't matter where I start.'

Now he had it.

'Correct. The position isn't important. You just have to enter the dimension.'

'And is that Hilbert Space?' Nick asked.

'It might be.'

'Or not.'

'There's always that possibility. That's the beauty of it. Everything is possible.'

'And are we still talking about the quantum world?'

'We're talking about all possible worlds. And this is them.'

And it was. And it is. Or are. Timelessness is hard to pin down on the page in mere words. Multi-dimensions resist marks on paper.

Nick was in transition. Setting out. He wanted a map. A guide. He needed to know he was looking in the right dimension. The challenge was far greater than simple direction.

Up, down, in, out, may self-define as prepositions. They stand in relation to other words. From the Latin, to place before. In which case they mean nothing in and of themselves. Or do they?

What do words mean anyway?

35

When it comes down to it.

The definite particle third person singular is not a pronoun. Mission creep. Overload. *Reductio ad absurdum.*

Language is relative. And yet so much more than a game or games.

Can I ask whether in the best of all possible worlds, grammar would exist. Does grammar exist? And what does 'best' signify?

What does signify signify?
What do we mean by signify?
What do we mean by mean?

In the Cabrach Bunker there was some unpleasant business to attend to.
Torquil pointed to the barcode on Nick's arm.
'We have to get rid of that.'
'I thought you disabled it.'
'That's not good enough for where you're going. We have to remove it.'
'Will it hurt?'
It hurt.
Life hurts.
All transitions have a cost and the cost is pain.
'Where are we?'
'Don't you recognise it?'
Silence
'In this place we are safe because it is no-place.'
'Dad, why are you always speaking in riddles?'
Nick still felt a frisson of excitement when he said the word 'dad'. He wished he understood more. He thought that if only they understood each other, they would be closer.

He was wrong.

It's not about understanding, it's about love. Emotion not reason.

'I love to hear you call me dad,' Torquil said.

They were on the same wavelength after all. Again. Still. Man and boy. Together. Mind dancing. The stage deeper than word dancing. The place where nothing else matters and everything is encompassed in the moment.

All the moments.
Something to hold on to.
Those other times.

'Read this.'
Torquil gave Nick a battered old handwritten book. Nick got a thrill just in reading the words written by his father's own hand, the ink faded on the page. The pages crumpled from age.

Points of connection.

As one reads what the other wrote there is a sense of communion. Conjunction. Synchronicity. Of being together even when apart.
The Ancients call me Utopia or Nowhere because of my isolation. I am a rival of Plato's republic, perhaps even a victor over it.' Thomas More.
'So who was Thomas More?' Nick asked.
He would never outgrow asking questions. It was a fundamental part of who he was in all moments.
'It doesn't really matter,' Torquil said. 'He was a philosopher in the fifteenth century.'
'What happened to him?'
'He was killed by the King.'
'What for?'
'For being honest.'
Is that the truth?
'They call it speaking truth to power,' Torquil said. 'It's a

dangerous game. I should know. I've played it all my life.'

'Teach me.' Nick paused with the enormity of the word to come still fresh in his mind, 'dad.'

'One day I will tell you about Plato's Cave,' Torquil replied. 'Not today.'

'I know.'

'You do?'

'Nan told me.'

'And one day I will tell you about it from my perspective,' Torquil said. 'That's a promise.'

And a promise is not something to be given, or taken, lightly.

'Is this utopia?' Nick asked.

'Where are we?' Torquil replied.

'Nowhere?'

'And soon we will be beyond even that.'

The words beyond the words that they spoke at that moment, which are words you read now and in reading you may or may not understand the thoughts that characters who are and are not real at the same time, depending on perspective, think. These words are:

'Utopia has always been with us and is all around us. It is the place Ultimate cannot reach, cannot buy, cannot own. To live there, you simply have to recognise where you are. And perhaps, more importantly, who you are.'

'But what is beyond utopia?' Nick asked.

And perhaps you ask that too.

'Ask Thomas More,' Torquil suggested.
Nick picked up the notebook and read on: *'Deservedly ought I to be called by the name of Eutopia or Happy Land'.*

'You might say that eutopia is what there is outside everything

38

we have left behind,' Torquil said. 'Outside, beyond, apart from - these are all insufficient words with insufficient values to explain what it means. Another dimension entirely. But that's where we are.' He paused.

It was a lot for anyone to take in, he knew that.

'Is it Hope?' Nick asked.

'No. Hope is part of the aspirational pyramid. There is no need for hope.'

Hope is a craving for something
We are the moment.
We are in the moment.
We are the moments.
All moments.
All moments are one moment.

'Just let go.'

And, trusting his father, Nick let go...

...as Torquil reached out for his son, unable quite to let go himself. The pain was too deep. And so the transformation was a jolting, sickening one.

Nick came to in another place.

The hand that he reached out for was his grandfather's. His father was not there. Torquil had been left behind. He still had other moments to experience.

But he would follow. And be followed. The relationship between father and son was cyclical and infinite.

Nick felt no regret in that moment. He was moving, not stationary, and there is no time for grief when you are in the realm of actions not consequences.

He had no idea where he was. It didn't matter when or where, just what. Not even why. Just being in the moment. And knowing, finally, who he was. He was his father's son.

FORM 6

How To Escape

If you start from a false premise, don't be surprised when you reach
a false conclusion.

First Find the right cave	Find your cave
Then Sit in the right cave	Sit in your cave
Just Be in the right cave	Be in your cave

It is difficult to ask the right question. Or to frame it correctly.
Especially if one comes from the wrong perspective. Or from a
perspective where right and wrong are essentially meaningless.

Ask rather: How did we get here?

Ask rather : Where is here?

Brand Loyalty led to the Ultimate World. But the Ultimate World
was not the best of all possible worlds. 'Best' is a poor concept and
a much worse word. It's a word for a world of hierarchy.

It has no meaning to us.

The Ultimate World of Brand Loyalty might be described as
dystopia.

Or reality.
Or not.
Fact or fiction.
Both.

It's a part of 'all' that I don't want to inhabit.

And the only way I know how way to escape from a dystopia is into
a utopia.

There are places real and imaginary. There are boxes and caves in all shapes and sizes.

Suspension of disbelief is embracing the narrative.

Science forges its own narratives. From black holes to wormholes, to Hilbert Space. It's all just stories. There are even college courses which teach about evil numbers. Beware of evil numbers; they will check you in to the Hilbert hotel, which is a way to constrain infinity.

Check it out.   Check out.

Pick the flavour of your spin and dance with your mind beyond the words in the text boxes.

Head west, head east, head up/down/in/out/back/forth -

There is no waiting any more

Waiting is a fixed point/particle in the wave

Beyond waiting is being.

You still want to know how to escape?

Even as I learn the fifty six forms
I let go of the fifty six forms

From all the boxes in all the worlds and all the caves in all the minds, when we broke free from the constraints of the hierarchy and of the world of best and real and identity.

We found ourselves.
Yes FOUND ourselves.
And in finding we realised we were already here.

FORM 7

A Particular Cave

'Who are you?' Nick asked.
'Why do you want to know?'

To answer a question with a question was always Nike's way. Always Nick's way. What's a consonant or vowel between friends? What does it matter where a letter stands in a word? What's in a name? In any possible world the letters c or e made no difference to that feature of his personality.

Name, after all, is the thief of identity.
The name that can be named is not the name.

'Because we are creating your narrative,' the narrator replied.
'We?' Nick asked. 'Isn't that your job?'
'It's your lives,' the narrator replied, 'your responsibility and your creative choice.'

If you don't create your own identity it will be constructed for you and when you come to curate it you will no longer know who you are.
This is how we lose ourselves.
Our creativity is part of our infinite qi.

The question remains.
'What's the last thing you remember?'
'A bright light,' Nick replied.
'That's so passé,' came the response.
'But it's true,' Nick said. 'It might not have been the last thing that happened but it's the last thing I remember. Then I woke up. Here.'
'And the narrative continued in the other world,' said the narrator.

'What's the ending?' Nick asked.

'For you or the narrative?'

'I don't know the difference,' Nick said.

'Of course you don't. There is no distance between you and your narrative at present,' the narrator replied. 'That's one of the things we are creating.'

Nick was baffled.

'So, what happened to me?' he asked.

'To Nike?' the narrator asked but didn't wait for a response before reading out the story:

'What he didn't see was the vehicle approaching from behind. He didn't see it as it hit him and he saw nothing as he was thrown, doll-like over the bonnet, landing in a crumpled heap on the pavement. No light remained. Only blackness. Forever.'

'Cool,' Nick said.

'It's not a bad obituary as they go,' the narrator said. 'Though I could have written it better.'

Nick had had a moment to think.

'So,' he said, 'I'm dead.'

'In that world,' the narrator concurred.

'And that isn't the only world?'

'Clearly not,' the narrator replied.

There was a pause.

'And if you're about to ask if you're in heaven…'

'What's heaven?' Nick asked.

'Just a completely random and ridiculous narrative which should have been put out to grass long before it was,' said the narrator. 'Its strength to convince never justified the weakness of its plausibility.'

'But, my Nan?' Nick said.

'What about her?'

'She'll think I'm dead, and if she thinks that… and she thinks my

43

dad is dead…'

'There's a lot in these ellipses,' the narrator observed.

After a pause, more questions tumbled from Nick.

'Who are you?', 'What about Lucy and Eric?'
'Sorry?'
'Lucy and Eric. The gender bending sheep.'
'Don't you mean Bah and Humbug?'
'I don't think so.'
Nick paused again.
'I know who you are,' he said.
'The answer is always in the question,' said the narrator.

As the destination is in the journey.
As day turns to night and night turns to day.
All moments are one moment.

And in one part of the moment readers have no need of an author. Still, I exist. Living and dead. My creative intention guides but does not dominate.

You construct. We curate differently.

Beyond words while in another part of the moment, in another cave, the characters had no need of a narrator.

FORM 8

FIRE burns EARTH

A Tsilhqot'in Bear Cave

The next thing Nick knew he was waking up with the jolt of a truck. He thought he was in his grandfather's Landrover. He thought he was three years old.

At the sound of a familiar voice, he opened his eyes.

'Hey Nick.' It was his grandfather.

He saw a face he had not seen in so long, but one he would never forget.

And then he looked out of the window, as if expecting to see his childhood.

It wasn't.

The trees were bigger, the road was straighter and the clear felled forests seemed to stretch on into infinity.

'Where⋯?'

'You're awake,' Callum said. 'We'll be there soon. You must be hungry.'

He was.

The landscape overpowered his senses. The smells and sights and sounds were all familiar and strange at the same time.

The mountain ranges spread over an expansive horizon. In front of the mountains, the rising morning sun framed a river which flowed sparkling and eternal over rocks and boulders, between banks where no cows drank but where bears and beavers made their homes and came out in the dark, or when no humans were near.

Looking out of the window, Nick said, 'This place is so cool. 'Where are we?'

Callum smiled.

'Don't you recognise it?' he said.

'I've never been here before,' Nick said. 'Have I?'

Suddenly he was not so sure. Everything was strange and familiar at the same time. He was coming home to a place he'd never been before.

He tried to orient, to make sense. He failed. Sometimes there is no sense to be made, especially when one experiences a sense of place.

'Life is full of moments,' Callum said. He paused. 'Well, actually it's just one moment,' he continued. 'And we approach it from a range of perspectives. You have to connect into the right part of the moment and···'

'Like···' Nick wanted to grasp at it. But it was just out of his mental reach. Beyond questions.

Everything is connected.
We're part of it all.
The question is in the answer.
The narrator doesn't always tell the story.
And certainly not the same story.
It's all a question of perspective.
In which we are all implicated.

All moments are one moment.

It's riddles again, Nick thought. He wondered whether he would ever understand any of this. He wondered whether he would ever understand himself. Was understanding even possible? Or desirable.

Callum saw Nick's confusion. He wanted to help. He wanted to explain. But they were in the middle of a landscape too big for any map to navigate. They could see so far into the distance that perspective was impossible. The canvas was too broad. It was too bright.

'You get to the moment by focus. Find a place to focus. Join the wave.'

Nick looked blankly at his grandfather.

'You're a long way from the Cabrach now,' Callum said.

'Are we in Hilbert Space?' Nick asked.

'It doesn't matter where you are, it matters that you are,' Callum said.

'And you are.'

His father's voice came like a memory, sneaking into his mind, like Infinitely Small's breath from a time and place beyond his own personal experience.

Many miles down the road, deeper into the story wilderness, they met a roadblock. Callum stopped the engine. They had to leave the truck. It was only when he felt the ground firm under his feet that Nick believed he was not dreaming. They walked, side by side, following the path of the river. It danced and played across the rocks, the rocks which were part of the mountains up above. It was a bigger range of mountains than he could possibly have imagined. Snow covered. Winter was coming.

Callum stooped down and picked up a handful of water. He let it trickle between his fingers.

'What is this colour?' Nick asked. 'I've never seen it before.'

'If we have to name it, I'd call it glacial blue,' Callum said. 'What does it remind you of?'

Nick knelt down beside his grandfather. He ran his fingers through the water as the water ran over his fingers.

'Her eyes,' he said.

Without words they shared the knowledge that she was here. The connection was fleeting.

'There should be trees,' he said. 'A forest.'

'There is,' Callum replied. 'Just not in this part of the moment.'

The sun shone down on the sparkling rocks which lay underneath the water as it ran and bubbled along on a journey he could not even imagine. He looked up towards the mountain. Amidst and

47

beyond the clear felling, he could sense more than see that creativity was curating new identities. Trees were growing again despite the destruction that had sold itself as a constructive action.

Oh Canada. You are the smallest part of the moment. The stories and lives are bigger than you will ever know. You can give a place a name but you cannot own a place by naming it. You did not create this place. You do not curate this place. Your construction is a destruction by any other name and it does not smell as sweet as the wildflowers in the meadows, or the blueberries and fir-pine scent in which all sense of identity is lost and found.

Nick looked down at his arm, where the implant had been. It was not there. There was no sign it had ever been. And there was no pain.

The sun followed them as they walked towards the entrance to the dilapidated buildings of a disused mine. It was literally the end of the trail. It was beyond the end of the trail. Junked trucks and signs and debris littered around, causing dissonance with the beautiful natural landscape. A practical paradox.

Two men awaited them. They were dressed in the garb of a First Nations band. Their jackets and trousers were made of caribou.

It was cold. The men were both wearing mittens, which they took off to extend a hand of greeting.

Nick shook their hands.

Their hands were warm.

They reminded him of something he could not place··· of memories between his father and grandmother··· of things he could never have known. Unless···

Introducing themselves as Jimmy and Joe, the men led Nick and Callum into the building.

'Are you hungry?' Jimmy asked.

'Yes,' Nick said, though he had lost all thought of it till he was asked, his immediate senses all having been diverted into the overwhelming landscape.

'We will eat,' Joe said.

48

'And then we will take you to the cave.'

He pointed high up the mountain. Nick could see nothing. But it was there.

Perhaps that was the point.

On a full belly, the trek up to the cave was almost pleasant, with the last of the sun beating down and the smell of the trees offering a full bodied resinous assault on the breath taken into lungs unused to this level of physical activity.

'But still,' Nick thought, 'a cave?'

'Do you live here?' he asked.

Jimmy smiled and nodded.

The building below, now fading from sight, was somewhat decrepit, but Nick couldn't believe that living in a cave would be a preferable alternative.

As they approached the entrance, he turned and looked down. It was, he had to admit, a place that offered a good vantage point. Below, he could see the light playing off the river. The water dancing down the mountainside. And he knew there were worse places to be.

FORM 9

Debts and promises

Did you pass through a transition?
The Cabrach.
Was it death?
Of a kind.
Was it to be feared?
No, because I was shifting from one state to another state
From one way of being to another way of being
Being is constant flux.

And so you woke up and found yourself by the river

With a cave for safety and many caves to explore

And a new understanding of light and darkness

I owe you a debt.

What does this mean?

Something owed. Usually (in Western tradition) money.
But it can be gratitude or appreciation. That is what I owe you.

What does 'owe' mean?
It is an obligation.
A commitment or responsibility

And a commitment is a responsibility.

So you see we can get to promise from debt in five simple steps of
linguistic separation.
    A promise is a serious thing to give
    And to receive.

A promise is relational. It confers responsibility on both sides.

We cannot use formal syllogistic logic on these statements. At least I cannot.

A debt is paid by a promise.
A debt is a promise monetised.

Nothing of value should be monetised.

Money is not real. It is a metaphor at best.

And, knowing all that, I will make you a promise.

We will make a promise together.

I will give and you will receive this promise.

In all possible worlds. Best and worst.
In all dimension of Qi and for all moments.

And the promise is?

Love.

Beyond word and action and consequence.

Infinity.

And like the way, it cannot be named. It certainly cannot be monetised. Though it often is. But if you sit in the wrong cave for long enough the writing does not appear on the wall. Instead you find yourself throwing mud at the wall to make a picture. That is the monetisation of the caves of narrative and philosophy.

FORM 10

When Particles Collide

'Of all the stories in all the worlds you walk into mine.'

It used to be that we believed that all good stories began 'once upon a time'. We know differently now. We know that narrative is more flexible and mutable than that simple sentence allows. One man in his time plays not just many parts but lives on many stages – each of them a dimension in a multi-verse – and this world is part of an infinitely complex system.

'Tell me the last thing you remember.'

A line from an absurdist play.
A line from an absurdist play?

In that part of the moment when Stoppard shared a cave with Shakespeare, two men shook hands and they both knew that context is everything.

There was a moment, just before all that, when Nick looked into the eyes of a man and didn't know. And then he recognised him. But neither of these moments was once upon a time, though both of these moments marked a beginning.

It began before then. You can go back right to the moment of birth, or even conception, from which time while everything was not certain it was at least possible.

But there were many paths, many roads not taken, until the quantum leap with which the words 'welcome home, son' were spoken and Nick and his dad were together again.

But that time also had passed.

There was darkness all around. He was in transition. Moving but still. No place, no time, no space. Pure thought and pure emotion. Mind and memory in balanced harmony.

He was in a narrative cave. And so are we.

FORM 11

EARTH generates METAL

A Singular Cave

Somewhere in a conversation, characters spoke. And listened. Readers stepping into the cave may hear the voices before they see the writing on the wall.

> 'We met even before you were born.'
> *'How can that be?'*
> 'You were a possibility.'
> *'If so then I must have been one among many others?'*
> 'That's true.'
> *'And when did we meet?'*
> 'At the family trees.'
> *'Where?'*
> 'We used to go there for picnics. We'd sit and tell stories. And some of the stories became truth and some of them remained possibilities. That's life.'

And that was life. In the early twenty first century in rural Scotland life could still be told by stories. And life lived by seasons. And families still went on picnics. Before reality was virtualised, there were sunny days at the beaches. Private spaces and family places, known only to them. Meaning created by shared memory.

They lay under the cover of the leaves, ate 'negg' sandwiches and followed them with 'napples' instead of crisps, and told each other things they imagined as if they were the truth. And some of the things became truths. Simply because they were imagined and then spoken about.

> 'When I grow up I'm going to marry a man.'

That was Catriona's chosen version of the once upon a time opening sentence.

'I've heard it all before,' was always Torquil's reply.

Callum and Helen wondered where life would take their children. Life was wonder. And danger. But on a sunny afternoon in peaceful space under the family trees, looking out onto the biggest field in the world, the wonder was to the fore.

'How?' Torquil asked his father.

'Why' Catriona asked her mother.

And between and beyond the hows and the whys was the where and the when. But the questions come thicker than answers. It is always the same in the company of free-thinkers. Word dancers and mind dancers. Storytellers and philosophers.

And if you took a completely different path, you might end up at the same place, or a completely different one.

And what if there is no 'end'?

How do you explain such things to children? The answers you give at eight and ten become the paths they explore when they are eighteen or twenty. Or is that quite irrelevant? When everything is connected, how far can we be said to follow our own path?

The stories of the Odyssey and the Iliad and the Argonautica were staple fare for such summer afternoons when the family took time just to be, away from the farm and before Ultimate spoiled everything by taking it all and repackaging it, then demanding Brand Loyalty. Callum and Helen knew the stories and thought they understood the value of the stories, or of story itself. The value of narrative as a map is both limited and limitless. And we are all part of the infinite narrative.

'When I grow up I'm going to marry a man called Jason, and this is his family tree,' Catriona continued. She patted the tree next to her own.

And she did.

They met at University. There's nothing strange about that. The context, however, was more prose than poetry.

Catriona had a friend, a girl called Lauren. Lauren had a boyfriend. He was called Jason. They had a fight. Jason and Lauren. And then Lauren and Catriona. No one could remember what either fight was about. Before long it didn't matter. War is war. And young people will always test the theory that all is fair in love and war.

To begin with Jason wanted Lauren back. He had to develop a strategy. Form an alliance. So he hunted out Catriona, to help him in his task. The machinations of the University student are multi-dimensional. Too much study and too much alcohol and too many hormones and too many love songs and⋯

One thing led to another and Catriona and Jason fell in love. And instead of the conversation they thought they were going to have with Lauren, the one they'd prepared for all those long nights in the pub which were the precursor to the longest night on the beach before the sun came up during the kiss that sealed all their fates along a particular path, they went to tell her they were a couple.

And later, much later, Lauren, wanting to get her own back, made 'cow eyes' (as Helen would have called it) at Torquil. But Torquil, much as he knew the ways of cows, did not know the ways of girls - except his sister - and he fell for Lauren behind the byre. Hook, line and sinker. It's a familiar enough rural story. Boy meets girl⋯ and soon enough he was chasing her to the ends of the earth. Which in this case was Edinburgh.

And later on, he brought her home as his wife with child. And Nick was the child of the fragile union. But it was a union of opposites and never forged to stand the test of time. So Nick got left behind when Lauren realised the error of her ways and went on to pastures new. To a grass that looked greener but somehow didn't taste as sweet.

And all this is an archetypal story which has no less value because it is true in one possibility of a world. Lives lived and changed because of actions that might have been different had any particle of the wave functioned in an opposite spin cycle. Or the story taken another turn.

Reader, she married him. Catriona married Jason Pryce. Was it a marriage made in heaven? *Ah, but a man's reach must exceed his grasp or what's a heaven for? It's the damage that we do and never know, it's the words that we don't say that scare me so.* The full weight of western culture weighed heavy on them. Let's call it a happy ending. At least part of it was a happy ending. They had two children. Let's call them Lucy and Eric. Or you might call them Omo and Flora. A boy and a girl. The perfect nuclear family set free from the shiniest vision of utopia or dystopia you can imagine. Wave. Particle. Context is everything in the best of all possible possible worlds.

In the land of memories Callum remembered Jason Pryce asking for his daughter's hand in marriage. It was one of those dates that stuck in his mind. May 2nd 2009. A big moment, pushing its way to the perspectival foreground of meaning and memory. The day they got the swine flu pandemic leaflet. His thoughts went back to the same day if not date, eight years previously. The day which changed their lives forever. The day of death. Now another virus would change their lives again. All life is change. Viruses know that even if people don't. Viruses are just better at exploiting that change and harnessing it and directing it.

'Have you asked her?' was Callum's response to the proposed proposal.

'I wanted to do it properly,' the earnest young man replied.

'Properly, huh?' Callum removed his hat and scratched his head.

Properly was not a concept that came easily to him. Somewhere between the illusions of right and wrong it got lost in a melange of reality as hope and was something you couldn't pin down any more than you could control the washing on the line on a breezy day, or the determination of a cow to calve in the middle of the blackest night. At least, for a moment, his mind was taken away from the death of animals. And the poisonous properties of the virus looking for a host.

'Do you know Catriona?' he asked, a smile playing round his face as he imagined her response to Mr 'Properly.'

'I love her,' came the perhaps inevitable reply.

'Yes, but do you know her?'

And that, of course was the unanswerable question. Would love be enough?

It was of course unfair, both question and answer. Knowledge might be power but it is only a component of understanding and somewhere beyond understanding is the place love sits - if it sits at all.

Jason Pryce and Catriona Christie were married under the beeches which formed the family tree. Metaphorically his name was carved into the bark of the tree next to hers, where she had always known it would be, as the branches entwined and the possibility became a moment in time from which another path was generated.

They married in June on the longest of longest days, and the world was about to turn. As it always was. And then they went on their honeymoon. They were headed to Wuzhen in search of the total eclipse of the sun. It was to be the longest solar eclipse of the 21st century. Or so he believed.

That seemed to matter to Jason. He told Helen,

'It'll last nearly six minutes and forty seconds, the longest in all our lifetimes.'

She didn't know what to say so she said, 'that's exciting,' though she doubted that it was.

'Don't say, wrap up warm, mum,' Catriona laughed. 'I've got Jason to take care of me now.'

'Take care of you?' Now Callum laughed.

'Do you have any idea what you've let yourself in for?' he asked Jason.

'I hope not,' Jason replied. 'It's an adventure we're writing together.'

And she kissed him.

'He's like the brother I never had,' Torquil said to Lauren as they drove back to Edinburgh. It was not quite Wuzhen, but it had its own appeal - then, to them. He kissed her.

'Are we now empty nesters?' Helen asked Callum, as she kissed him that night.

'Be careful what you wish for,' he replied.

'Are we still writing our own adventure?' she asked.

'Writing is just living in another context,' he replied. 'Our story is our story.'

'Did our story start with 1984?' she asked later that night, as she took the book down from the shelf, blew dust from it and opened the first page.

Even after 1984 there are still so many stories untold,' he replied. 'And the clock still strikes thirteen.'

Callum sometimes wondered if 1984 had been the narrative virus which found them as unsuspectingly perfect hosts. But he never said that out loud. He didn't want to spoil Helen's story. From Troy to Big Brother, she was right. Unknown stories abound. The stories are infinite and we are all parts of a narrative we cannot ever fully comprehend, because we are part of the context we write and read and live.

Stories are curious things. The beginnings and endings are clouded by the leaves of the trees. Nick had been at the wedding before he was even born. He was rooted to the family tree long before the fences were erected in the field that split the family from the forest. No one knew he was there. Apart from his mother.

Long before his sister became a mother, Torquil's own status changed. The leaves came off the trees and transient nature prepared for new life. The son became the father of a son. Unto them a child was born. Unto them a son was given. And what a son. He lit up the skies and asked all the questions that had no answers and answered all the questions no one knew how to ask.

Born on his grandmother's fiftieth birthday, his roots to the family trees were vital. However far he went, he was bound to something beyond himself. He nourished and was nourished by his roots. His breath blowing out the candles on a birthday cake when he was four blew out his grandmother's on her fortieth and again on her seventieth. He reached back and forward through the mists of time and made no sense of anything. And finally, he found his place in a world. His world. Lost and found. This is the way the world turns. Like a circle in a circle, like a wheel within a wheel. Bang the drum, yin and yang.

Nick was fire. And fire burns. In any and all possible worlds, Nick's fire was like the sun. It shone on all around him, but to look directly at it was dangerous, even in an eclipse.

Some trees are chopped down early. In the possible worlds of the family trees, Lauren never made it past the sapling stage. She had a canker in her that no one could heal. She was planted but she never tapped into the root system of the trees who would have offered nurture. She was lost. She could not embrace the sun, even the part that was part of her. It burned too bright in her eyes and she turned away. She craved an alternate reality and there is a ready supply of alternative realities available in the ultimate expression of brand loyalty. She let go too easily. Nick held on too tightly. They shattered each other because the story was not to be of mother and son but of father and son.

FORM 12

Paradox and Meaning

No longer worried by what paradox means

a seemingly absurd or contradictory statement or proposition which when investigated may prove to be well founded or true.

the uncertainty principle leads to all sorts of paradoxes, like the particles being in two places at once

    Is paradox 'true'
    Is truth true?
    Is truth paradoxical?

What is the form in which you express, communicate, be.

    Some call it poetry. We call it word dancing.
    But word dancing is only thought dancing fixed

    The Ancients did not need to fix their words or thoughts
    That is the oral tradition.

    It is like the river.
    It can be dammed and it can be damned
    And in both ways it stops flowing for a time

    But rivers move.
    Rivers and trees understand quantum states of being
    We have to 'fix' this into something we call 'life'
    Which is only a part of the whole
    A staging post in the journey.
    The journey is Qi.

FORM 13

A Tsilqot'in Bear Cave

Inside, the cave was warm. Surprisingly. You'd expect a cave to be cold. At least that was Nick's expectation.

There was only a faint light, until Joe drew a curtain made from animal skins across the entrance and then it was dark. Nick's eyes struggled to adjust. His mind struggled along with his eyes. He said nothing but Jimmy caught his thought.

'We are not primitive. We know how to stay alive,' he said.

'Mostly we live in the disused mine buildings, utilising all the technology we have been given and all that you have brought. We share our understanding, co-mingling it in order to benefit optimally.'

'And most of the time that is fine. Most of the time no one cares. No one is looking for you and no one bothers with us.' Joe picked up the thread, seamlessly.

He spoke slowly, calmly, and his words wafted into Nick's very being as he listened.

'When we sense danger. When time dictates that people encroach, we go to the cave. No one looks for a man in a cave,' Jimmy said.

'And the cave is the place we meet to tell stories. So yes, in one sense, we live in the cave,' Joe added.

Like a song or a word-dance, Joe and Jimmy's voices ran back and forth. Their speech was accompanied by the beat of their drums - or was that just Nick's imagination?

'Bears live in caves.'

'No one living in the wider world wants to come across a bear.'

'A bear may kill you.'

'Can you outrun a bear?'

'You can shoot a bear with a gun.'

'But we don't shoot bears.'

'So when we live in a cave we have to live with bears.'

'The bear is not in the cave with us. Do not mistake me.'

'We have to live with the understanding of bears. With the acceptance of bear-reality. With an appreciation of bears.'

'Respect and reverence is the correct attitude for bears. And people too.'

Nick was sure he heard them say, 'Bears are people too.'

He felt a laugh bubble up inside him.

Bears are people too? What were these men talking about?

He looked at his grandfather.

'Do you have a problem with that?'

是不是

Deep in a cave, Torquil's mind went back to the awful year of Foot and Mouth. Of burning cattle. And further. To the naming of Lucy and Eric. And later, to Bah and Humbug. The sheep who had turned up, unexpected, uninvited, overnight on Christmas morning. No one knew where they came from. No one wanted to claim them. Except Catriona. His sister. She thought it was Lucy and Eric come back. She might have been right.

Nick and Torquil and Callum were together in the dark, lost in their family story. Lost beyond Hilbert Space.

是不是

'We do not fear the dark. We embrace the shadows. They are our stories.'

'A fire at the door to keep bears at bay, saying, this is my cave, my place, my space; is the same fire that might show us to those from whom we seek refuge.'

'Respect and reverence and welcome. Never fear.'

'But we are never cold, because we carry the fire with us. Inside.'

Jimmy was not speaking metaphorically. This was not so much sophistry, it was practical talk, aiming at practical living. At staying alive. At being alive. In a better way. Beyond linear dimensions.

'We take the embers of a fire lit during daylight and put them in stone. We place the stone under the beds on which we lie, and they warm us,' Jimmy said.

Nick sat on the stone bed. He could feel the heat. He remembered being with Nan. She had a name for a bed-warmer. What had she called it? A stone pig. Like a rubber hot water bottle but better. He began to relax.

'We have many ways of bringing light here,' Joe said. 'Old ways and new. Light is never a problem for us. We know how to see. When we are here, we do not hide. We are not in fear. We choose to absent ourselves from the dimensional reality, that is all. We go to a different place.'

'We lie here, in the dark, or in the light from the batteries. We tend to prefer a half-light as it reminds us of the older days, the days before.'

Jimmy and Joe were off again, that sing song, back and forth way they had. It was calming and compelling at the same time. They understood narrative.

'And in the cave we tell stories.'
'It has ever been thus.'

Joe picked up the thread.

'Stories are a ways to make sense. To make meaning. To share.'

'The story of infinity is told in many ways,' Jimmy said.

'Call it Socratic dialogue, or physics, or yinyang. Energy that is stored must be expended and then more work undertaken to store it again,' Joe added.

'Even renewable energy needs work to replenish it.'
'Look for the writing on the wall.'

Nick looked. He could barely see the wall. There was no writing. No shadows. No real light.

Nick had a question burning up inside him like fire. He was not yet a stone pig person. He could not reserve the energy within. When he had a question he had to let it out, like a flame.

'I have a question,' he said.

They waited for him to formulate it. Time, if it existed, stood still for a moment.

It was about infinity.

Those are often the hardest questions to frame.

'Can a word be infinite?' Nick asked.

No one laughed. They took him seriously. This was far from the world of Pryce and the Project House and Productive Work. This was 'real' life.

'You have to understand space differently,' Jimmy said.

'Are you ready for some cave art? Joe smiled.

It was his idea of a joke.

Then he drew his story on the wall.

'In 'my' perspective of space we have to allow that (p)= particle and (w) = wave,' he said.

'Then we have (wp) = wavicle – where particles and waves 'reside' together in a dimension. Accepting always that = does not mean equals in any real or meaningful sense.

'So as you want to know it, Words are (p) that can 'fix' – thus name is the thief of identity.

'Each word fixes. A string of words fixes, but the more words you use the less fixed you become. Meaning becomes divergent as you build the sentence. And before long there are so many meanings, options, nuances, readings, that you have lost the fixity and perhaps the identity.'

'Does this matter?' It was a rhetorical question. A question that is not a question. Revealing a deep paradox.

'Only if you live in a fixed world. A fixed mindset. And we cultivate fluidity. That is wu wei.'

'Hang on, that's a Chinese concept.' It was a thought. Maybe Nick's thought. Maybe not.

Jimmy continued: 'It's a story. We all have our stories. Our own myths. Our own ways of connecting and describing. And sometimes it is easier to step outside the known, outside the culture we think we know, the things we have fixed as belief and reality. Sometimes we have to go somewhere else to know where we are. Only then can we see the perspective we seek.

'So let us not worry about who thought it first or who said it first or who discovered or invented, or where it came from – none of that matters. All that matters is how you come to be in that part of the moment. And where you find your home.

'Words are (p) but they can become a portal if you look beyond the fixed dimension. Take them into (wp) wavicle status and through that immerse yourself; because it's not as simple as entering. Entering requires a fixed point to start from and we are trying to get away from points.

'Immerse yourself in what is behind the word – the 'wave' if you like, but the wave of infinity. If you see it from the perspective of linearity you are caught up in the world of mathematical infinity which will not help you at all. That is maths as language and the language is fixed (and, if I may say so, faintly ridiculous). It is a story but it is not THE story. The way that is named – or enumerated – is not the way.'

'And what about Hilbert Space?' Nick thought he remembered it had seemed important back at the other cave.

'Hilbert space takes you away from Euclid,' Jimmy said.

Euclid. Ah Euclid. Good old Euclidean geometry. A fixed world which made rational sense in the language of mathematics. Hallelujah.

'However, not 'true.' Not infinite. No use to us now,' said Joe.

'Hilbert space is a story for scientists. For mathematicians. For those number theorists who like to think of themselves as mathemagicians. Who create evil numbers as part of their narrative - but they are all just storytellers in a cave. And it's not our cave. Never,' said Jimmy

The answer to Nick's next question came before the question was asked. In the darkness, his grandfather spoke.

'You'll know it when you're there.'

'How?'

'She'll be there too.'

'And you?'

'Yes. But you may not always see me. It depends what part of the moment you're focusing on. But I'm always there. We all are.'

'So, like, you were always there? Watching me?'

'Always there,' Callum nodded in confirmation.

'Always will be?'

'Of course. As long as you live in the moment.'

'Believe in the moment?' Nike was puzzled by the word live. He thought he had a grip on belief··· but then···

'No. It's bigger than belief. Belief is the doorway but you have to walk through the door to reality.'

'Reality is what you choose to believe, right?'

He spoke the words he remembered hearing somewhere, in another dimension. He couldn't remember who said them. His nan, perhaps. It was the sort of thing she might say.

'Yes and no.'

Silence.

Finally broken.

'I have to go.' Callum spoke.

'It's not safe.'

Nick didn't know why he said it, or how he knew it. The words came unbidden from somewhere deeper and darker.

'Nothing is ever safe. Safety is just a word. It has no power over me,' Callum said.

He was going to fetch Helen. Nothing and no one would stop him.

FORM 14

METAL enriches WATER

Magnolia Walls

'Of all the birthdays in all the world, you send a cake to mine.'

She could do nothing but thank him.

'It wasn't me,' Pryce said.

'Oh, but it was,' Helen replied.

'You just didn't know it.'

They had just moments together, but sometimes a moment is all it takes.

'I wanted to come before,' he said.

'It wasn't your fault,' she replied.

And as he left the room, he remembered his promise and whispered in her ear,

'Your son wants me to tell you he loves you.'

The words were said and accepted.

'Is he alive?' she could hardly get the words out.

'I can't say any more.'

'It's enough.'

Though it wasn't. But it was a start. From a world where her son and her daughter and her husband were all dead, the cake offered something beyond ultimate hopelessness. The words offered something more.

If the cake had been a message from the past, this was a message from an urgent present. Which pointed towards a future choice. A possibility. Beyond hope.

And who sent the cake? Well, that depends on how you relate to the narrative. On how you construct the narrative. Mystery is just clouded perspective. Until you are in the right cave you will not see the writing on the wall.

Helen's mind could not fix perspective by looking at the magnolia wall. 'The Bubble Tree' wall might have held the answer.

But her daughter was dead.

Unable to believe that any of the people who were dead to her in the magnolia cave had baked and sent a 'real' cake, she accepted the more rational view that it must have been a real man, And Pryce was such a man. But Pryce was just the conduit.

It was another version of the story in which he had said he would take care of her daughter. Another version of the story in which her daughter did not die. She was in the wrong narrative cave in 2030. The conclusion came long before an understanding that the end was nigh, yet was infinity staring her in the face.

2005

In 2005 Helen and Nick were out in the biggest field in the world. It was February. Gloves were being worn. Happily.

'Is it really the biggest field in all the world?' he asked, still full of wonder at the enormity of life in all its aspects.

'It is the biggest field in our world,' she replied.

And family names are significant. Despite his avowal that name is the thief of identity, Callum led the way in the naming of things in the family geography. The reason being, it was quicker to find your way around if you created a family map. So 'scone top' and 'the biggest field in the world' and 'badger bottom' and 'bullock brae' each had their own stories attached and the stories aided the memory and helped the family ground itself in place and space if not in time.

The biggest field in the world took an hour to walk round when Nick was four. When he was eight it took only forty minutes and when he was eighteen it would have taken less than thirty or more than all the minutes in a day. Because he was no longer there to walk it, hand in gloved hand with Helen.

On the day they walked the field for his fifth birthday she had been talking to him about his twenty first birthday, which she imagined in the glorious sunshine of a snowy day of sharp flinty blue steel, unlike todays damp earthy brownness whose cold bit with loose, dank jaws not sharp teeth.

'We'll walk round the biggest field in the world and it will only take half an hour. Unless there is snow, then it might take as long as it takes now.'

It was her way of explaining the relativity of time and the phenomenon of growth and the impact of the seasons.

'And will we wear gubbs?' he said.

He laughed because by the age of five he could choose to wear 'real' gloves instead of mittens, and his choice was invariably to wear mittens. Fathers and sons only share so many traits. Or maybe Helen had learned a trick or two in the intervening years. She had knitted Nick's mittens herself. They looked like Beltie cow puppets. He loved them.

On that day, however, he took off his Beltie 'gubbs' and said, 'Nan, please put your hand in mine.'

So formal. So polite
She smiled and took off her glove. She put her hand in his. She felt his warmth and his love as they intertwined her fingers.

'Happy birthday, nan,' he said.

'Happy birthday, Nick,' she replied.
It was the thing they shared, above all else. A birthday.

'Are we twins?' he asked her.

'Why do you ask that?'

'Because my teacher says that only twins have the same birthday,' he said. 'But I told her I have the same birthday as you. And so we must be twins.'

In the rational world, explanation is everything.

'There is a perspective in which we are twins,' she said.
'What's a persp⋯ perspective?' he asked. 'Is it the kind of glass that grandad uses⋯?'

She laughed. 'That's perspex.'

'And is it not the same?'

She thought. 'No, perspective is how you see things.'

'If I see through perspex then I see things differently,' he said.
He was right.

She knew it. She just didn't know how to tell him the difference.

And there was no time. The gloves were off. The hands were being

71

held and they reached the gate. They left the biggest field in the world and headed for the family trees. Bleep and Booster, not long out of puppyhood, ran on before them, eager to drink from the hollows at the base of what was then known as the 'drinking' tree. Helen's tree.

'Why are birthdays important?' he asked.

He knew they were. He knew they shared this important day and it gave them a special bond. A bond that allowed them to go out in the February snow and walk through the biggest field in the world and stop at the family trees where he would sit in her lap up the thinking drinking tree and look at the world from a different perspective. So many words in a language that only they could understand because it was only their moment and we can experience such moments only if we live them.

She tried to answer him. In terms a five year old would understand. Terms a fifty five year old struggled with.

'Why are birthdays important? They are the one unique day we have. The one thing worth celebrating. You are only born once. That's the special day. And commemorating that day each year is an appreciation of your uniqueness in a world of homogeneity. That's why it's important.'

She waited for him to pull her up on words like commemorate, and unique and homogeneity. She was never one to indulge in baby talk. The 'gubbie gubbies' were part of the family story.

'Your father hated to wear his gubbies, he said they made his hands like sweating pigs,' she said.

'I know this story,' he replied, solemn. 'You told me last year, when I was a little boy.'

She remembered she had told him some time last year, when they were out on a walk and he had dropped one of his Beltie mittens and been inconsolable at the loss. Even sending the old dog back scenting had failed to find the lost glove. She had knitted him a replacement. He had been lost in love and admiration and promised never to lose a gubb again. He was happy to wear them on strings. Strings helped him keep his promise. And he knew, even at five, that a promise was something to take seriously.

That day, as they sat up the thinking tree, Nick voiced his thought.

'It *is* like sweating pigs,' he said. 'I never thought of that before.'

So serious. So young. So much to learn. So much to unlearn.

He had no need for the difficult words she had used in telling about birthdays. He simply transformed them into words that made sense for him. And that made it simple. We might all learn that lesson.

Birthdays were important because they were a special day. Cake and candles. A walk in the field. Making memories. Just him and her. And the dogs. Of course, always the dogs.

The sun came out. Nick smiled and shifted on Helen's lap. The dogs had finished drinking the tree dry.

'Are you cold?' she asked him. 'Do you want to go home?'

'So many questions, Nan,' he laughed at her. 'You ask too many questions. Questions are for people like me. Not for ones like you.'

'And what is the difference between me and you?' she asked.

'Young and old,' he said, as if he had solved the answer to the universe.

'But we share the same birthday?' she said.

'We are twins of different ages,' he said. 'So I get to ask the questions and you have to give me all the answers.'

'I'll do my best,' she replied. 'But you know I don't know all the answers.'

He smiled at her.

'Never mind, Nan,' he said. 'When you are old as the hills you will.'

She wondered when she would be old as the hills, and whether he was right.

'Tell me about what it was like when you were born?' Nick asked. After all, asking questions had been claimed as his right.

'I don't remember, I was very young at the time,' she replied.

73

'I mean, tell me a story about it.'
And so she did. As they walked home.

1960

When I was born my world began. Not the world, it was there before and it will be there long after. But 'my' world.

And in my world my dad and mum gave me a present when I was five years old, the same age you are now.
'What was it?'
'A napple tree,' she replied.
'That's a lovely present,' he said. 'And did it grow?'
'It did,' she said.
'As big as the thinking drinking tree?' he asked, looking back.
The tree looked smaller with each step, but he knew it was big. He understood something of perspective.
'Not as big as our tree,' she said. 'Our tree is hundreds of years old.'

2005

He smiled that she said it was 'their' tree. One word with so many happy feelings attached.
'How old was the napple tree?' he asked.
'When?'
'Now.'
'Oh, now, it would be fifty years old,' she said.
'And fifty isn't hundreds, is it Nan?' he said. 'I know that.'
He thought for a moment.
'What happened to the tree?'
'When?'
'In the story.'
'It grew and grew and···'
'And in the end?'
'The end?'
A pause.
'I don't know,' she said. 'I haven't seen it in many years.'

74

'Where is it?' he asked.

'In the garden I grew up in,' she said.

'Can you take me there?' he asked.

'One day, perhaps.'

She knew she never would.

But the half promise was enough for him.

'And tell me about what it was like when I was born,' Nick said.

'It? Do you mean the tree?'

'I mean the world,' he said, 'Everything.'

'Oh, everything,' she laughed. 'Is that all?'

She took a deep breath. It was easy to remember. The feelings flooded back.

'When you were born I saw the world through different eyes. New eyes. Your eyes, which came from my eyes but moved us forward to a new and different reality. New dreams. New possibilities.'

New pain, she thought but did not say.

'Was I a good birthday present?' he asked.

Still, at five, the world revolved round his own perspective. Everything was framed with him as centre. But the centre would not hold and he was learning to hold hands to stop someone else from falling, not just for the security it gave himself.

'The best,' she said.

'What happens after the best?' he asked.

'I don't know,' she said. 'I hope we never find out.'

'Do you know what my best ever birthday present is?' he asked.

'No.'

He turned round and kissed her.

'You, nan,' he said. 'Just you. And I am lucky because I got my best birthday present before I was even born.

She offered to help him put on his mittens.

He declined.

He took her hand again.

'I will never let you go,' he said.

And he meant it.

But he couldn't see the future, even the near future. And time makes liars, if not cowards, of us all.

Beyond time, however, there is another dimension.

At another part of the moment, the best birthday cake ever was made by a son and a daughter. And also, delivered by a husband and eaten by a grandson - even when he didn't remember those times in the biggest field in the world and the questions and the holding of hands and the promises made.

'Are promises made to be broken?' Nick asked Helen in 2005.

She wondered where he got his questions from.

'Nothing is made to be broken,' she replied. 'It just sometimes happens.'

'Like gubbs?' he said.

'Sorry?'

'If we drop them, like gubbs.'

She laughed. As usual. He was right. It all depended on the perspex of life.

2030

In 2030 these were memories she held close. The Ultimate screen was not a friendly screen to her. She kept these memories close in her mind. It was a promise she had made herself. Some things are not for sharing.

When Pryce left Helen their stories parted but there were no endings in sight.

Time moves in cycles, not in the linear patterns of beginning, middle and end. No more do narratives have to. The cycle of Helen's sixty years did not start with physical birth in 1960 but with narrative birth in 1984. And so the end, should it come, was due in 2044. In that respect, 2030 just marked a solar eclipse. On Saturday

June 1st. Literal and figurative. Narrative fiction and fact combining. There is always another point in the moment.

The next significant solar eclipse came on Monday November 25th in 2030. By which time many, many worlds would have turned and many, many changes would have occurred.

And Price and Helen would come to recognise each other through many different prisms of kaleidoscopic light.

FORM 15

Mind the Gap

It's time to open the circle.
It's time to look into the cave of your choice.

Do not fear the gap at the entrance to the cave. Respect it, as you step carefully.

One thing is certain, you will walk this way more than once.

And what you see will determine what you think.
And what you think will determine what you see.

As all good quantum theorists will tell you; the act of observing interferes with and irreversibly changes what is being observed.

Entanglement is the essential property of quantum systems.

And what does this mean for narrative? To get personal, what does this mean for you, hey, yes, that's YOU - reading this book, now! You are part of this as it is part of you. Even if you stop reading. Even if you burn the book. Even if you keep it hidden from your waking mind, now it's part of you. You are part of it.

A lesson from quantum mechanics is that we can't understand the nature of reality. We should learn to live with this realisation and accept we only have partial knowledge of what reality is. We must learn to let go.

Yet this lesson was taught thousands of years ago. It has been repeated in every place and at every time. It is the moment revealed in parts.
Western eyes don't want to hear.
Western ears don't want to see.

They cannot understand or accept the darkness of the Western Enlightenment.

Scientists spend too much time trying to explain, when all you need is to experience.

After all, at the end of the clichéd day when push comes to shove, science is just another grand narrative. Scientists know this. Science is a story, predicated on answers. To measure is to create. But what kind of a creation are they selling us? There are many gaps to mind out for and many people fall into the trap of thinking it is our purpose to fill them all. Some try to fill the gaps with the theoretical language of mathematics.

As the sun should not be looked at with the naked eye, so maths is the language of those who would wear, if not blinkers, then at least sun glasses. Of those who are afraid to be burned by the sun they are obsessed with harnessing. Who want to count and measure and fix. Not content with naming the unnameable, they want to count the infinite. They geld the stallion and call it 'horse'. They put a size on infinity. Their only poor achievement is a fixed 'reality', created hypothetically outside of the system it constrains by measurement. The act of measurement defines what is being measured. At least this is mathematics in the Western tradition.

By putting layers between the unknowable reality and their world, Western culture strives to contain and control and rationalise and fix that which cannot be caught. And so the gap becomes a black hole. A vortex into which we fall headlong, all the while demanding that our box is not a box and our system is not of our making. And that the world should bend to our will and all things bow down before us.

The desire to hypothesise out of the system we created is a will to power. We are just things among things. We are part of nature not the rulers of nature. We have no position of privilege unless we make it so. The world is as we make it And if we create it as a system, we live within that system. How many times and how many ways can one say this.

This is the reality paradox. Be mindful of gaps. Especially the gap between
      language and thought
      Words and ideas
      言 和 思想

If you step over them into the cave which houses the walls of discourse on the nature of linguistic meaning, you may find that the only reality of linguistic science is the word. Its embodiment is its reality.

  书不尽 言　shūbùjìnyán
  Writing cannot fully express words

  言 不尽 以　yánbùjìnyì
  Words cannot fully express what is in my heart

This is truth in any version of language.

In this cave you will find angels dancing on the heads of pins, who are also wont to argue/disagree that Chinese does or doesn't have a written alphabet. They are lost in symbols and signs and they try to box up alpha-beta- para-doxia in shiny packages that only the intellectually wealthy can open.

That these angels cannot agree on language and its purpose surely serves as a great example that 'the way that can be named is not the way.'

But the cave of Western linguistics is every bit as dank as the cave of Western philosophy. The walls drip with symbol and sign and signifier and sleazy sentences struggling to survive, all of which are lost in the translation beyond words into the moment beyond meaning.

Which brings us to the gap of truth -or is it a gap of credibility?

Truth might be defined (in a box) as a recognition made in any culture by any generation.

And yet. Over timeless time we discover the same questions. The same needs. Progress is impossible in a timeless environment. So if you must aim, aim for depth not direction. The destination is in the journey. All moments are one moment. Perhaps the same thing is said in many ways because there is only one thing to say and that is everything. And the journey is finding your place in the moment, where everything you feel is everything you are; where you become part of the dao. This is life. Some consider it a burden they carry. Some wear it lightly. Either way, what you are looking for is what you carry with you, mostly afraid that somehow what is behind you will catch you up and crush you, until one day the load is lifted and there is no way back. In that moment you may find you are not tapping yourself on the shoulder or patting yourself on the back.

From small to big, from dark to light, from lies to truth.

When you look behind and come face to face with yourself, there is no more fear.

If you let go.

You just are.

In all dimensions.

This is Qi[M]

Not all questions have answers.
Do all questions have answers?
Is this the question paradox?
And does it matter?
Is this a question?
Quantum entanglement is timeless infinity.
Nothing matters except while you are doing it.

These are not answers.
Nor are they questions.
Or statements.

They are cave writings.

FORM 16

A Quantum Cave

In the cave of quantum hermeneutics, it is written: The world of Philosophical Relations is one of interpretive boxes, literary and philosophical.

Imagine that Laozi and Heraclitus, two men who are not allowed to exist, met in a cave.

What would that conversation be like?

What would they talk about? Certainly not their existence or otherwise.

Grand words like ontological and existential and hermeneutic are just graffiti to their minds. These are words that obscure, as they promise to clarify, but they are not used productively as paradox or analogy, or to shine lights on potential paths home.

Herclitus says: you cannot step in the same river twice.

Laozi says: Am I Zhuangzi dreaming I am a butterfly or a butterfly dreaming I am Zhuangzi?

Heraclitus says: Language is slippery.

Laozi says: The writing is on the wall. Who can see it?

And the crowds nod their heads sagely, thus proving not only that they are not sages, but that they exist even less than these men, who we can never know until we listen to the parts of the moment beyond the words, with our heartmind.

'Is Laozi Zhuangzi?'

You might as well ask

'Is Heraclitus Homer?'

Name is the thief of identity.

A flexible author once said: - or perhaps we should just say; 'it is written', which covers the same ground: Language is a tool to hold ideas. Once ideas are conveyed, language is forgotten.

The ancients understood the value of the open circle. Of the flexibility of chapters. They understood that the text is open, not unstable. That the meaning of words is found in their mutual spirit. That behind the author is a person. Many people. That 'behind' is simply a positional word. A perspective. A preposition which is also an adverb. Grammar is not the be all and end all. Language is not just a game. Metaphor fills the gap between language and thought. The roles of speaker and listener are as endlessly reversible as the pronouns that depend on them.

A voice in the dark shouts out: How croaks the raven?

And the shadows on the wall ask if hermeneutics is simply an attempt to take the text out of the box.

What do we mean by raven?

The creator. The destroyer. The trickster.

It's culturally relative.

A bear might as well ask, What do we mean by bear?

The bear knows.

And you, if you meet a bear, you too know what it is and who you are in relation to it.

When you meet a bear you understand that the ancients transmute fear to reverence.

We might show such respect for the ancients.

The writing on the wall says:

Reverence is fear let go.

Respect is an acknowledgment of one's own insignificance.

Behind the author is a person. Many people. And sometimes they are editors.

In a light-filled cave once we asked: Did the Pearl Poet write The Pearl? Or not?

That is a question worthy of Laozi and Heraclitus. They applauded us from the cave of non-existence which paradoxically is the cave of daoist literary hermeneutics. If you must put a name to things.

We did not need to name names.

We just laughed.
What if written language is a metaphor?
Is there a quantum raven in the box?
The destination is in the journey
The question is in the answer

So we do not need to know whether Zhuangzi is a fictionalist, or indeed what philosophical fiction is - like a bear - you'll know it when you meet it head on. Reading is an interactive process between reader and text, and reader and author and reader via text. As Shakespeare said and didn't say: 'remember the narrator.'

Questions of authorship are like words blowing in the wind.

Heraclitus and Laozi and Zhuangzi simply lead us back to ourselves in their games of paradox. Only connect.

Laozi said it all, even though he probably never existed and two thousand years later, Li Zhi said much of it again - and people, real and imaginary, have been saying the same words ever since. In every language. And yet the ears are still blind and the eyes are still deaf. Language is a paradox. Heraclitus knew that. He knew the only dao to follow was to search the selfso. All this happened long before Heidegger alerted us to the instability of meaning. People fear paradox as they fear chaos. Even Schrodinger kept his cat firmly alive and dead within a box. In Chasing Waves we opened the box, all the boxes. And flew back to ourselves.

Zhuangzi said the author was dead, long before Barthes had his moment in the sun. Heraclitus knew that there was no way to verify whether the reader's understanding matches the author's intention. And anyway, this is just part of the process. The temporality is not important. The 'order of things' is not important.

Long before? It's just a metaphor for a different part of the moment.

85

However long you try to gather Bamboo Strips and fragments, you will never read them all. You cannot step in the same river twice. The way that is named is not the way.

The writing on the walls are shadows, when you look with your eyes open.

Sometimes we see most clearly with our eyes closed.

Because all the answers cannot be written,

Nor yet all the questions.

Each culture and age has its own stories and its own ways. Ultimate social media was early identified as soma. And we called this our freedom. Our democratic right. To speak without being heard. To share without giving. To befriend without knowing. To use words as we like, to fight and sell and consume and proclaim and never, never to consider whether all that we really know is our ignorance of where and who we are and what and why. And all the questions in the world are lost in the pictures of cute cats and the process of selling the shiny new brand of loyalty demanded in the ultimate dystopia.

The writing is on the wall and those of open and complete spirits can read that bears and ravens and non-existent philosophers and everyone with hearts to see and eyes to hear will find a way out of dystopia through the cave of utopia.

And this is where we live without fear.

And this is a cave I would happily sit in to hear the stories of all moments.

精神 舞

Meanwhile, in another cave, the literary theorists set up camp. They deal in instability. Their boxes are, as we might say, on shoogly pegs. And in their instability, they are grasping. They grab at the bamboo strips. They grab at any part of a text they can hold. They limit texts and creativity itself by attributing value and structure and reason. They create words and signs and symbols and beat everything to death with their intellectualising of meaning and their fixing of meaning in fetish words like semiotics and signifier. Sneakily small sounding substance soaked symbols.

Intertexuality is the battleground of meaning. The Postmodernists are our own Terracotta Warriors made flesh. By championing radically plural texts and liberating the disruptive force, that which they seek to disrupt becomes its own code.

In this sense literary theory is a metaphor for capitalism, the giant which consumes itself.
   Is that analogous enough for you?
   A simile stands between is and becomes.
   A metaphor leads to the paradox path.

Barthes tried to recreate the box - changing reader from consumer to writer. Barthes was dancing round paradox but his eyes were not fully open. He was trying to create a new language. He railed against the predictable cultural codes of readerly texts while creating his own version of Schrodinger's box. All the while breaking paradox into para and doxia and thinking he was doing something more than missing the point.

Still, the paradoxical text admits that culture is a contested term. But the radicalism of what may be called the 'post-perfect' world is not the same as speaking truth to power. Not even analogous.

The privileging of intellectualism is the act of creating power in one's own image.

And we should know that humans are simply things among things.

Literary criticism is so much stumbling around in a dark, dank, slightly musty cave.

Analytic philosophy is no more than making boxes to sit in and on and throw at other people.
Quantum physics is a desire to write on the walls while sitting inside boxes made by analytic philosophers.

If you happen to find yourself in these caves, I suggest you don't sit on the box or open the box. Look at the shadows for the writing on the wall left by Laozi and Heraclitus, beyond fiction and/or fact:

> You can't find Dao in the words
> The way is not in the words
> Not even in the pattern of the words

In the world of the empirical author, a literary text is ontologically an empty structure which derives its meanings from the omnipresent Dao.
> Which simply stated says:
> You can't get there from here.
> We do not need to lose ourselves in the words.
> To find ourselves, we need to lose the words.

FORM 17

WATER puts out FIRE

Magnolia Walls

Memory plays tricks on you. That can be a good thing. Invented memories can be re-purposed as the stories we want to have told ourselves. The worlds we want to have inhabited exist and are shared simply by using words as tools.

As Zhuangzi said, 'words are not just wind; words have something to say.'

It was Nick's twenty first birthday. Helen's seventy first. Imagine. Just imagine.

'We should have a cake, nan,' he said.

'Of course we should. And a party.'

She wanted so much to have a party.

'Who will be there?' he asked her imagination.

'They will all be here,' she said.

If she wished it hard enough, it would be true. In some possible world, there would be a party. Just not this one.

He listed the people who would be at the party. He gave them their individual names, not their family labels. Helen, Callum, Torquil, Catriona and Lauren,' he said.

He was about to start inviting all the dogs they had ever owned, when she stopped him short.

'Why would you want your mum at your birthday party.'

'Because she is part of my story. Part of my life.'

'Not the best part.'

'But from another perspective.'

The conversation of the imagination was an easier one to have than any reality would allow. But still Helen feared she was putting words in his mouth by bringing them from her mind into being.

Beyond memory. After truth.

She stood back and allowed father and son to talk. Was it in her mind's eye? Or was it in a version of reality she had no real access to? It was as if she was behind a perspex sheet. In a magnolia cave.

There was another cave, in another dimension in which father and son were sharing words and thoughts she felt belonged somehow to her.

'You loved her once,' Nick said.

'And I hated her once,' Torquil replied.

'Can't we get beyond that?'

'She killed my sister. She stole you away.'

'Yes, but.'

'There's no yes but,' Torquil was firm.

'It's my party.'

'I know.'

'So let me have this. Maybe she'll surprise you.'

What father can deny his son even this? Whatever the personal pain. However much he did not want to believe that part of his treasure could never be wholly his.

But how to let go?

'I don't imagine she would even come.'

'Would? Don't you mean will?'

There's a huge gap between those two words and concepts. It's bigger than linguistic form or moral value. It's··· possibility and reality. Wave and particle.

'If you stare at the wall for long enough···'

Lauren and Catriona turned up at the party. They brought presents.

Catriona fell into the arms of her father and Lauren fell into the arms of her son.

'I am so sorry,' she sobbed.

'It's okay mum,' he replied.

'No it's not okay,' she said. 'I should never···'

'Forget it,' he said. 'I have.'

'He hasn't,' she said, looking at Torquil.

'You can't forgive what you can't forget, right?'

'We have to be beyond that.'

We don't cover ourselves in glory with every moment we live and we all do things we will regret. Some of us live to regret them. Some of us don't. Does it matter who dropped the glove? Or how or when or even if?

Forgive and forget.

But do you have to forget in order to forgive? Or do you forgive in order not to forget?

The truth of the matter lies deep beneath and beyond the cliched version of living.

Does it matter who made the cake?

You can't have your cake and eat it. This is a more false proposition than its original idiomatic construction; you can't eat your cake and have it. But the thing about cakes is this: Just blow out the candles and make a wish.

The party doesn't matter. It's the people who matter. We forget that. We argue over the detail and lay blame when we should just accept.

If you free the memory from the specific moment of error and shift perspective to all the moments, you will be invited to the party.

The sum of all the moments is bigger than even the biggest single moment. The wave encompasses the particle but we tend to let particles blot out the wave. In doing so we eclipse the sun. We need to open ourselves to the possibilities. Otherwise the loss will shield us from the thing we most desire.

And so, a birthday party in the mind. And in the memory.

Helen told herself: 'It could be like that. In my imagination it is. It's a possibility. And so it's a reality. Of sorts.'

In some time and place Helen spoke to Nick. The future and the past were meaningless in the context.

'Do you have the watch?'

'Which watch?'

'Your grandfather's watch.

'Yes.'

It's a time piece. It tells the time. Or a version of the time. Not a very useful one. While you look at the hands of that watch, you cannot be anywhere but in linear time. You have to stop looking at the passage of time like the hands on a watch before you can really experience time.

And she was hanging on to time.

Time to⋯

Let go.

In the darkness of the Cabrach bunker, out of which he could see even with his eyes closed, Nick told himself, 'It could be like that. In my imagination it is. It's a possibility. And so it's a reality. Of sorts.'

'Can't I at least tell her I'm okay?' Nick asked his father. 'Surely⋯'

'I mean, you sent the cake⋯ you're tapping into her memory⋯'

'I didn't send the cake,' Torquil replied.

'Then who?'' Nick asked.

Torquil decided to go the extra mile. Troy would harness the Immortal Horses one more time. He had got his son back. He did not want his mother to suffer the loss he had felt all those years⋯

In the magnolia cave Helen's screen lit up.

'Nan, It's Nick.' For the first time Nike didn't mind saying that name out loud. Standing next to Troy, he finally felt a sense of belonging, purpose, identity, family. He wanted to share this with Helen.

'Nick, how⋯ where are you? Is something wrong?'

Something didn't seem right but Helen couldn't work out what it was.

'I'm with dad,' came the response.

'What?'

'My dad. Your son⋯ he's here⋯.'

The connection was lost.

He reached out and felt her hand.
She reached out and felt his hand.
They both wished the perspex gloves were off.
She opened her eyes.
He opened his eyes.
They were alone.
In different caves.

FORM 18

Space and Time

You can be in another place. Just not at the same time as you are here. But of course that depends on your understanding of time.

Lost a thought
Lost a memory
Got it back

Can you see the shadows on the wall?
What are they doing?
Shadow dancing

Why?
It's what they do.

There is a cave for all time and all people. You just have to find it. Its name is Legion because there are many.

It was to a cave up in the mountains Laozi went, because he realised that people would venerate the likes of Confucius as a philosopher. Because they love order and hierarchy and don't understand that it isn't the answer. Or the reality. The theory of everything might be staring you in the face every day but people only see what they want to see.

The only limits are my imagination.
Imagination is limitless.

For me the only limit is my creative communicative competence.

Meaning?
That others have to find their own way. Coming together is a rare thing. And it's not equivalency. Or metaphor. But we live in those

worlds because most of the time we can't reach beyond those dimensions of fixity. We can't let go. First accept. Then let go. Then find.

You control yourself by letting go.

The quantum paradox of entanglement is as old as Chinese philosophy.

If you are counting time and space.
There are no numbers to count beyond infinity.
Quantum is the language, the alphabet, the story of the way.
Shouldn't that be ways?

When one can resolve the way with the ways, that's Qi[M].

The implied reader might ask the unreliable narrator the following question:

I wish you would explain to me what the symbol means.
What it means to me isn't what it means to you.
Are you sure about that?

We can only experience it how we express it.
We are stuck with metaphor and meaning and myth.

What is a 'real' character?

Beyond the death of the author, still the author exists as part of the narrative web. The paradox of authorship is part of the way of intentionality. Which is entangled with agency. Do you see?

The text escapes from the box and the author, reader and characters (both those in search of an author and those happy to be fictional) go along for the ride. Pandora opened a box.

I kicked my way out of every box I found by redefining it and in doing so, became a person, real and fictional, in and out of stories whose reality is in my mind. Is my mind.

There are multiple worlds inside my head. Boxes in the box from which I have been trying so hard to escape at the same time as yearning to be a brain in a vat. To be lost in the story of my own existence and non-existence.

Why have I felt the need to share these worlds - these thoughts? They seem to make up my identity - to validate myself in space and time.

And what I've learned is that externalising the interior landscapes is a dangerous path. In trying to validate myself through sharing I somehow lost the wholeness of my own identity.

The whole person is in the cave. The cave is all moments. The reality of identity lives in the worlds in the head which are a box without shape or form.

So what is this sharing thing all about?

Is it better simply to 'be' in one's own reality? How does one step outside of the worlds in one's head?

And is it really worth doing?

I had a friend. I called him a friend.
He didn't need to step outside of his head.
His communication needs were minimal.
He was happy where he was.

He would share on his own terms
But he was complete in himself and
Uncompromising as such.

Is this the lesson I need to learn?
Is this the person I need to become?

You lose something of yourself when you externalise your thoughts.

Finding the balance is the art of life.

And plot can get right in the way of the story. This happened. That happened. You said that happened before so this can't have happened. Open your eyes. It's all possible. All paths lead not to Rome but to ⋯ balance. If you let them.

Balance is not about teetering, it's about relaxation. It's not about being on the edge it's about being in the centre of reality.

And reality is what you choose to believe.

So when Wittgenstein says 'The limits of my language form the limits of my world,' he issues a paradox about the fixity of meaning.

An obsession with meaning will not help you to attain balance.

FORM 19

More False Premises

If you start from a false premise, don't be surprised when you reach a false conclusion.

'What if Plato was wrong?'

'What do you mean?'

'Well, the story is about how the people in shackles look at the shadows on the wall and then some of them get out into the light. Then they try to come back and the people refuse to leave the shadows.'

'What if the light was the Ultimate world and the people who went out there got caught up in it. What if the people who stayed and looked at the walls made the best choice?'

'And never see reality?'

'That suggests that outside that particular cave was a reality worth seeing.'

'Sight isn't everything.'

'No, but a sunny day⋯ who can resist a sunny day?'

'Perhaps learning to accept the dark is a better choice.'

She shuddered.

'I don't think I can ever accept the dark.'

'You do it every time you shut your eyes.'

'Yes, but that's 'my' dark. Not an external darkness. It's my choice. And I can always open my eyes.'

'But you can't control what you see when you open them.'

'That's true.'

They sat for a while.

'What if it's just the wrong cave?'

'Meaning?'

'There's many different caves.'
'So can you take me to the best of all possible caves?'
'Of course I can.'

What is the relationship between actions and consequences?

Watching the waves collapse on the beach. It's a metaphor. But what really is a metaphor?

What is equivalence?

You have to leave metaphor and mathematics behind. Or aside. Or apart.

We will go into many caves where philosophers meet. Where bears sleep.

And we will stare at the wall until the writing becomes clear.

Sometimes you see most clearly with your eyes closed.

And when your eyes are open, sometimes you don't see at all.

It was a beautiful view.
It was.
From that room.
I know that room too.

We shared it. Over time.

It was the best and worst of times.
Somewhere between good and yellow, I thought I understood. As they spoke about game theory, my mind wandered. I didn't realise then that if you learned game theory and played the game and gamed the system you won in the system.

The system only rewards the players who play according to the rules. It's a fact in the factual world which claims to be reality.

I think we shared the same cave for a while. A cave where light and darkness were less important than truth and lies.

Between belief and knowledge
Between you and me. Or you and I.

I feel that the logical analytical philosophers are in a dark, dank cave.
They throw light around in an attempt to reduce the fear
But I did not need their light.
Light comes from within.
Not from rules.

Their rules and reason and logic lead to hierarchy and to brand loyalty and that leads to the Ultimate world. They were as much a part of Ultimate as the paradox of the Glass Bead Game.

There they were, playing that game, every Tuesday at 11am. Thinking they were changing the nature of the world. Thinking they were explaining and understanding but really they were ruling the world by creating themselves in their own image. Gods of philosophy. The cult of analytic philosophy worships at the altar of logic and laughs in the face of those who take their metaphysics in a different direction - who find truth in paradox and whose points of reference are simply points.

Mostly they were clever young men. And one of them was a particularly clever young man. He had the temerity to take on the masters and he spoke their language. But it was only the words of a clever young man who wanted to be accepted by challenging the status quo from within. By adding his light to the sum of their light - by being in their cave. He knew he was not the biggest bear in the cave, not yet. In time he would game the system and rise in the system. But no one beats the system.

They all love Big Brother in the end.

Looking from another perspective I understand that in the hierarchy of the philosophers cave the biggest bears win.

And I was Goldilocks.

I was a quantum being in a world of analytical logic. They failed to teach me the self-referential aspect of failure. They tried. Repeatedly. And when we failed, they shut me out.

I was not welcome in that cave.

It was not my cave.
I learned that.

People who were in that room and people who had never been in that room, but were still in that room because we put them there, they are all the philosophers of the analytic cave. They dance on the heads of pins and think that makes them angels. It does not. It makes them people who dance on the heads of pins.

Dancing on the heads of pins is as pointless an endeavour as naming the Higgs Boson. Which leads, strangely enough, to 'finding' the Higgs Boson and that is the pattern of rational, reasonable science in the Ultimate world.

Some came to tell us that. I think Derek tried to tell me. I was so lost in the light I couldn't see his words or his thoughts. I could see that he scared them. Perhaps that was his appeal for me. To me. His wave rolled from East to West. My wave takes me West to East. Perhaps that is inevitable. Your wave must collapse in a direction away from where it began. If it can be said to begin.

He still scares them. Not wanted. Dead or alive. That much I understand. Though he scares them so much they have to let him into their cave. Sometimes they hold their enemies close. Sometimes not.

It was different for me. I was not a clever young man. I was not a philosopher who could sit in an analytic cave and criticise. I was beyond that. My face did not fit. My identity did not fit. My direction of travel was so much wave interference. How could I not believe in numbers? How could I not believe in money? How could I not believe in hierarchy? How could I not believe? I wanted to sing with Peter. In his cave. I did not know about caves. I thought we had left Plato in his cave and were chasing waves not putting labels on boxes.

They pushed me out of their cave.

From a different place now I see it simply. With no regret or recrimination. No darkness, only light.

I was always in my own cave.
And they are in their cave telling their stories

My story does not fit with theirs.
Until I inhabit a story it is not mine.

I am not interested in the naming of things
Being not naming.

I had no need for naming and necessity.
I was beyond the possibility of altruism even then.

Some enlightened people at one point gave ten percent of what they had. They called it effective altruism. I called it the identity of tithing.
In the caves of identity through economics

I gave and I give a hundred per cent of what I am.

Not every cave dweller welcomes that way of being.

Sometimes I wonder whether a cabin in a meadow is just a light-filled cave.

FORM 20

FIRE softens METAL

A Tsilhqot'in Bear Cave

In the cave Joe and Jimmy set up a chant.

And if we sit in the cave long enough···

The ancients used to say that if you stared at the wall for three
years, the writing would appear.
But what is three years?
What is time in relation to space?
And where am I?
Do you need to ask?
Yes.
When you don't need to ask, then you will have found yourself.

In the dark, Nick heard their voices, as if waking from sleep.
'The cave is the place we meet to tell stories.'
'No one looks for a man in a cave.'

Nick looked at the wall. There was no writing on it. There were no
shadows. There was nothing except the noise inside his head.
Nothing except the moments after death.

Transformation.

Nike and Pryce both felt it.
Nick and Jason both felt it.

There was no white light,

There was just word dancing.

There is a time when you are out of place.
There is a time when you are out of time.
There is a time when you are out of space.

When everything you are is everything you have.

And you have nothing.

Then you understand.
Perhaps you begin to understand.
But beginning is temporal.

In the beginning was the word. The word is danger.

Before the word was before the beginning.

Before the beginning was the infinite.

The shadows on the walls spoke out:

We have no concept of before so we need no concept of beginning.

We are beyond
Beyond beginning
Beyond word

In the darkness Nick and Pryce were the same and different. They faced the same experience but in different guises. Their paths were the same and different. Nick wanted to reach out to Pryce, to tell him it would be all right. That there was something beyond, after, outside··· but he had no words and the shadows dimmed.

Pryce heard a voice: 'We have to go different ways. I have already gone one way and you have to go another. It's all a question of perspective. And perspective is less about where you stand and what you see and more about who you are.'

Nick reached out beyond the words. He wanted to hold Pryce. But he knew he could not.

Pryce had his own questions. He must ask them of the shadows.

'By leaving danger will I find safety? Or is this just another kind of danger?'

Words played like shadows on the walls. The drum beat yin and yang.

So why did I have to leave?
You have to move to find stillness.
I don't understand.
Not to find stillness. To become still.
Stillness is infinity.
Immortality is beyond words.
Words bring legacy.
Music is movement but immortality is stillness.

Be careful of words. Use them wisely. They are tools.
Thoughts become words. Words become actions.
Actions have consequences. Consequence brings unexpected change.
Change explained by words is not change.
The vicious cycle. Or the virtuous circle.

You cannot always choose.
But I had to leave my home.
You cannot leave your home.
You are part of the family trees.
Always moving in order to be still.
Blowing with the wind.

Nick closed his eyes. Pryce was in the Cabrach Bunker. He had been there himself. He understood the confusion. The fear.

A people without a place are in danger.

106

The danger is when you are told 'seek and you shall find.'
I tell you, do not seek and you will find.
You are already in the place you want to be.

Desire as craving is dangerous.

The Cabrach was too close to the 100 men. Too close to the world of Ultimate. It was a place where there was something to steal and something to own and people to control and beliefs to requisition.

Nick could not clearly remember leaving the Cabrach Bunker. He knew it had something to do with an eclipse. He remembered the words from somewhere in the dark saying,

You are in more dimensions than you have awareness of. Become aware. Change the perspective.
And then the words in another part of the darkness saying,
When where am I becomes who am I?
And knowing that the words that spoke in the darkness were his own.

The chant continued:
Even in beauty there is pain.
We were rooted in the land.
We were forced to move.
We came back.
To another place that we recognised as home.
Home is where the heart is.
A whole Heart is spirit.
A fractured heart is so full it has burst open and the spirit bleeds into the world.
What is the matter?
What is matter?

When you know who you are
You will be where you are.

I wish. I hope.

In the darkness:

(Nick reached out to Pryce)

These are all dangerous dances to do with words.

(and he was gone)

Better be still.

He was back in the Bear Cave.

'Hilbert space takes you away from Euclid,' Jimmy said.

As if Nick had never been away. As if he knew who or what Euclid was.

'To understand Hilbert Space you have to begin with allowing non Euclidean geometry. Accept infinite dimensions,' Joe said.

Is it even possible? A thought. Not words. In his own head Nick was in the paradox of trying to hold on and let go with each breath. With each beat of the drum. Yin. Yang. Word. Thought. Action. Inaction. Wu wei.

'Wittgenstein, and you, want to hook yourselves onto a dimension, to 'fix' it with your point – your particle point – and yes, that will be the limit. Because that's the one word we let loose. LIMIT. Is that the key word in the sentence?' Joe said.

Nick understood then that philosophers and caves come in many forms and the philosophers in this cave were dimensions away from Plato. And Wittgenstein. And words and equations. And language and reason.

What do we mean by Enlightenment? East and West are never further apart then in this word as concept.

'You see what I'm saying,' Jimmy pressed. 'The more words you use the less certain your meaning becomes.'

So even an aphorism or an epigram are fixed in relativity,' Joe continued.

'The meaning of aphorisms and epigrams goes way beyond the

words.'

Nick looked at the wall, he saw writing appearing from the shadows. Symbols, not words, as Jimmy explained:

'Words are trigger points, stepping stones, jump off points, into the Qi[M].'

'First you must understand Qi[ ] and by that I mean you must allow the space to exist in every dimension between the brackets which are our understanding of limit.'

Lying in the half-light with warmth suffusing his back into his body through his spine, Nick was unclear which of the philosophers was speaking. It didn't really matter. The drum beat yin, the drum beat yang. The story was multi-dimensional, coming at him from all angles. He let go, and let the story wash through him. Not over him. Through him. It became a part of him as he became a part of it.

'Welcome to quantum infinity.' Joe said.

And the drum ceased to beat.

'When you inhabit the space and do not see the [ ] as any form of boundary, then you will find [M]

'If you seek to place your own 'm' into the brackets, you are being Wittgensteinian. You place limits when you possess.'

A pause for correction, or effect.

'I said 'find' m and of course you cannot 'find' it. You have to become part of it. One with it.'

'First you will try to view from your perspective. That is natural.'

'You try to find your way into the 'M''

Nick opened his eyes. He saw the writing on the wall

Qi[M].

It was even more elegant than that most lauded equation which had travelled through spacetime even beyond GRsΩHist or E=mc2. This equation had more dimensions. Can it be an equation without equivalence, he wondered. Then let go again. But let go with his eyes wide open. Now he would begin to learn.

'You will note that for this notation we capitalise M to mean 'all moments are one moment' and 'm' is the stage before this, think of it as a 'particular' moment.'

Was it Jimmy or was it Joe? Did it even matter? The words came from beyond a particular man, beyond a particular place.

'And this must be beyond wave - But it is also beyond the 'limit' of language and world. Here is how I choose to render it,' the voice said:

$$Qi[\quad] \quad \text{Quantum Infinity}$$
$$Qi[m] \quad \text{A moment in Quantum Infinity}$$
$$Qi[M]$$

You might see the first as the 'words' or the language.

Next is your approach –beyond the 'words' into the 'reality' or 'existence'

Then there is understanding that Qi[ ] 'is' all Moments.

'But even here you have to have moved beyond thinking of the [ ] as bounding or containing. It frames. Multidimensionally. But there is no boundary of [ ] or in [ ]. It is just a way to help you while you still need a place to enter. When you are there you will not need it any more.'

'You have to learn to look at symbols/language/words as simply a conduit.'

'The Way that can be named is not the Way. The Way is Infinity.'

'Does infinity exist? Nick couldn't hold the question in.

The drum beat yin - the breath is out.

'What else exists apart from infinity?'

The drum beat yang - the breath is in.

The light flickered. The warmth invaded. Time held no power.
Infinity existed.

FORM 21

Not Waiting but Being

Am I looking at a version of the Ultimate screen? I don't want to live through a screen. I don't want to look at shadows on the wall.
 So shut your eyes
 Go beyond memory

Prepositions aren't guides. They are just words that go before.
 Staring at the wall...but not waiting.
Time is different for waiting and for reflecting, thinking, acting
 (embrace the darkness)
The problem of personal identity over time can be resolved simply by time passing.
 (You are part of our family tree)

When we were young we approached it from the wrong perspective. We spent all our energies trying to understand and resolve pi. It was time which was the more relevant part. Not the definite particle. The wave. It took time to understand that!

 So what is this thing called meaning?

First we name it, then we find it, then we revere it, then we question it, then we abandon it, then we revile it.

 This is capitalism. Aspirationalism. Ultimate world.
 It is not the best of all possible worlds.
 It is not the cave I dwell in.

 I went back to the naming of things.
 How can it be that you find something only after you name it?
 Do you not find it first, then name it?
 Do you have to name it at all?

FORM 22

Possible Caves

In a cave. In the darkness.
Where you have to choose your point of focus. Where anything is possible.

Trees, like words, don't stand in isolation (except in forests where no one is listening)

Our family tree was known to our family as the beech. But it was really the beeches. And we all relied on each other.

There were six of us. But one day, long ago, two of the trees got put on the wrong side of the fence. That's because a field boundary was being established and ownership of the land was disputed and no one understood the relationship of the trees. At that point in the stories no one knew about the trees, and even you would wonder why there were six.

Our family, you say, is five. Callum, Helen, Torquil, Catriona and Nick. That's because you are looking into the story at the wrong point.
Who is the sixth tree?
We'll call him Pryce. Or Jason. It doesn't matter which. His name isn't who he was. Jason Pryce will do.
And who ended up on the wrong side of the fence?

Assuming there was a 'wrong' side.

Catriona and Jason Pryce.
Why?
There are many stories that will tell you an answer to that.
But which of them is true?
All of them are true.
At the same time?

Not at the same time, no.
In the same space?
Remember your quantum theory please.

One day in one of the possible worlds of the story a man came and chopped down the trees in the field. To make way for more barley, I suppose. Or just because he could. There was a reason, possibly many reasons. But from our family point of view, none of them were good.

In the best of all possible worlds, Catriona marries Jason Pryce and together they build happy endings. No trees would be cut down. But in the best of all possible worlds would Lauren cease to exist? Without her there would be no Nick. And when a tree is felled in a distant forest, even unobserved, it is said the butterfly effect is felt. An element is lost and without all the parts of the whole there is no whole.

What happens when characters and authors and narrators and readers real and implied sit in the cave together?

'Who is Godot?'
Godot is who or what we are waiting for.
The narrator?
Is the narrator a part of the story?
Is the narrator Godot?
Or Qi.

They can't all be in this cave.
So some things are impossible in the best of all possible worlds?
Impossible is such a difficult concept.

'Let's just say some things aren't. At the same time,' the narrator said.

114

So what you're telling me is that we can't all be in the same cave at the same time, because someone mucked around with the order of things (or the disorder of things) and chopped them down and displaced them, or changed their being, or trajectory or part in the story…

If that's how you can best understand it, let's go with that.

Okay.

Infinity allows all possibilities but the space-time continuum of the stories we are able to imagine in the space of the thoughts we can convert into words at any time we fix them means, effectively, no.

Once upon a time, when that happens, the easiest thing is to accept that you don't know. That you don't understand. That it's not where you are just now. Which is the equivalency of saying - it's too difficult for you to process or engage with, or deal with. Let go. Just let go. Then you'll be surprised what happens. If you never let go you'll never be surprised and if you're never surprised you always know what's going to happen and so only a very few of the things that could possibly happen ever will, because you are bound by what you expect to be the case. Which is a case but not all the cases in all the dimensions of quantum infinity.

She was lost. Outside and inside.

I used to love the light, because I could see most clearly. But there's something in the darkness, something else that you can see. Like looking up at the stars, pin points in the distance but burning so brightly.

'Always moving,' the narrator said.

Sometimes when you leave the cave it leaves with you. Sometimes the sun and moon are both blotted by clouds.

Sometimes on a clear, starry night, when anything is possible, all connections are there to be made. On such a night, if you take stars into the darkness of the cave, you will find the family trees.

'But I will not be there,' Helen said.

FORM 23

METAL chops WOOD

The Cabrach

'Have we met before?'

Something about the voice seemed familiar to Pryce. He just couldn't place the man.

'Quantum question theory. Nike asked you about it. Do you remember?'

Pryce felt like he remembered everything about Nike, right up till the moment··· he hated to say the words. He hated even to think the thought. He steeled himself: Up to the moment he died.

He noticed he was sweating.

'You remember?' the man pressed.

Pryce was captivated by his eyes. They were so familiar. So··· so like Nike's eyes.

'He was like a son to you, no?'

Pryce wondered if the man could read his thoughts.

'Who are you?' he asked.

'He made you feel like a father.'

It was a statement not a question.

And what is it to be a father? It was a question Pryce had asked himself many, many times. He remembered how Nike had made him feel. Proud. Trusted. Good. And the grief when he died. Nothing had ever felt like that. He had not let it show but it was like it had killed a part of himself. Or maybe it had brought a part of himself alive. The desire to fight back. Even when he knew it was pointless. Even when every part of him wanted to give in. Somehow he knew that he had had to continue. Even when it made no sense.

And now, here he was. Facing the unknown. Waiting for Ultimate.

Pryce had assumed that a father would be prepared to do anything for his son. To die for him if necessary. But Nike had not been his son. He had been a boy who shone bright, and for whom he had taken risks; who had amazed him and confused him and charmed him and aggravated him. In whom he saw much of himself and something far beyond himself. But he was not his father. He knew that. He had not been prepared to sacrifice himself. And Nike was dead.

Out of the darkness the man spoke again.

'Do you remember the tutorial on Quantum Question Theory? "So, what is the purpose of UTheory $\sum$ ®?"'
It was not just Nike's question.
That's when we met.'
'We met?' Pryce was confused.
The aim of Question Theory is to produce data which helps the ULTIMATE® system refine itself.'
The man quoted the definition Pryce remembered working on with Nike, just before···
'You felt like a father then.'
Again, not a question, a statement.
'How did you know?'
'I was there.'
'But how?'
'Cogs in a wheel, right?'
'Why am I here?'
'Our boy.'
'Our boy?'
'Nick.'
'Nike?'
'In one world he is Nike, but in my world he is Nick.'
'He was your son?' Pryce asked.
'Nike is your son.'
'I was never his father,' Pryce said.

118

It was only when he said the words that he realised how much he had wished it had been true. To be a father. To be Nike's father. That would have been something worth living for. Something beyond the pain and bitterness and emptiness. In a split second he had an idea what being a father meant. The emotion all but overwhelmed him. He added:

'If I had been, I would have sacrificed myself.'

'What?'

'I was not prepared to sacrifice myself for him.'

The admission impacted like a bullet in his chest. Pryce felt sick. And somehow more real.

'It's not about sacrifice,' the man said. 'It's not about whether you would die for him. Whether you would try to trade your life for his. Life isn't a transaction. It's about love. And love is not about sacrifice. You can't trade your way into and out of emotions.'

'But Nike is dead.' Pryce felt that for all the man's sophistry, this was a fact that had to be acknowledged. It was a truth. His truth.

'That is just one part of him. The same part of you has died. Think of it like trees… death is just part of a larger process.'

Pryce struggled to take it in.

'Oh, come on. You taught the theory: the principle of UTheory $\sum$ ® is the acceptance that the theory changes as the system changes. The system has changed. We have changed. The theory, therefore, changes. It's not about life and death. It's all a matter of perspective. Of where you are. Of who you are. Of the choices made and not made.'

There was a silence. An expectation to respond.

And so Pryce looked firmly into the man's eyes, even though he felt a fear.

The man reached out. Pryce braced himself for the hit. This was the man he had let down. The man he had dreamed of being but failed to live up to. How could he be forgiven? Ultimate had stolen this man's son, and he had been responsible…

The father grasped Pryce's hand and shook it hard.

'And now it's my time to thank you.'

'I don't need thanks,' Pryce said, shocked. 'Your son died. You told me. I remember.'

'It was part of the deal. You told my mother. You kept your part. Now I'll keep mine.'

'What is that?' Pryce asked.

'Opening the door to choice.'

'What choice is there?'

'Reality is what you choose to believe,' the man said. 'Do you believe that?'

'Are you going to kill me,' Pryce said.

He had assumed the man was there to kill him. He was ready for that. But that was when he thought he was from Ultimate. Now···

'You're already dead,'Torquil said.

Pryce was stunned.

'Feels good, doesn't it?' Torquil laughed.

So death was not the end. Or even an end. Or this was not death. Nothing made sense. He had no idea where he was, but even more he had no idea who he was any more.

'So what is my name··· now?' Pryce asked.

'You want a birth name or a given name?'

'I can pick?'

Torquil smiled. 'We can all pick who we are,' he said. 'It's the one choice they can't take from us, no matter how much they think they can.'

'I don't...' Pryce was overwhelmed.

'To them, now, you have ceased to exist. So now you really live.'

'Without a name?'

'We can call you Jason,' Torquil said, 'because your journey is not yet over. There is unfinished business for you···'

'Jason?' He tried it over in his mind and his mouth.

'Yes, I can live with that.'

It had a familiarity about it.

Jason paused, understanding the ridiculous enormity of what he had just said. Live. A small word, but he felt more alive than he had for decades. Here, in the darkness, with a stranger.

'And now what?' he asked.

'Take yourself back to the world before Angela. To the man you might have been. If you had followed another part of the story. In that world you might have had children. A boy and a girl. There's a boy and a girl who need you. Who have also been uprooted. You need to plant yourselves somewhere new. You have to lead the way for them. They are young.'

'So am I not coming with you?'

'You have another place to be. With them.'

'And Nike?'

Jason, as he now was, knew as soon as he had said the name that he had let go of 'his' boy.

'Nick's safe with me,' Torquil said.

'And who am I to you?'

You are part of our family tree. The words were never said, but whispered like the wind words they were.

In the deep light of the darkness an answer was unnecessary.

They were brothers. They had both been father to a boy.

But their paths were now different. They had come together just briefly, to pursue a greater aim, but now was the time to part.

'Can I see him again?' Struggling to identify as Jason, Pryce felt he could not leave without at least asking this question.

From behind him, out of the darkness, a voice came. A recognisable voice.

'Hey man··· you're here···'

He could feel the boy standing right beside him. He wanted to look, but he knew that if he did, Nike would not be there. He could almost taste and smell his presence. But he dared not look. He tried to stay light.

'You got any questions for me?' Pryce asked.

'Got some answers,' the boy replied.

'You don't need me then,' Pryce said.

'They need you,' the boy said.

'They?'

'Omo and Flora.'

Of course. He knew it.

'We all need each other,' the boy continued. 'Will you..?'

He didn't need to finish the sentence.

'Of course I will.'

'It means you can't see me again,' the boy continued. 'But hey, sight isn't the most important sense now, is it?'

'No? When'd you get so wise?'

'Spend enough time staring at a wall in the dark and you learn some stuff,' the boy replied, laughing.

Pryce wanted so badly to turn round. To see Nike. He had never felt so close.

'Don't do that,' Nick said.

'What?'

'You know.'

Jason looked up. Before, it had been completely dark. Now he was sure he could pick out some lights. Pinpricks in the sky. All the stars in the sky shone down. Every one a possibility.

'Hey, did you know? There's a flaw in their theory of everything.'

Jason laughed, 'I never knew that.'

'Well it's true. Cool, huh?'

Typical Nike. He had so missed the boy.

'But what does it mean?' Jason Pryce asked.

It was more a question to himself, he wasn't even sure if it came out in words or remained in thoughts. But he got an answer, almost before he had asked the question.

'It means that Ultimate does not control the random element. Which means there's a hole in their system of everything. You could call it a worm hole if you like. Actually, it's more like a sieve. There are holes everywhere. You just got to find them. And you don't find them by looking. You find them by understanding. So now you know. Theory only takes you so far. You have to live. Go find Omo and Flora.'

He finally realised he had been offered a choice. A chance. It was still hard not to feel it like a sacrifice. But that might be because he craved love so badly and yet understood it so tentatively. He still wanted to turn and embrace Nike. But Nike was gone. Nick had given him a path to follow. A purpose. Beyond Ultimate. Beyond Pryce. He was Jason.

FORM 24

Butterfly Dreaming

The relation of things.
A caterpillar cannot understand a butterfly.
Am I a butterfly dreaming I am a man or a man dreaming I am a butterfly?
I am both and neither, until I flap, or do not flap, my wings.
  Waiting, not being.
I am now only slightly connected to that person I was. And that does not scare me. Person is quantum.
  I am like water that flows.
  But I am also the definite particle
  This is selfhood

I used to fear non-consistency. Thinking that constancy somehow it meant permanency.

And death - the ultimate non-existence was a thing to be feared.

Now I begin to appreciate the relationship between part and whole

  First find your whole.
  Then be in it.

FORM 25

Best of all Possible Caves

There is no need for God in the best of all possible worlds.

That's quite a revelation.
Quite a shadow to wipe from the wall.

Let's just be clear. Leibnitz was wrong. The best of all possible worlds was not discovered by a Frenchman in a wig in the 18th century. Enlightenment values run so counter to any best of all possible anything, except to those with wigs and money. We can discount his version.

And so God has had his metaphorical chips?
Yes, or his jotters.
Depends on your cultural bias.
No God then.
No need.

As for Voltaire?

Well Candide was comedy, right?

But there are other books.

And some of them were written by men I knew. Clever young men. Philosophers in training.

I read their books. And I lived the writing of them, second hand.

I remember sitting in a room with one clever young man talking about the best of all possible worlds. Before he had written the book. Maybe even while he was writing it. In his head. Before the words came onto paper and became something you had to read.

Passage from oral to written tradition. From wave to particle. No more.

However much he argued against the gods, he was still well trained in the analytical tradition.

If only I knew it then, I was a quantum being in a light filled cave. I watched the waves collapsing on the shoreline and was wondering - what happens to snow where the sand becomes water - just as a philosopher said; 'and if you don't look, it collapses into a wave'. I thought he meant what I was physically looking at. He wasn't. He was talking logic.

And the clever young man was only concerned with the 'strictly philosophical' in his clever young book. He saw personal identity as an abstract thing whereas I always took it personally. Too personally perhaps.

In my cave, personal identity was my only security. It was the light and the fire and I was scared to stare at the wall and I didn't like the darkness if I looked out. When I looked in, I found light. But I always wanted to open the box. Not so much to unwrap it and find out what was inside, but to let what was inside out. I thought the cave was a prison. Of all the caves in all the world, there is nothing good or bad but thinking makes it so. You'll have read your Hamlet? You'll have had your tea?

And so clever men, young and not so young, spoke of identity being strictly numerical. The distinction between numerical and qualitative identity is crucial in the fifty six forms. And I did not believe in numbers. So I was lost. To them and to myself.

The clever young man nearly found the paradox. He understood that twins are not the same, they are two different people. But he thought that this was purely a numerical conclusion. Or, at least, that it was only numerical conclusions that mattered in matters of identity.

But hey, what did he know?

I called him Fardles the Bear. After Hamlet.
After Hamlet?
After Hamlet.

I gave a paper entitled: Who was Fardles the Bear?
It was a joke. We all did it. It was what made philosophy 'fun.'
So I gave a paper, I can't remember what it was about, referencing 'who would fardles bear?'
We all took ourselves so seriously in the world of philosophical jokes.

It's a by-product of thought experiments.

Let's not give the clever young man a name. He doesn't deserve to be part of the naming of things. Or even a number. Do we then deny him his identity? Does he then cease to exist in any meaningful way?

In a different part of the moment I found out that he wasn't who I thought he was, even then. I thought he was a doctoral student when I was an undergraduate. But I discovered that he was just a year 'above' me. The difference was, he knew game theory. He had the Western aura. Confidence. We sat in the same seminars. In light filled rooms where ideas collapsed into waves. He talked. I listened. There was a hierarchy in our philosophical tradition. Not always well earned but always well observed. Except once.

The one time I spoke out of place, the writing was on the wall… and my 'fate' was sealed. The fate that narrowed my possible worlds and had me standing in Tottenham Court Road in 1984 where we first met. Oh, no, that was not me. That was another version of me. The one I learned to call Helen.

An author in search of a character meets
A character in search of an author.
What is being sought?
What is lost/found?

Perhaps that moment, of speaking when I should have stayed silent, was what made me retreat back into my cave - alone. Into a world of my imagination. My own box.

Perhaps it was that I didn't speak when I should have. That moment happened too.

It was all part of the game. Or a game. The game was tennis. And the player was Smart. A man who had a careless yet significant relationship between name and identity.

He wrote about Time in 1963. He wrote that all moments are one moment, though he didn't say it as simply of course, perhaps because he was a tenured philosopher.

But I never knew. Not at the part of the moment when I knew him.

He came half way across the world to play tennis with me. No. He came half way across the world to do philosophy and in his down time I was detailed to play tennis with him. We played games. But it turns out, not the same game. A tennis court is also a box.

At that time he was in his seventies and I was in my teens. And he beat me hands down every match.

Was it style over substance?

It was simply experience of how to be in the right space at the right time. Made concrete in the practical world.

You can run but you can't hide. And you don't have to run if you know where you are or where you will be at any point in the moment.

I used to say to him, lamely, as a joke: 'I'm better at philosophy than I am at tennis.' I don't know if it was true and I doubt he worried about the truth conditional of my statements. We were just playing tennis after all. He was a philosopher relaxing. I was a student trying not to make an impression - oh, how the clever young man would have dealt with this situation differently - not trying, or just trying not to get my ass whipped. To salvage some shred of what I thought was credibility.

I have since learned, and forgotten and learned again, the danger of cool. Put paradoxically, it is not cool to be cool. Or perhaps it is that it is not cool to try to be cool. The further you go the less you know. The more you try, the less you succeed. Dao has all the answers. If you know where to look. Or more quantumly, if you know not to look.

Back in the story of 1983. A man called Smart was one of the authors of our text book. And that author was made flesh on the tennis court as box. He became real in a different way. I did not understand enough about anyone's personal identity to connect to him in the reality beyond the text book as box.

If I had known then how to do my research I might have found his earlier book (a book deemed too difficult for me by the gods of analytic philosophy and certainly not on my reading list) in which he states that time is tenseless. And then we might have had a really interesting conversation, given that my obsessive preoccupation at that time was not tennis, or making an impact, but the relationship between personal identity and time. Then I might have stopped running and met him at the net. Confluence might have been achieved. And it was. Just not in that moment.

Forty years later, and thirty years after he died, I read his book and converse with him again. I play tennis with him again in my mind, and the experience itself suggests to me that he was right about the tenseless nature of time.

We are together again. He still beats me hands down. But this time we meet outside all the boxes.

And Mr Smart's contribution, in case you have lost the plot, or thread of what is where and where is what, is that time is tenseless.

Thank you Mr Smart. Then and now, and in many parts of the tenseless moment you have come to my rescue, even while you beat me. Good humour, calm spirit and friendship. Then and now. I have brought you into my cave - but you were there all the time after all, weren't you? You didn't need me to invite you. Or to serve.

If just once I had said, 'in the best of all possible worlds I beat you at tennis' my life might have been very different. I would have entered a totally different part of the moment.

And now we are free to leave the cave.
To open all the boxes.
Mind dancing.
Wingless. Without shame.

I thought it was the possibility of altruism that would save me. I thought that clinging to the freedom of anarchism was my way. They were all particles but someone Smart showed me the wave. In the confluence of then and now.

I have been in many caves. I have opened (and closed) many boxes. We have shared. Those others whose names defy their identities. They know who they are.

Nothing else matters. Because nothing matters. Because nothing does not exist in infinity.

I discovered (when I stopped trying to understand) the part of my story that no longer seems to be real. The person I no longer am. The identity that has turned into a shadow of a self. And the paradox is that beyond this shadow - which cannot be soaped back onto a body - is ziran. Self-so. Am-ness, if you will. Deep am-ness.

I discovered that deconstructing boxes can be another way of building boxes. That all the world is in and out of the box at the same time. When Wittgenstein and Schrodinger fight it out, the dim light on the wall is of quantum entanglement.

And the ancients say:
If you stare at the wall for three years···

But you do have to be in the right cave!

First find your cave.
Then,
Go deeper into the cave, without fear.

Then open your eyes to the darkness.
Open your eyes in the darkness.
Accepting the paradox that the darkness leads into the light.

In learning the fifty six forms,
I stepped out of the wrong cave.
I sat in the right cave with my eyes tight shut
Thinking that all I could see was in my box
Making boxes of memory and metaphor.
No wonder I could not see the writing on the wall.

I had pinned all my thoughts on 无为 (wu wei) for many a year. It was my brand of choice. But as the fifty six forms deepened I encountered 自然 (ziran).

I understand that everything is lost in the translation
That even in sharing we have to let go.

I am learning a new language
And
I am learning language in a new way.

There are many translations to be found in many places - in the words and the symbols and also the places between the words which are more enlightening even than metaphors.

When I find these words, translated by another, I learn that from my beginning, from the beginning of my world, from the day of my birth I was a quantum being. In an atomic, deterministic, logical, analytic world.

In simple metaphorical terms: a fish out of water.

I used to try to be the best little particle I could be.
But I was never comfortable as a particle.
I have always been part of the wave.

The question remained. How was I to be in the river?

When I learn to translate for myself, beyond the language, then I will be in the river and more than that, I will be the river.

FORM 26

WOOD stabilises EARTH

There's a bond between a father and a son which even a mother cannot fathom.

The roots of the family tree spread many ways and nurture comes in many forms.

Even on the darkest of nights, a father and son can feel each other standing shoulder to shoulder. Sometimes they do not need to look each other in the eye. And however much they want to hold each other in their arms, they keep a distance. The embrace is saved for the women. When a father and son are men, especially when they are men who have lost each other along the way, their strength is shown in different ways. Their love is shown in different ways. Just as strong. But different.

Torquil and Callum Christie were a father and a son who could not face each other.

Words had been said. Actions had been taken. The words and the deeds spun through time make the web of existence on every level we cannot even imagine.

'I lost a daughter and you lost a son. Let's not lose each other,' the father said.

And off they went.

Before the sunset. Into other worlds.

Worlds of war as they both raged against the system.

After fifteen years of death on a farm and ten years of trying to deal with the consequences of these deaths, they took actions.

They both needed to learn of the seasons of infinity.

They both had the same question: 'Why must we sacrifice our children?'

But the answer was different.

Now they stood together, side by side, together as long as they did not come face to face. And they talked.

We lost our way.
Our pain isolated us, father and son.

Remember when we functioned as a family?

Torquil smiled at the memory.
'Dad, remember mum's birthday that time. You took her out and we made a cake. Before the decades of death.'
'I remember.'
'We were apart and then we came together again.'
'And will that happen again now?'

Twenty years of death and dying.
Twenty years of life and living.
Twenty years of transformation.

'Just remember, dad.'
'I have so many memories I don't know where to start.'

Callum had nothing left but memories, it seemed. The burden of the years had weighed heavily on his shoulders. The loss piled upon loss had the stench of death he had first smelled in 2001. He had never really recovered from that smell.

Then he lost his daughter. Then his grandson. Then his son. Then his wife. Then himself. Then hope. And so he stood, beyond hope, in the darkness, looking up at the sky. Beside the son he had taken with him. And then lost. Or who had lost him.

A father had to ask his son a question. It was not right. The ways of the world told him that as father he should provide answers, not questions. But he had no answers. He had given his life and the lives of all those around him to find the answers. And answer came there none. So now he had to ask.

'I'm asking you for us to be reunited. As a family. Together again.'

He wondered if his son had that power. He doubted and had faith all at the same time. And he knew that doubt and faith were the wrong language. But he had no words for what he wanted to say. So the son spoke first.

'Dad, if you can only have one person to be with, the rest of your life, who would it be?'

'How can I choose?'

And as he said it, he knew that he had already chosen.

The answer, as always, lay in the question.

There was one more question.

'Did you have to kill me?'

It was a question Callum felt he should have asked man to man, face to face, but he knew that if he turned, his son would be gone and all hope of a future would go with it.

'You came to the Immortal Horses. You wanted me to do something. I did something, dad. I did all that I could.'

'That was then. Now you are still killing people but bringing them back to life in another place. If you've done it for them you can do it for me.'

'Casablanca, dad.'

'What?'

'How did it end?'

'Sacrifice.'

'But we are better than that, right?'

'Are we?'

'Dad, I'm *your* son. I'm better than that.'

'So what can you do? Breathe life into us? Make us all immortal?'

Torquil smiled.

'Dad, it's already done. You just have to go get her. She's

waiting for you.'

Could it be that simple?

'Just let go, dad.'

Is it that simple?

'Where are we?' Callum asked.
'You know where we are, dad,' Torquil said.
'I only know where she is,' Callum said. 'And that I cannot reach her.'
'You can, dad, you can.'

We are scattered, like seeds on the ground, but seeds that have died because they were not watered.

'She's the river, dad.'

And he knew he just had to follow the river.

But before he went on his Odyssey, beyond his own understanding of name as the thief of identity, he had thoughts to resolve.
He had to learn to see time differently. Then he would be able to reach her.

And so he learned. His son taught him. And he learned.

A pattern emerged in his being. A pattern which would take him beyond the dimensions he knew of. And when he found himself, he would find her. And when he found her, he would take her and by letting go he would never let her go again. And he would never let go of himself. By letting go. The paradox of infinity cannot be completed. It is not faith or hope or trust or truth. It just is. Enter infinity. Be.

FORM 27

Personal Identity

When I was young I lived in a world. Call it a real world if you like. A world of philosophers. And I was obsessed with personal identity over time while others were concerned with the best of all possible worlds. Forgive me for repeating myself, it's a hazard when multiple parts of the moment come into focus in the timeless time.

The irony was that I was focussed on the wrong part of the equation (focussing on equations is wrong minded anyway).

And university tried to alienate us from our own culture, indeed our own being, by feeding us the literature of the intellectual; the alienation of modernism in a deliberate attempt to mould us into their characters. But I was always built from radicals.

Free radicals at that.

In looking for something I thought I had not learned or did not know, I discover I have known it since I was a child. More than forty years ago I read the very words but their meaning for this part of the moment was obscure.

Now, with a different perspective I read these words again, as if for the first time, and it is like coming home. All it took was time and space - spacetime to be in a different part of the moment and I am here, fully in the moment.

In order to understand personal identity over time I did not realise that what was needed was time. It was not all that was needed, but it was part of what was needed. As they would have said so proudly (if they had noticed this) it was a necessary but not sufficient condition.

When I was young I held onto my personal identity, close round me like a cloak.

Young people wear hats to frame their identity. Some people never get over that, or past that, or beyond that. Some identities never grow. They become fixed and fused and atrophy. And this is called safety, and security.

But I realised, after many years, that while my focus had been on Personal Identity over time

It should be
Personal Identity through Time.

And even then⋯

Over is hierarchical.

So - Through. Or should it be across?

The difficulty of words like through, beyond, over, beneath, before, is that one gets lost in prepositions and adverbs and classes and grammar and⋯ trying to follow the rules is the quickest way to lose your creativity. If you are me. Which I am. Now. And then

I suspect it has to be personal identity IN time.

Depending, of course, on your interpretation of time. Whether, for example, it does or doesn't exist. A wise man once said 'a text has both entering and departing strokes' and I am not about to argue with that. Whether the statement was made by a man who lived, or an author (dead or alive) or a narrator (real or implied) does not change my relationship to the words.

Open and close. Entry and exit.

Yinyang

138

As I have lived through the fifty six forms my grasp on personal identity seems much more flexible. I am more flexible. I am not the person I was who clung onto that identity. That identity is gone, even while parts of it remain. Identity is like skin. You slough it off in your sleep. You change without even knowing it. Till one day you are nothing like your old self, even though you are still your selfso - if you believe in ziran, that is. Otherwise··· I don't know.

It's your skin. It's your identity. You choose.

Am I an author or a philosopher?

These are labels. And in so far as they are just words I deny them.

I am all moments.

All the world is caves and all caves are boxes.

I always thought my way out of the cave was through characters.
But here's the irony.
I misread the writing on the wall.
Or at least, I read the writing correctly but I was looking at the wrong wall.

I thought it meant characters in fiction
It meant characters instead of alphabet.
The characters which are the gateway to the open circle.

I misread the writing on the wall.
Because I was afraid of the dark
I stayed in the light too long.
I explored and opened boxes.
I shared what I found.
I gave it away and because I placed no price on it
I was not valued.
It was not valued.

There is no value to lightshadows.

It was in the cave of literary theory that I learned I am not an author - living or dead.

It was in the cave of philosophy that I learned that name is the thief of identity.

I didn't sit in the right cave for long enough for the writing to become truly clear.

The message of short sightedness, the lesson learned by failing eyesight and the flickering of light taught me to shut my eyes in the dark and learn to see the writing clearly at last.

And the writing said MIND DANCING
And the writing said ALL MOMENTS ARE ONE MOMENT
And the writing said LET GO

I've gone so deep into the cave of Western thought that I have to throw out first principles. And with them I throw out the alphabet.
Start again from the character.
As you are reading these words.
They are simply the writing on the wall.
Sometimes we see most clearly with our eyes closed.

The narrator smiled. And said to an implied reader, 'I want to thank you for reminding me I am a philosopher.'

Now I see that I am a part of all that I have been and all that I have been is simply part of all I am in any particular moment.

I am wave and particle. Collapsing into a wave is a transition which no longer hurts. It is transformation.

Death holds no fear.

Self is not important.
At least, it holds no primacy.

And as the fifty six forms become clearer and more achievable I begin to see the relationship between individual and society, self and time, self and other, now and then.

And I see that paradox is the way.
At least paradox is my way.
Embracing paradox.
Being paradox.

I do not need to explain it to myself and if I do not need to explain it to you, we are together in the moment.

Explanation is negotiating our relative positions.

Sharing stories is meaningful communication in multiple dimensions.

We share our stories in caves.
And when we open the boxes
we share our stories in the river.
And we are the river.

FORM 28

Caves of Enlightenment

Sitting in a cave, we come to understand that there is more than one enlightenment.

What shall we say of them?

All the worlds are in the caves and all the caves are all the world. And all exist between possibility and probability.

Is it a question of West meets East?

Western views of Enlightenment are tied up with economics. Adam Smith. THE Enlightenment.

The definite article.

That should provide a clue to the error straight away.

It was an historical period in which science and reason were constructed as the pinnacle of human achievement. Skepticism and liberty were principles but founded on ideas of progress. The hierarchy shifted but it was still a hierarchy. From Enlightenment came Intellectualism.

There was some good in the thoughts of the Enlightenment. But they threw the baby out with the bathwater.

It led to individualism which leads to selfishness and unequal power.

Eastern enlightenment is much more fluid. Much less fixed. It is a journey, a path. It is unknowable except to the inner spirit. It does not manifest in architecture or profit and it dances to the tune of a different drumbeat.

There is relativity beyond culture.

God is an answer for a question that has no answer. In religion people strive for enlightenment as in reason they strive for it. However, true enlightenment is no more and no less than awakening to the natural state of being.

You do not need to seek to find.
You just have to let go.
Open. Accept.

To talk of enlightenment is to talk like a child. I want to be a farmer. I want to be an astronaut. If you talk of enlightenment you do not have it.

And where is enlightenment to be found?

Ultimate will feed you forever.

Ultimate has all the answers to the questions it is pointless to ask.

But you will never find enlightenment however hard you look for it. Seek and you shall NOT find.

Be and you are.

All we have is all we are.
All we are is nothing.

We are all we have.
If you have many possessions
this is your identity.
Nothing is everything.

Caves are crowded places. The walls are covered in writing.
  Inside the boxes are the stories.
  Open the boxes and the stories fly out.
  And you become the story and the story becomes you.

  If you let go.

The symbol for the river $\approx$ is also part of the non equation
$$Reality \approx *Qi\ [M]$$
  It is not the answer, or even an answer.

It is just a way to understand boxes and moments and caves and people and places and facts and fictions and beginnings and endings and··· infinity···

If you are looking for an ending at the end you are looking in the wrong place. And in the wrong way.

  We are beyond endings and beginnings.
  We are mind dancers.
  We are.

  Just let go.

FORM 29

EARTH blocks WATER'S flow

If stories don't have a beginning then they don't have an end either. But they do have a point where you can be lost.

And Callum became Randall became Odysseus and went on his journey.

He learned as he travelled.

Branches get broken and limbs are chopped off.
Beech trees are not bamboo. They have different root systems.

It may be significant.

He learned as he travelled.

Figure out what kind of tree you are.
How do you move out of the wrong forest?

Find your cave.
Follow the river?
No. Step into the river.
Become the river.

He went to the magnolia cave.
She knew him.
Not by his name but by who he was.

He took her away from there and they went together to places they had been before and places they had only dreamed of.

They sat together at the mouth of the cave. Together in the moment. In all moments.
'You know I didn't send you the cake,' he said.

'Then who?'

'If it wasn't you, and it wasn't Torquil···'

He smiled.

'Where is she?' she asked.

'I don't know,' he replied. 'But she is somewhere, out there, out on a limb as always.'

And Helen cried. But they were tears of joy not tears of sorrow.

'They are all somewhere but we cannot always see them,' he said. 'It is different now.'

'But it is freedom,' she said.

'Letting go is the price we pay for freedom,' she said. 'I see that now.'

'It doesn't follow the path of logic or rational thought,' he said.

'We are way beyond that,' she agreed.

'But then we always were,' he said. 'We just forgot it for a while.'

'A long while.'

'It's all relative,' he said.

And it was. It is.

Whatever you think about time. It passes.

She held his watch.

'I gave it to Nick,' she said. 'Because I thought it was a way to get back to you. If I let go of it, I would let go of you and if I let go of you, I would let go of myself···'

'And that is when I found you,' he said.

'We found each other,' she said.

He stood on a boulder above the river and threw the watch with all his strength. It glinted in the sun as it spun through the air and crashed into pieces on the rocks in the river. A kaleidoscope of timeless time, flowing as part of the river.

'You loved that watch,' she said.

'It has served its purpose, he said. 'Now time is no more.'

'The watch is just a symbol

To keep time in place

But we know time

We have no need of a watch.

We know how to keep time in our pocket.'

And she knew that he was right.

是不是

We have to find new ways to think about things. New ways to get beyond the naming of things. New paths and new patterns and new ways of engaging with ourselves in all possible worlds.

You might put a date on it. And if you did, it would be the total solar eclipse on August 22nd, 2044. At 18.31, if you are so wedded to time.

All moments came together from the Cabrach to Canada and the darkness fell. It was possible to look at the sun because there was no sun. And in the light of that darkness anything is possible. Day becomes night and dark becomes light to pinpoint a moment in all the moments.

是不是

Helen and Callum were found in that moment outside timeless time, he in the mouth of a cave, looking down at a river. She in the river, looking up at the mouth of the cave. Apart but together in the dog-eared day which usually passes from sunset to sunrise without so much as a whimper.

Of all the sunsets in all the worlds, you walk into mine.

'I never know what day it is,' she said.
'And it doesn't matter,' he said.
She understood.
'Remember the old story?' she asked.
'The fishing line?'
'Yes.'
'The one part of the story we didn't think about was the river.'
And the truth is in the river. The truth is the river. Our truth.
The answer was always in the question.

To look for more is futility.

And in the moment when all moments became visible she said

'Do you know my favourite?'

'Favourite what?'

'Time.'

'Time?'

'Moment.'

He drew her closer to him and breathed her in.

'It's when you can see the sun and the moon in the sky at the same time,' he said.

'How did you know?' she asked.

He smiled.

'Because it's my favourite too.'

是不是

We all see the sun in different ways. The beauty found in sunset and sunrise is surely the transformation in front of our eyes. The connectedness through spacetime seen every day but individually unique. You can't truly capture a sunset. You never fully hold onto a sunrise. You can't make sense of them by counting them, any more than by recording them. They just are.

They are and we are.

As a game, they shared a private language, giving Wittgenstein a chance to turn in his grave.

'You came'

'You called'

Lines from another story, and our story, and every story that ends well, especially stories which recognise there is no ending or beginning, only moments which are part of the moment.

Paradox is the path.

是不是

I want to be with them all again,' she said. 'But I'm afraid of caves. I can't go in.'

She stood in the river and suddenly he felt she was slipping away.

'Why?' he asked though he already knew.

148

'Sometimes we see most clearly with our eyes closed,' he said.

'Perhaps, but I love the light,' she replied.

'Dusk leads to darkness but twilight leads to early dawn.'

'I know that, but in between is darkness. Real darkness. I hate it. I've lived too long in the darkness.'

'You have just been in the wrong cave,' he replied.

'Some of us are just not cave-dwellers,' she said.

And she was right.

'If I have to go into the cave to see them…'

'You don't,' he said.

'I cannot stand being dead,' she said. 'Even if that's the only way to be with you. I can't do it.'

'You don't have to,' he said.

What frightened her about death was not dying. Not the concept. It was the actuality and the waste and the void.

The sense that it was the final inner darkness. Fear of an endless total soular eclipse. No more sun. No more life.

Philosophers deal in threshold arguments. But this was one threshold he could not carry her over.

'If I step into the cave, I will die,' she said.

'Reality is what you choose to believe,' he replied.

'It's what I believe,' she said. 'I can't follow you there. I can't be with them there. Whatever it costs.'

As the light faded on the mountain, she understood that it is never truly dark in the cave.

He turned and led her away from the river, past the myriad shining pieces of a watch which now was not a watch and for whom time had shattered into more dimensions than could be imagined.

是不是

There is always the river. She was the river. Quantum entanglement in action.

And when they were both dead, or characters, no one would ever know or care that

149

He loved the twilight.

She loved the dawn.

Or even that they were united in their appreciation of the moments when day and night co-mingled.

It didn't matter

It doesn't matter

What mattered was they had this part of the moment entirely to themselves,

是不是

And all the parts of moment come together in the river.

'I love you Helen,' Callum said.

'Don't fight it,' he added gently. 'Just go with it.'

And so she did. She accepted it wasn't about coming and going and waiting and leaving and living and dying. Or dark and light. It was about so much more than that. Beyond caves and boxes were acts of creation experienced in something infinitely more than the best of all possible worlds. He took her by the hand and felt her with him, by his side, at the mouth of the cave. And yet still in the river.

And another voice spoke:

Sitting in the mouth of the cave the warm sun encloses me in a cotton wool daydream. I can hear laughter coming up to me from the river. I can just see her through the trees, running like a hare and he is close behind. She's jumping up onto a big boulder beside the river and has her arms out, turning and turning. Her head looks up towards me at the cave looking and laughing. He stands still. I can't see his face from here but I think he's laughing too. He joins her on the boulder. They embrace. No, more than that, they fall into each other. As they touch, they change form and photons of light replace their humanity with multi-coloured streams - colours such as I've never seen before. I raise my hand to shade my eyes. The light gets brighter and brighter as photons collide with the most amazing bursts of energy as they scatter away into infinity⋯

the river. Beyond their words, in their world, I have found my way.

舞蹈无翼 无耻

We are all together and I have broken out of all the boxes and all the stories in all the worlds. Where everything is relative, everyone and everything is related. And all moments are truly one moment. We just call it here and now because here and now is where we are in our particular part of the moment. We sit in the cave until we understand that being in the river is the quantum leap that allows us to be what and who we are beyond space and time. When we do not need to cast the rod to catch the fish because we are the fish and we are the river.

Letting go is realising that all the worlds are not in the box and caves are not boxes. They are simply places of refuge until we can all dance in the waters of the river. And to suggest that that which cannot be spoken of should be passed over in silence is the prison for those who believe that the limits of language make the limits of their world.

'Nan, hey, Nan, remember life is but a dream.'
'Mum, I'm going to make you a napple pie.'
'Mum, look at the bubble tree.'

She was finally able to thank Catriona for the birthday cake.

The confusion lifted. She held hands with her family. One by one and all together.

They understood, in that part of the moment, that the only escape from dystopia is utopia. And utopia is simply an allusion to guide us beyond equations.

They realised that beyond the Ultimate world is Qi[M].

And that

Life is but a dream whether you are a man or a butterfly.

FORM 30

Endings

If you are looking for an ending, you will not find one, especially at the end.

Here, in what might be called the middle, unless you wish to make it the end, you are free to pick what endings suit you at whatever time you need one. Or walk away from the concept of endings entirely.

Open your eyes and you will find endings everywhere you look. They are like flowers in a meadow. Or pebbles in a river. Bend down and pick whichever one you need.

The end does not exist.

Endings are simply opinions gift wrapped in a box.

And when you open the box, the endings fly free.

Consider that a story without an ending may be part of an act to free intertextuality from its postmodernist box.

An ending is only valid as the culmination of a narrative hierarchy. And if the narrative is an open circle, then ending becomes meaningless.

By making your own meaning you become part of the story as you read it. And in doing so you come out of the cave and open all the boxes in all the worlds.

Embrace paradox.

Do not fear words,

Respect the meanings.
They are just particles.
They are just moments in the wave.
Go beyond the rules.
Because rules are restrictions on infinity.
Rules say that expectations must be met.

The ancient East says 'A text has both entering strokes and departing strokes.'

The modern West says 'A work is finished if it answers the purpose for which it is intended.'

When things are said they cannot be unsaid.
When things are known they can be forgotten
but
When things are understood they cannot be lost.

Do you still seek an ending?
Do you ask
What kind of a story is this?
What kind of a story is that?

This and that
Is and was
Are all as Chinese whispers
Or the flowing of a river

There are so many shadows on a wall

Pick a moment
Any moment
Be the river
You are the ultimate narrative.

Go word dancing

Beyond Rules of law
Beyond Rules of grammar

Beyond prose
Beyond drama
Beyond narrative
Explore wuxing
And find Wuji

As you write your own endings, you find your answers in the questions you seek.

When you spend enough time in your cave, if you close your eyes, you will see your writing on the wall. You will discover that instead of reading an ending you are writing a story in your own mind.

Writing is flow
Thinking is flow
Being is flow
Flow is flow

And nothing is not but what is.
Paradoxically.
Meaning is created out of whatever we have to hand.
Creativity not necessity, is the mother of invention.

Meaning is being
Being meaning
That's all there is and
All you need to know.

FORM 31

Moments

If all moments are one moment, you are part of that moment and your story is part of the story you read as it is written and before and after it is written, in words or characters.

Within all moments

Choice is our individuality

The choice is yours.
The choice is always yours.
Choose what to look at
Choose what to hear
Choose who to be
Choose which cave to sit in
Choose to open or close the box
Choose to open and close the box
Choose your box/es.
Choose life
Choose all moments.

And what is a life in all its moments? It's the load you carry with you until one day it is lifted from your back. It is the darkness you fear will catch up with you. It is not tapping yourself on the shoulder or patting yourself on the back. It is when you look behind you in fear and come face to face with yourself, fearless.

If you still need instructions,
First find your cave.
Sit there.
Wait.
And when you have learned that waiting is temporal and time is relative

Become.

What do you see when you open and close your eyes in quantum infinity?
Moments.
Moments when you dance wingless without shame.
Moments when you let go
Until you embrace Qi[M]

The End.
Or Not

Here are some moments. To you they are random. To us they are our lives. Real characters live in the space shared by author, character, narrator, text and reader. Our name is legion for we are many.

The words conceal as they reveal.
The paradox of being.

Spin up - A plane. A spitfire. Wings dipping in the clouds.
It's your freedom.
Your perspective.
You in space/time in a fictional reality.

Spin ahead - you see a bear. You run, it runs. Lucky if you both run away. Safe if you both run in opposite directions. Respect the bear for the ancestor it is.

Spin down - you are at one with the water. Your feet are in the water and are the water and the water is - just is. And you know this is all moments in that one moment.

Spin behind - while the world celebrates the clock ticking, we made a camp and drank champagne from pint glasses and filled our boots metaphorically with the joy of living and slept and dreamed such dreams. We saw their fireworks but the light we shared was deeper and longer lasting. They went out with a bang. Our friendship endures.

FORM 32

Intertextualities

I lost the plot
And found my story.

My storied self went on a journey. Through fifty six forms of
intertextuality. Beyond the words and meanings and caves and
boxes, in letting go a new way emerges.

These days it might be called curating a life.

Deep in the cave of Western thought, first principles are chains.

The alphabet is shadows on the wall.

The heroes journey requires the bravery to break the order of
language and narrative progression and to rebuild using analogy,
embracing paradox.

Beyond an ending, the possibility is to start again, from character.

But you read words
As easily as you speak words.
With as little thought of meaning
As fear of being eaten by a bear.
Fear is a lack of respect and reverence.

For some these words are simply scribbles on the wall.

In the caves of intertextuality some sit on theoretical boxes, looking
at the wall. Turning chaos into order and losing the meaning of
value in the process.

For others the moments beyond the words speak truth to power.

Resist the binary.

Find creative balance.

Dao is not a journey from a to b in spacetime.
It is in coming home to 'being'.

Understanding your own dao in the context of wuji is an adventure and a trial.

Eternal return is an inevitability - a cave drawing - a cartoon sketch, confirming Qi[ ]

Forget irony. Favour honesty
Abandon intellectualism.
Feel emotion. Fearless sentiment.
There is infinite depth to be found in moments.

In a state of flow one loses track of time.
In a state of wu wei, one loses time itself.

Between and beyond curators and editors there are infinite voices of author/reader creating infinite characters and narrators.

Seeing narrative as unstable suggests some failure. Narrative is flexible, perhaps infinitely so, but this does not mean there is no authorial intent. It's a good example of a misunderstanding of the concept of relativity. Each reader creates their own meaning as an affirmation of infinite perspectives, not as a suggestion that the author has no meaning or intent.

Postmodernism lurches towards an extreme individuality of meaning - which is an essential part of its problem. The postmodernist paradox is that announcing the death of the Author is a revolution which supposedly gives power to the reader - at the expense of the author. A by-product is that it allows without an intent to get away with narrative murder. It is a political gesture. It doesn't overturn the hierarchy, it just allows authors to be lazier. And the lazy books fly and the books with real heart and soul are lost 'like tears in rain'.

Living has been replaced by curating virtual lives and critical reading has been replaced by searching and collecting texts.

For most there is no time left to read, there is too large a choice, too long a journey. The caves of choice are swipe right silver screens.

I say, honest thought is the truest guidebook.
Find your philosophy on bamboo strips.
Create it, not in your own image.

To discover my intention, read what I write in the spaces beyond the words.

Because writing is only part of the deal.
Because thinking is a part of writing.
Because words on a page are only a gateway
and there are other doors and windows to open.

These are places more multi-dimensional than subtexts or marginalia.

The fifty six forms goes beyond words and numbers and beyond Ultimate reality.

I had a dream which was not all a half baked dream. I reached out into dimensions I could not imagine. By exploring the texts on the walls of the caves of my creative mind and the boxes I have made and opened and closed and sat in and carried and destroyed. I learned not to wrestle with bears. I abandoned the destination and embraced the journey and found myself in the meaning of 56.

Beyond number.

Number beyond measurement. As symbol. Number as analogy. More than effective metaphor. Reducing numbers to characters whose purpose is to count or measure or sell is pointless and directionless. I smiled at the excesses of 88. Two fat ladies is number theory taken to extreme. Evil numbers and the numerical concept of infinitely small are unstable texts. They are stories. I lurked in the margins of physics and went past the theory of everything where all the stories come together. Are you there too? Will we meet and share laughter? Will our parts of the moment connect? Are we characters in search of an author or authors in search of a narrative?

Who draws stories? Who writes pictures? We all do.

If we let go

We are all word dancers
We are all mind dancers

Reaching into the river we find oral history and chronicles. I went beyond East and West and beyond direction and time.

Guodian strips offer a vision of ancient intertextuality and alert us to the flexibility of chapters. They teach us to stop looking for stability in text. To look beyond stability of texts, behind formal patterns. The structure of rational discourse is a destination without a journey. An answer without a question.

When you let reason go then you find what you were looking for.
    When you stop trying to find - there you are.

All paths are permissable

This is either the hardest thing you will ever read or a place of safe-haven, where we meet and share through all the moments.

If you choose to open the circle

Instability becomes openness.

Disrupting becomes embodying.

The open circle is author/not author inviting you to find your dao in the adventure of the story of all moments in the ultimate narrative.

And the narrator said; 'Thank you for reminding me that I am more than a philosopher of fictions.'

24 FORMS
Creative Balance

WUXING
无形

FORM 33

HELEN feeds TORQUIL

Galloway

'I don't want to.'
'I don't care.'

It was a battle they played out every day. It was winter. Cold out. Helen wouldn't let three year old Torquil go outside to 'work' with the sheep until he was properly dressed. That meant wearing a hat and gloves. He didn't mind the hat, he took pride in that. Dad wore a hat. But he drew the line at the gloves.

The battle had been played out so many times. So many times Helen faced the challenge that she could not outsmart a three year old.

Defeated by a three year old. It's a situation familiar to all parents. Helen felt it keenly. It was not that she wanted to outsmart him but she felt uneasy about the fact that, somehow, in all their interactions, Torquil always triumphed. It suggested an imbalance.

Her excuse, then, was that she was restoring balance - not the balance of power, just relational balance. She resorted to the master strategy her own mother had employed on her. We learn from the ancestors. Sadly, she'd forgotten how much she had resisted that same strategy in her own youth. Now, the boot was on the other foot – or to be more precise the glove was not on the other hand. And the battle lines were drawn.

We might observe that a strategy is only a good strategy if it stands a chance of working, not just because it resolves a problem. And some problems resist resolution. The intractable problems are always with us. Parent and child. Solve that puzzle if you can.

And if you're wondering about the strategy, as well you might, she had put the mittens onto a string that ran through the back of Torquil's jacket. They dangled there, emerging from the sleeves like dead woollen mice.

Torquil hated it. As much as she remembered hating it. And still he refused to put his hands into them. The gloves were off, and not just metaphorically, even before he'd left the front door open in his hurry to get out to the yard and 'help' dad.

'Don't like gubbs' he said.

'What about if I get you some 'big boy' gloves?' she said. 'Work gloves.

A pause.

He remained unconvinced.

'Like dad wears when he's doing something important?'

It was her best shot. An appeal to his desire to be like dad.

Torquil shook his head.

'No gubbs.'

Helen now faced a choice. She could force his hands into the hated 'gubbs' or let him go off with them dangling free which would leave his hands exposed to the biting winter cold.

If the dilemma was comfort or safety, Helen knew she would choose safety every time.

She didn't really have a choice. Not now, not ever. He was her heart's reflection. The facts were simple; Torquil would always win.

This problem *was* intractable. The relationship was not defined by power but by love. That most complex of emotional attachments.

Helen brought herself down to her son's level. She squatted down and kissed him on the nose. Looked him in the eyes. With love.

'Why do you hate gubbs so much?' she asked, her tone palpably more loving than she remembered her own mother's had been.

The moment was marked by an understanding that 'you can't fight City Hall.' Instead, Helen tried to get into the head of a three year old. Perhaps if she could simply see things from his perspective.

Sometimes you only have to ask.

'They make my hands like sweating pigs,' he said, voice firm and clear.

A roar of laughter came from Callum who had been standing outside the door, waiting for the power struggle to be over. Like father, like son.

He held the door open, letting the chill inside.

She wondered, did none of them understand that an open door let in the cold? Did none of them feel the cold?

And while she was distracted with wondering, Torquil won.

Who could not laugh at the inevitability of the particular.

Torquil won because Callum intervened. A dad has rabbits a mother cannot pull out of the hat, after all.

'Well we can't have that now, can we son,' Callum said.

'No dad, we can't,' Torquil affirmed.

For that moment, in his mind, they were men, together. Torquil felt respected. Ten years later he would have added, 'see, dad gets it.'

All moments are one moment.

'Are you ganging up on me?' Helen said.

She knew when she had lost. As always, in reality, Callum was the cavalry and she thanked him for it.

If only he would shut the door...

'Tell you what, Torquil,' Callum added. 'Bring the dead mice along with you in your pockets,' he quickly tucked them in, 'and if your hands get cold we'll both put on our gloves, right?'

'No sweating pigs?'

'No sweating pigs. Just toastie hands if we need them. We don't want to clap the sheep and kye wi' cauld hands now do we?'

'No dad.'

Torquil was pacified. For a moment. Until another thought struck him as they left Helen at the doorstep.

'Does Catriona have to wear gubbs?'

'If she comes into my yard she does,' Callum said, 'But she's at school just now. So don't worry about Cat eh?'

'Okay dad.'

And with the matter cleared up in his three year old mind, Torquil proudly followed his father into the yard.

It was perishingly cold.

They went, man and boy, into the 'cow palace.' It had been recently built to overwinter the hundred strong herd - thirty Belties and seventy Charolais cross-Limosins. These were 'the princesses'. Their name stemmed from another family moment.

'Don't be a princess,' Callum had told Catriona one day. She was complaining about a leak in her wellies as she waded through the muddy sludge of the yard. She had been given the responsibility of helping direct the cows back to their new home after a regular session being checked over in the crush. And yet, she was complaining.

She had thought he was suggesting she was a cow - not in that bad, adult way - but in the way that meant her attitude was bovine. The problem was, that for Catriona, bovine was good. Cows were her friends.

A joke can only work when there is shared linguistic awareness. Similarly an insult. Perspective is everything.

So when Helen later asked a muddy Catriona, sitting on the chair by the kitchen range as she pulled off her socks, where she had been to get into such a state, the girl replied; 'taking the princesses back to the cow palace.'

'The princesses?' Helen asked?

'Yes, and daddy told me not to be one,' Catriona said. 'But I want to be.'

'A princess?' Helen was surprised and not a little bit fearful that her muddy six year old was about to turn 'pink'.

'A cow,' Catriona laughed. 'Moo-ve over Torq,' she added, pushing him away from the range where he was warming his hands.

'I love cows,' she said.

'Me too,' Torquil added.

'Who is your favourite cow?'

There followed a long conversation between the children on the various merits of the various cows··· until it was agreed that while Teeny and Tiny were great, and Amber was 'precious', the best of them all was Infinitely Small.

Listening to them chatter gave Helen pause for thought about the interactions between parents and children.

Who teaches who? There's so much to learn. Not just right and wrong, good and bad, but how to see things. How to understand them and how to explain. Making meaning through creativity with words. As a family.

Was this what set them apart from other families? Was this their uniqueness? Were they all part, a contributing, essential part, of something bigger than any one of them? Were they family trees even then? Even before.

There was a moment in 1991 when Callum and Torquil stood in the cow palace, warming their hands in the deep, rich fur of Torquil's favourite calf. It was one of 'those' moments. We all recognise them. We all have them. And if we are lucky, we remember them for the rest of our lives. They place us in spacetime. They are part of us and represent when our moment is in harmony with something bigger. All moments.

The family agreed that of all the cows in the cow palace, the Belties were the real princesses. A hardy breed, they could easily have spent the winter outside. But when the weather turned really poor, everyone agreed they deserved to be indoors if they wished. So Callum gave them the choice and usually, as he turned for home, several of them followed along into the byre. He didn't even need a feed bucket. They took little to no persuasion.

And in the moment Callum and Torquil shared in 1991, a particular little Beltie calf was special. He had a name. A back story. And he was loved. He was Infinitely Small.

'He'd like it if you put on your gloves and stroked him that way,' Callum said.

Unlike Helen, he was confident that he was smarter than a three year old boy. At least his three year old boy. Fathers and sons have a bond that is mostly secretive, but strong and secure.

'Would he?'

Callum nodded.

'Did he tell you that?' Torquil asked.

'Sure did. He'll tell you if you listen very carefully.'

Torquil put his ear close up to the calf's mouth. He felt warm breath. He felt slobber. He heard the in and out and the snuffle and nuzzle of living breath. The calf nibbled at his ear, looking for the bottle which served as a teat - his mother having died in the process of a difficult labour some days before.

At that, Torquil jumped back, amazed.

Wide eyed he told his father, 'He did tell me,' with a seriousness reserved for the under fives.

'Then put them on,' Callum said.

'Help me please, dad.'

Father and son worked together to get the dangling woollen mittens onto the small, freezing hands so that a boy might give solace to another boy - a boy who had lost his mother. Because for Torquil, species wasn't important.

There was one thing the family agreed on. Animals were people too. Humans didn't have the exclusive right to be called people.

'Does he miss his mummy?' Torquil asked.

'Who, Infinitely Small?'

Torquil nodded.

'Aye, he probably does, but if you are very kind to him, he'll forget.'

'Forget his mummy?'

'No, forget his sorrow.'

Torquil blinked.

'I won't ever forget my mummy,' he said.

These days don't last. They grow up so fast. Everything is change.

But the memories are as permanent as they are fleeting. They exist in more than one place at more than one time. They are always infinite. They are pain and pleasure combined.

On that particular, particularly cold February day in 1991, it wasn't long before the familiar cry came out;

'My hands are sweating pigs. Get the gubbs off, dad.'

And the shadow of a memory yet to come, played over the cow palace.

A birthday cake. Forty candles. A birthday present. A grandchild. And a message from another dimension for a seventy year old woman who had given up all hope.

All moments are one moment. It all depends where you stand.

Form 34

TORQUIL builds NICK

The Cabrach Bunker

'How can you possibly imagine a utopia?'

'What can you do but imagine a utopia. I mean, a Utopia, by definition, isn't real. Is it?'

Torquil looked his son square in the eye and realised that this was the moment he had been waiting for all his life.

Since that last moment.

The moment of his son's birth.

It was a time when both their names were different.

A moment when everything changed.

With one loud, lusty cry, his world had transformed for ever. A birth-day.

And now, twenty years on, contextuality had been achieved. If you followed the pattern of linear time. He understood that it was a pattern they had to break to stay alive.

∞ ∞ ∞

'Let me ask you a question Nick.'

'What?'

'When did you last see your father?'

Nike was trying to work out whether it was when he was six or seven and shut his eyes momentarily to concentrate. While they were shut Troy's voice invaded his thoughts.

'Use emotion Nick, not reason. Think outside the ULTIMATE® box.'

Nike opened his eyes, and found himself enfolded in an embrace from his father.

'Welcome home, son.' Nike could see the tears in Troy's eyes, blurred through the tears in his own.

∞ ∞ ∞

'My childhood wasn't idyllic,' Torquil said. 'But it was real. It was what I wanted for you. To be part of something.'

'Of family?'

'More than that. Family in nature.'

He continued, 'I wanted you to have memories. Then Ultimate came and stole everyone's memories.'

'I have memories,' Nick said. 'And we can make new ones, now, can't we?'

'But they won't be the same memories.'

It was a shared thought. Spoken or unspoken. Sometimes these things matter.

And what is a story? A shared memory. A construction giving life to meaning. An act of creation in which we make and find our own meaning.

And share it if we dare. Or if we can.

'I wanted you to be a real boy.'

'I am a real boy. Now.'

Torquil shook his head. 'No. Now you're a real man.'

Nick felt pride for the first time in his life.

'So what are we talking about here?' Nick pressed him.

'We're talking about what happens in the quantum gaps when you enter the Qi[ ] space.'

'Huh?' Nick was way out of his depth.

Author, character, narrator, reader. All are broken the moment we move beyond comfort and safety. Definitions as names and words as explanations are not fixed. Not any more. Or less.

'Let me tell you about Quantum Infinity,' Torquil said. 'It is the places you long to be. They are there. They are particles in the wave of life. The points we have lost contact with. The points we forget how to find. You need a map of a different dimension to find them.'

'And you're going to show me that map?'

A point of connection was made, and felt.

Torquil took his time.

Troy had shown Nike.

But Torquil could not show Nick.

Not in a true paradox.

'You'll find it for yourself. You have to.'

'Or?'

'Or you die.'

The choice was stark. Nick turned round. He was alone in a dark bunker far below a place that he barely recognised as home.

'Remember that everything is connected.'

Word as thought and feeling.

He took a breath. Deep. In and out. In and out. Open and close. Proving to himself he was still alive in some world, even if it was a world he didn't know. A world that didn't feel real. In which his status was not fixed. Who was he?

And what is reality? Away from the Ultimate world, he struggled to remember. He had lost his place, if not his life.

Grasping for something more important than air, he sensed there was another moment. Was it futile to say earlier? It was just another moment. Another memory. Another part of the story. When and where he was negotiating ways of being.

Beyond thought.

Nick remembered feeling the connection.

As she blew out the candles.

Was he back?

He opened his eyes. It was dark. He opened his ears. He heard nothing. He opened his mouth. It was the last resort.

'Is utopia just another version of the virtual world?' Nick asked.

There was no response.

Either Torquil wanted him to think for himself or he was alone, with only breath and memory to tell him he existed.

'Can we reach it through productive work?'

He asked another question of the silence. Questions were his path. His fundamental nature.

He opened all his senses
and he was back.

'No. Only through 'unproductive' work.'

His father had not abandoned him.
His breath came more easily.

In the dark, unseen, there was the hint of a smile as Nick asked, 'What's that?'

'When you go beyond.'

'Beyond what?'

'Beyond the Ultimate lifestyle experience.'

'And so, I···?'

Nick still couldn't bring himself to ask the question. To face the reality. That this was the world beyond The Project House and Ultimate and··· all this. It could not be real.

Troy was Torquil. The leader of the Immortal Horses was none other than his own father.

Nike was Nick. Alone or not alone in a cave. And he

wondered, as we all wonder: All this. It could not be real. How could it be?

No one had taught him how to have an existential crisis. Certainly not how to resolve it. In the Ultimate world such things were unimportant. Life itself was unimportant.

An explanation came. From father to son.

'As far as the world is concerned, you are dead. You have been killed by the 100 men. It is time to move into another dimension. Live in a totally different way.'

The father was calm in the delivery of this most incredible of statements. The son was grasping beyond breath.

'Utopia?'

'Have you heard of Hilbert Space?'

Nick shook his head.

"The virtual life is easy to sell", Torquil said, quoting another part of the moment. Another memory. Another mind making meaning.

'It was a version of reality. You did not buy it, you were sold into it. But that's not our reality. I'm offering you reality. In another dimension.'

'Cool.'

If only it were that simple.

'You'll have to make a choice. A real choice. The kind of choice that has been eliminated by Ultimate.'

'How?'

'Ah, now that would be telling.'

'So tell me.'

Nick couldn't stop himself. He turned to face his father. But it was dark. He felt alone. All that was left was breath.

'The Birthday cake. That's the moment.'

It was impossible to know whether this was a thought inside his head or a voice putting the thought into his head.

'The moment?'

He felt saved by a memory. Something to hold onto. Beyond his father's voice.

'The moment we have to get to.'

Torquil gave Nick time to process this information.

'What do you mean?'

'You have to understand context,' Torquil said.

He was patient in the face of questions.

'The question is: Is it possible that, independently of which is the quantum state, the quantum observables each possess definite single value, regardless of whether they are measured or not?'

'That's really a question?'

'It really is.'

'And the answer?'

Nick was impulsive. Like all young people.

Torquil remembered it well. The fact and the feeling.

'Never mind the answer, work on accepting the meaning,' he replied.

'Which is?'

'That Quantum theory exhibits contextuality'

'Which means?'

Even as he was asking the question, Nick knew this was how they were together. How they were meant to be together. How they lived. They were question and answer to each other. It was like looking in a mirror. It was what he saw beyond the mirror.

More than questions and answers. More than words. Mind dancing. The perfect challenge. Father and son together as one. Part of something bigger than both of them.

We all live in caves. Sometimes we make the caves. Sometimes we find ourselves in them. Sometimes we lose ourselves in them. Sometimes we are the cave.

Birth and death are just the most recognisable entry and exit points. They are the easiest and the hardest way to tap into memory.

'A context is a set of mutually compatible quantum observables.' Father.

'And?' Son.

'From Birthday cakes to Plato's cave, even things that appear to be, no, even things that are state-independent, are

177

contextualisable.'

Go beyond the words.
Dance with me.

Think with me.
Be with me.
The world of words is only one world.

'There are thirteen observables realizable on a three-level quantum system and this is the smallest quantum system allowing for contextuality. According to the Yu-OH set.'
'If you say so.'
Nick was in danger of letting go.
'It's just a question of where to start.'
Torquil didn't want to lose him.

In the world of probabilities there is always scope for the unthinkable. The story has many endings, even before the beginning.

'So where should I start?' Nick asked.
'Where do you want to start?'

The way that can be named is not the way. Each person has to follow his own way. Every path is individual, though not independent.

'The birthday cake?' Nick said.
'Question or answer.'
It was hard to define.
Nick felt himself slip-sliding away.
Would Torquil let him off the hook?
Would Torquil let him fall?
Of course he wouldn't.
They were Father and Son.

In all possible worlds.

'Does it have to be one or the other?'

Nick reached out.

Help me. Catch me. Don't lose me. Don't let me go.

Torquil smiled. His son had a natural instinct for this.

'What do you think?'

The door was open. The shadows began to emerge on the walls of the cave.

'Surely, according to what you say, they must be joined···
contextually? And so it doesn't matter where I start.'

Now he had it.

'Correct. The position isn't important. You just have to enter the dimension.'

'And is that Hilbert Space?' Nick asked.

'It might be.'

'Or not.'

'There's always that possibility. That's the beauty of it. Everything is possible.'

'And are we still talking about the quantum world?'

'We're talking about all possible worlds. And this is them.'

And it was. And it is. Or are. Timelessness is hard to pin down on the page in mere words. Multi-dimensions resist marks on paper.

Nick was in transition. Setting out. He wanted a map. A guide. He needed to know he was looking in the right dimension. The challenge was far greater than simple direction.

Up, down, in, out, may self-define as prepositions. They stand in relation to other words. From the Latin, to place before. In which case they mean nothing in and of themselves. Or do they?

What do words mean anyway?

When it comes down to it.

The definite particle third person singular is not a pronoun. Mission creep. Overload. *Reductio ad absurdum.*

Language is relative. And yet so much more than a game or games.

Can I ask whether in the best of all possible worlds, grammar would exist. Does grammar exist? And what does 'best' signify?

What does signify signify?
What do we mean by signify?
What do we mean by mean?

In the Cabrach Bunker there was some unpleasant business to attend to.
Torquil pointed to the barcode on Nick's arm.
'We have to get rid of that.'
'I thought you disabled it.'
'That's not good enough for where you're going. We have to remove it.'
'Will it hurt?'
It hurt.
Life hurts.
All transitions have a cost and the cost is pain.
'Where are we?'
'Don't you recognise it?'
Silence
'In this place we are safe because it is no-place.'
'Dad, why are you always speaking in riddles?'
Nick still felt a frisson of excitement when he said the word 'dad'. He wished he understood more. He thought that if only they understood each other, they would be closer.

He was wrong.

It's not about understanding, it's about love. Emotion not reason.

'I love to hear you call me dad,' Torquil said.

They were on the same wavelength after all. Again. Still. Man and boy. Together. Mind dancing. The stage deeper than word dancing. The place where nothing else matters and everything is encompassed in the moment.

All the moments.
Something to hold on to.
Those other times.

'Read this.'
Torquil gave Nick a battered old handwritten book. Nick got a thrill just in reading the words written by his father's own hand, the ink faded on the page. The pages crumpled from age.

Points of connection.

As one reads what the other wrote there is a sense of communion. Conjunction. Synchronicity. Of being together even when apart.
The Ancients call me Utopia or Nowhere because of my isolation. I am a rival of Plato's republic, perhaps even a victor over it.' Thomas More.
'So who was Thomas More?' Nick asked.
He would never outgrow asking questions. It was a fundamental part of who he was in all moments.
'It doesn't really matter,' Torquil said. 'He was a philosopher in the fifteenth century.'
'What happened to him?'
'He was killed by the King.'
'What for?'
'For being honest.'
Is that the truth?
'They call it speaking truth to power,' Torquil said. 'It's a

dangerous game. I should know. I've played it all my life.'

'Teach me.' Nick paused with the enormity of the word to come still fresh in his mind, 'dad.'

'One day I will tell you about Plato's Cave,' Torquil replied. 'Not today.'

'I know.'

'You do?'

'Nan told me.'

'And one day I will tell you about it from my perspective,' Torquil said. 'That's a promise.'

And a promise is not something to be given, or taken, lightly.

'Is this utopia?' Nick asked.

'Where are we?' Torquil replied.

'Nowhere?'

'And soon we will be beyond even that.'

The words beyond the words that they spoke at that moment, which are words you read now and in reading you may or may not understand the thoughts that characters who are and are not real at the same time, depending on perspective, think. These words are:

'Utopia has always been with us and is all around us. It is the place Ultimate cannot reach, cannot buy, cannot own. To live there, you simply have to recognise where you are. And perhaps, more importantly, who you are.'

'But what is beyond utopia?' Nick asked.

And perhaps you ask that too.

'Ask Thomas More,' Torquil suggested.

Nick picked up the notebook and read on: *Deservedly ought I to be called by the name of Eutopia or Happy Land'.*

'You might say that eutopia is what there is outside everything

182

we have left behind,' Torquil said. 'Outside, beyond, apart from - these are all insufficient words with insufficient values to explain what it means. Another dimension entirely. But that's where we are.' He paused.

It was a lot for anyone to take in, he knew that.

'Is it Hope?' Nick asked.

'No. Hope is part of the aspirational pyramid. There is no need for hope.'

Hope is a craving for something
We are the moment.
We are in the moment.
We are the moments.
All moments.
All moments are one moment.

'Just let go.'

And, trusting his father, Nick let go...

...as Torquil reached out for his son, unable quite to let go himself. The pain was too deep. And so the transformation was a jolting, sickening one.

Nick came to in another place.

The hand that he reached out for was his grandfather's. His father was not there. Torquil had been left behind. He still had other moments to experience.

But he would follow. And be followed. The relationship between father and son was cyclical and infinite.

Nick felt no regret in that moment. He was moving, not stationary, and there is no time for grief when you are in the realm of actions not consequences.

He had no idea where he was. It didn't matter when or where, just what. Not even why. Just being in the moment. And knowing, finally, who he was. He was his father's son.

A Particular Cave

'Who are you?' Nick asked.
'Why do you want to know?'

To answer a question with a question was always Nike's way. Always Nick's way. What's a consonant or vowel between friends? What does it matter where a letter stands in a word? What's in a name? In any possible world the letters c or e made no difference to that feature of his personality.

Name, after all, is the thief of identity.
The name that can be named is not the name.

'Because we are creating your narrative,' the narrator replied.
'We?' Nick asked. 'Isn't that your job?'
'It's your lives,' the narrator replied, 'your responsibility and your creative choice.'

If you don't create your own identity it will be constructed for you and when you come to curate it you will no longer know who you are.
This is how we lose ourselves.
Our creativity is part of our infinite qi.

The question remains.
'What's the last thing you remember?'
'A bright light,' Nick replied.
'That's so passé,' came the response.
'But it's true,' Nick said. 'It might not have been the last thing that happened but it's the last thing I remember. Then I woke up. Here.'
'And the narrative continued in the other world,' said the narrator.
'What's the ending?' Nick asked.
'For you or the narrative?'

'I don't know the difference,' Nick said.

'Of course you don't. There is no distance between you and your narrative at present,' the narrator replied. 'That's one of the things we are creating.'

Nick was baffled.

'So, what happened to me?' he asked.

'To Nike?' the narrator asked but didn't wait for a response before reading out the story:

'What he didn't see was the vehicle approaching from behind. He didn't see it as it hit him and he saw nothing as he was thrown, doll-like over the bonnet, landing in a crumpled heap on the pavement. No light remained. Only blackness. Forever.'

'Cool,' Nick said.

'It's not a bad obituary as they go,' the narrator said. 'Though I could have written it better.'

Nick had had a moment to think.

'So,' he said, 'I'm dead.'

'In that world,' the narrator concurred.

'And that isn't the only world?'

'Clearly not,' the narrator replied.

There was a pause.

'And if you're about to ask if you're in heaven…'

'What's heaven?' Nick asked.

'Just a completely random and ridiculous narrative which should have been put out to grass long before it was,' said the narrator. 'Its strength to convince never justified the weakness of its plausibility.'

'But, my Nan?' Nick said.

'What about her?'

'She'll think I'm dead, and if she thinks that… and she thinks my dad is dead…'

'There's a lot in these ellipses,' the narrator observed.

After a pause, more questions tumbled from Nick.

'Who are you?', 'What about Lucy and Eric?'
'Sorry?'
'Lucy and Eric. The gender bending sheep.'
'Don't you mean Bah and Humbug?'
'I don't think so.'
Nick paused again.
'I know who you are,' he said.
'The answer is always in the question,' said the narrator.

As the destination is in the journey.
As day turns to night and night turns to day.
All moments are one moment.

And in one part of the moment readers have no need of an author. Still, I exist. Living and dead. My creative intention guides but does not dominate.

You construct. We curate differently.

Beyond words while in another part of the moment, in another cave, the characters had no need of a narrator.

FORM 35

NICK burns CALLUM

A Tsilhqot'in Bear Cave

The next thing Nick knew he was waking up with the jolt of a truck. He thought he was in his grandfather's Landrover. He thought he was three years old.

At the sound of a familiar voice, he opened his eyes.

'Hey Nick.' It was his grandfather.

He saw a face he had not seen in so long, but one he would never forget.

And then he looked out of the window, as if expecting to see his childhood.

It wasn't.

The trees were bigger, the road was straighter and the clear felled forests seemed to stretch on into infinity.

'Where···?'

'You're awake,' Callum said. 'We'll be there soon. You must be hungry.'

He was.

The landscape overpowered his senses.. The smells and sights and sounds were all familiar and strange at the same time.

The mountain ranges spread over an expansive horizon. In front of the mountains, the rising morning sun framed a river which flowed sparkling and eternal over rocks and boulders, between banks where no cows drank but where bears and beavers made their homes and came out in the dark, or when no humans were near.

Looking out of the window, Nick said, 'This place is so cool. 'Where are we?'

Callum smiled.

'Don't you recognise it?' he said.

'I've never been here before,' Nick said. 'Have I?'

Suddenly he was not so sure. Everything was strange and familiar at the same time. He was coming home to a place he'd never been before.

He tried to orient, to make sense. He failed. Sometimes there is no sense to be made, especially when one experiences a sense of place.

'Life is full of moments,' Callum said. He paused. 'Well, actually it's just one moment,' he continued. 'And we approach it from a range of perspectives. You have to connect into the right part of the moment and···'

'Like···' Nick wanted to grasp at it. But it was just out of his mental reach. Beyond questions.

Everything is connected.
We're part of it all.
The question is in the answer.
The narrator doesn't always tell the story.
And certainly not the same story.
It's all a question of perspective.
In which we are all implicated.

All moments are one moment.

It's riddles again, Nick thought. He wondered whether he would ever understand any of this. He wondered whether he would ever understand himself. Was understanding even possible? Or desirable.

Callum saw Nick's confusion. He wanted to help. He wanted to explain. But they were in the middle of a landscape too big for any map to navigate. They could see so far into the distance that perspective was impossible. The canvas was too broad. It was too bright.

'You get to the moment by focus. Find a place to focus. Join

188

the wave.'

Nick looked blankly at his grandfather.

'You're a long way from the Cabrach now,' Callum said.

'Are we in Hilbert Space?' Nick asked.

'It doesn't matter where you are, it matters that you are,' Callum said.

'And you are.'

His father's voice came like a memory, sneaking into his mind, like Infinitely Small's breath from a time and place beyond his own personal experience.

Many miles down the road, deeper into the story wilderness, they met a roadblock. Callum stopped the engine. They had to leave the truck. It was only when he felt the ground firm under his feet that Nick believed he was not dreaming. They walked, side by side, following the path of the river. It danced and played across the rocks, the rocks which were part of the mountains up above. It was a bigger range of mountains than he could possibly have imagined. Snow covered. Winter was coming.

Callum stooped down and picked up a handful of water. He let it trickle between his fingers.

'What is this colour?' Nick asked. 'I've never seen it before.'

'If we have to name it, I'd call it glacial blue,' Callum said. 'What does it remind you of?'

Nick knelt down beside his grandfather. He ran his fingers through the water as the water ran over his fingers.

'Her eyes,' he said.

Without words they shared the knowledge that she was here. The connection was fleeting.

'There should be trees,' he said. 'A forest.'

'There is,' Callum replied. 'Just not in this part of the moment.'

The sun shone down on the sparkling rocks which lay underneath the water as it ran and bubbled along on a journey he could not even imagine. He looked up towards the mountain. Amidst and beyond the clear felling, he could sense more than see that creativity was curating new identities. Trees were growing again despite the destruction that had sold itself as a constructive action.

Oh Canada. You are the smallest part of the moment. The stories and lives are bigger than you will ever know. You can give a place a name but you cannot own a place by naming it. You did not create this place. You do not curate this place. Your construction is a destruction by any other name and it does not smell as sweet as the wildflowers in the meadows, or the blueberries and fir-pine scent in which all sense of identity is lost and found.

Nick looked down at his arm, where the implant had been. It was not there. There was no sign it had ever been. And there was no pain.

The sun followed them as they walked towards the entrance to the dilapidated buildings of a disused mine. It was literally the end of the trail. It was beyond the end of the trail. Junked trucks and signs and debris littered around, causing dissonance with the beautiful natural landscape. A practical paradox.

Two men awaited them. They were dressed in the garb of a First Nations band. Their jackets and trousers were made of caribou.

It was cold. The men were both wearing mittens, which they took off to extend a hand of greeting.

Nick shook their hands.

Their hands were warm.

They reminded him of something he could not place··· of memories between his father and grandmother··· of things he could never have known. Unless···

Introducing themselves as Jimmy and Joe, the men led Nick and Callum into the building.

'Are you hungry?' Jimmy asked.

'Yes,' Nick said, though he had lost all thought of it till he was asked, his immediate senses all having been diverted into the overwhelming landscape.

'We will eat,' Joe said.

190

'And then we will take you to the cave.'

He pointed high up the mountain. Nick could see nothing. But it was there.

Perhaps that was the point.

On a full belly, the trek up to the cave was almost pleasant, with the last of the sun beating down and the smell of the trees offering a full bodied resinous assault on the breath taken into lungs unused to this level of physical activity.

'But still,' Nick thought, 'a cave?'

'Do you live here?' he asked.

Jimmy smiled and nodded.

The building below, now fading from sight, was somewhat decrepit, but Nick couldn't believe that living in a cave would be a preferable alternative.

As they approached the entrance, he turned and looked down. It was, he had to admit, a place that offered a good vantage point. Below, he could see the light playing off the river. The water dancing down the mountainside. And he knew there were worse places to be.

FORM 36

CALLUM generates PRYCE

A Singular Cave

Somewhere in a conversation, characters spoke. And listened. Readers stepping into the cave may hear the voices before they see the writing on the wall.

'We met even before you were born.'
'How can that be?'
'You were a possibility.'
'If so then I must have been one among many others?'
'That's true.'
'And when did we meet?'
'At the family trees.'
'Where?'
'We used to go there for picnics. We'd sit and tell stories. And some of the stories became truth and some of them remained possibilities. That's life.'

And that was life. In the early twenty first century in rural Scotland life could still be told by stories. And life lived by seasons. And families still went on picnics. Before reality was virtualised, there were sunny days at the beaches. Private spaces and family places, known only to them. Meaning created by shared memory.

They lay under the cover of the leaves, ate 'negg' sandwiches and followed them with 'napples' instead of crisps, and told each other things they imagined as if they were the truth. And some of the things became truths. Simply because they were imagined and then spoken about.

'When I grow up I'm going to marry a man.'
That was Catriona's chosen version of the once upon a time opening sentence.

'I've heard it all before,' was always Torquil's reply.

Callum and Helen wondered where life would take their children. Life was wonder. And danger. But on a sunny afternoon in peaceful space under the family trees, looking out onto the biggest field in the world, the wonder was to the fore.

'How?' Torquil asked his father.

'Why' Catriona asked her mother.

And between and beyond the how's and the why's was the where and the when. But the questions come thicker than answers. It is always the same in the company of free-thinkers. Word dancers and mind dancers. Storytellers and philosophers.

And if you took a completely different path, you might end up at the same place, or a completely different one.

And what if there is no 'end'?

How do you explain such things to children? The answers you give at eight and ten become the paths they explore when they are eighteen or twenty. Or is that quite irrelevant? When everything is connected, how far can we be said to follow our own path?

The stories of the Odyssey and the Iliad and the Argonautica were staple fare for such summer afternoons when the family took time just to be, away from the farm and before Ultimate spoiled everything by taking it all and repackaging it, then demanding Brand Loyalty. Callum and Helen knew the stories and thought they understood the value of the stories, or of story itself. The value of narrative as a map is both limited and limitless. And we are all part of the infinite narrative.

'When I grow up I'm going to marry a man called Jason, and this is his family tree,' Catriona continued. She patted the tree next to her own.

And she did.

193

They met at University. There's nothing strange about that. The context, however, was more prose than poetry.

Catriona had a friend, a girl called Lauren. Lauren had a boyfriend. He was called Jason. They had a fight. Jason and Lauren. And then Lauren and Catriona. No one could remember what either fight was about. Before long it didn't matter. War is war. And young people will always test the theory that all is fair in love and war.

To begin with Jason wanted Lauren back. He had to develop a strategy. Form an alliance. So he hunted out Catriona, to help him in his task. The machinations of the University student are multi-dimensional. Too much study and too much alcohol and too many hormones and too many love songs and···

One thing led to another and Catriona and Jason fell in love. And instead of the conversation they thought they were going to have with Lauren, the one they'd prepared for all those long nights in the pub which were the precursor to the longest night on the beach before the sun came up during the kiss that sealed all their fates along a particular path, they went to tell her they were a couple.

And later, much later, Lauren, wanting to get her own back, made 'cow eyes' (as Helen would have called it) at Torquil. But Torquil, much as he knew the ways of cows, did not know the ways of girls - except his sister - and he fell for Lauren behind the byre. Hook, line and sinker. It's a familiar enough rural story. Boy meets girl··· and soon enough he was chasing her to the ends of the earth. Which in this case was Edinburgh.

And later on, he brought her home as his wife with child. And Nick was the child of the fragile union. But it was a union of opposites and never forged to stand the test of time. So Nick got left behind when Lauren realised the error of her ways and went on to pastures new. To a grass that looked greener but somehow didn't taste as sweet.

And all this is an archetypal story which has no less value because it is true in one possibility of a world. Lives lived and changed because of actions that might have been different had any particle of the wave functioned in an opposite spin cycle. Or the story taken another turn.

Reader, she married him. Catriona married Jason Pryce. Was it a marriage made in heaven? *Ah, but a man's reach must exceed his grasp or what's a heaven for? It's the damage that we do and never know, it's the words that we don't say that scare me so.* The full weight of western culture weighed heavy on them. Let's call it a happy ending. At least part of it was a happy ending. They had two children. Let's call them Lucy and Eric. Or you might call them Omo and Flora. A boy and a girl. The perfect nuclear family set free from the shiniest vision of utopia or dystopia you can imagine. Wave. Particle. Context is everything in the best of all possible possible worlds.

In the land of memories Callum remembered Jason Pryce asking for his daughter's hand in marriage. It was one of those dates that stuck in his mind. May 2nd 2009. A big moment, pushing its way to the perspectival foreground of meaning and memory. The day they got the swine flu pandemic leaflet. His thoughts went back to the same day if not date, eight years previously. The day which changed their lives forever. The day of death. Now another virus would change their lives again. All life is change. Viruses know that even if people don't. Viruses are just better at exploiting that change and harnessing it and directing it.

'Have you asked her?' was Callum's response to the proposed proposal.

'I wanted to do it properly,' the earnest young man replied.

'Properly, huh?' Callum removed his hat and scratched his head.

Properly was not a concept that came easily to him. Somewhere between the illusions of right and wrong it got lost in a melange of reality as hope and was something you couldn't pin down any more than you could control the washing on the line on a breezy day, or the determination of a cow to calve in the middle of the blackest night. At least, for a moment, his mind was taken away from the death of animals. And the poisonous properties of the virus looking for a host.

'Do you know Catriona?' he asked, a smile playing round his face as he imagined her response to Mr 'Properly.'

'I love her,' came the perhaps inevitable reply.

'Yes, but do you know her?'

And that, of course was the unanswerable question. Would love be enough?

It was of course unfair, both question and answer. Knowledge might be power but it is only a component of understanding and somewhere beyond understanding is the place love sits - if it sits at all.

Jason Pryce and Catriona Christie were married under the beeches which formed the family tree. Metaphorically his name was carved into the bark of the tree next to hers, where she had always known it would be, as the branches entwined and the possibility became a moment in time from which another path was generated.

They married in June, on the longest of longest days, and the world was about to turn. As it always was. And then they went on their honeymoon. They were headed to Wuzhen in search of the total eclipse of the sun. It was to be the longest solar eclipse of the 21st century. Or so he believed.

That seemed to matter to Jason. He told Helen,

'It'll last nearly six minutes and forty seconds, the longest in all our lifetimes.'

She didn't know what to say so she said, 'that's exciting,' though she doubted that it was.

'Don't say, wrap up warm, mum,' Catriona laughed. 'I've got Jason to take care of me now.'

'Take care of you?' Now Callum laughed.

'Do you have any idea what you've let yourself in for?' he asked Jason.

'I hope not,' Jason replied. 'It's an adventure we're writing together.'

And she kissed him.

'He's like the brother I never had,' Torquil said to Lauren as they drove back to Edinburgh. It was not quite Wuzhen, but it had its own appeal - then, to them. He kissed her.

'Are we now empty nesters?' Helen asked Callum, as she kissed him that night.

'Be careful what you wish for,' he replied.

'Are we still writing our own adventure?' she asked.

'Writing is just living in another context,' he replied. 'Our story is our story.'

'Did our story start with 1984?' she asked later that night, as she took the book down from the shelf, blew dust from it and opened the first page.

Even after 1984 there are still so many stories untold,' he replied. 'And the clock still strikes thirteen.'

Callum sometimes wondered if 1984 had been the narrative virus which found them as unsuspectingly perfect hosts. But he never said that out loud. He didn't want to spoil Helen's story. From Troy to Big Brother, she was right. Unknown stories abound. The stories are infinite and we are all parts of a narrative we cannot ever fully comprehend, because we are part of the context we write and read and live.

Stories are curious things. The beginnings and endings are clouded by the leaves of the trees. Nick had been at the wedding before he was even born. He was rooted to the family tree long before the fences were erected in the field that split the family from the forest. No one knew he was there. Apart from his mother.

Long before his sister became a mother, Torquil's own status changed. The leaves came off the trees and transient nature prepared for new life. The son became the father of a son. Unto them a child was born. Unto them a son was given. And what a son. He lit up the skies and asked all the questions that had no answers and answered all the questions no one knew how to ask.

Born on his grandmother's fiftieth birthday, his roots to the family trees were vital. However far he went, he was bound to something beyond himself. He nourished and was nourished by his roots. His breath blowing out the candles on a birthday cake when he was four blew out his grandmother's on her fortieth and again on her seventieth. He reached back and forward through the mists of time and made no sense of anything. And finally, he found his place in a world. His world. Lost and found. This is the way the world turns. Like a circle in a circle, like a wheel within a wheel. Bang the drum, yin and yang.

Nick was fire. And fire burns. In any and all possible worlds, Nick's fire was like the sun. It shone on all around him, but to look directly at it was dangerous, even in an eclipse.

Some trees are chopped down early. In the possible worlds of the family trees, Lauren never made it past the sapling stage. She had a canker in her that no one could heal. She was planted but she never tapped into the root system of the trees who would have offered nurture. She was lost. She could not embrace the sun, even the part that was part of her. It burned too bright in her eyes and she turned away. She craved an alternate reality and there is a ready supply of alternative realities available in the ultimate expression of brand loyalty. She let go too easily. Nick held on too tightly. They shattered each other because the story was not to be of mother and son but of father and son.

A Tsilqot'in Bear Cave

Inside, the cave was warm. Surprisingly. You'd expect a cave to be cold. At least that was Nick's expectation.

There was only a faint light, until Joe drew a curtain made from animal skins across the entrance and then it was dark. Nick's eyes struggled to adjust. His mind struggled along with his eyes. He said nothing but Jimmy caught his thought.

'We are not primitive. We know how to stay alive,' he said.

'Mostly we live in the disused mine buildings, utilising all the technology we have been given and all that you have brought. We share our understanding, co-mingling it in order to benefit optimally.'

'And most of the time that is fine. Most of the time no one cares. No one is looking for you and no one bothers with us.' Joe picked up the thread, seamlessly.

He spoke slowly, calmly, and his words wafted into Nick's very being as he listened.

'When we sense danger. When time dictates that people encroach, we go to the cave. No one looks for a man in a cave,' Jimmy said.

'And the cave is the place we meet to tell stories. So yes, in one sense, we live in the cave,' Joe added.

Like a song or a word-dance, Joe and Jimmy's voices ran back and forth. Their speech was accompanied by the beat of their drums - or was that just Nick's imagination?

'Bears live in caves.'

'No one living in the wider world wants to come across a bear.'

'A bear may kill you.'

'Can you outrun a bear?'

'You can shoot a bear with a gun.'

'But we don't shoot bears.'

'So when we live in a cave we have to live with bears.'

'The bear is not in the cave with us. Do not mistake me.'

'We have to live with the understanding of bears. With the acceptance of bear-reality. With an appreciation of bears.'

'Respect and reverence is the correct attitude for bears. And people too.'

Nick was sure he heard them say, 'Bears are people too.'

He felt a laugh bubble up inside him.

Bears are people too? What were these men talking about?

He looked at his grandfather.

'Do you have a problem with that?'

是不是

Deep in a cave, Torquil's mind went back to the awful year of Foot and Mouth. Of burning cattle. And further. To the naming of Lucy and Eric. And later, to Bah and Humbug. The sheep who had turned up, unexpected, uninvited, overnight on Christmas morning. No one knew where they came from. No one wanted to claim them. Except Catriona. His sister. She thought it was Lucy and Eric come back. She might have been right.

Nick and Torquil and Callum were together in the dark, lost in their family story. Lost beyond Hilbert Space.

是不是

'We do not fear the dark. We embrace the shadows. They are our stories.'

'A fire at the door to keep bears at bay, saying, this is my cave, my place, my space; is the same fire that might show us to those from whom we seek refuge.'

'Respect and reverence and welcome. Never fear.'

'But we are never cold, because we carry the fire with us. Inside.'

Jimmy was not speaking metaphorically. This was not so much sophistry, it was practical talk, aiming at practical living. At staying alive. At being alive. In a better way. Beyond linear dimensions.

'We take the embers of a fire lit during daylight and put them in stone. We place the stone under the beds on which we lie, and they warm us,' Jimmy said.

Nick sat on the stone bed. He could feel the heat. He remembered being with Nan. She had a name for a bed-warmer. What had she called it? A stone pig. Like a rubber hot water bottle but better. He began to relax.

'We have many ways of bringing light here,' Joe said. 'Old ways and new. Light is never a problem for us. We know how to see. When we are here, we do not hide. We are not in fear. We choose to absent ourselves from the dimensional reality, that is all. We go to a different place.'

'We lie here, in the dark, or in the light from the batteries. We tend to prefer a half-light as it reminds us of the older days, the days before.'

Jimmy and Joe were off again, that sing song, back and forth way they had. It was calming and compelling at the same time. They understood narrative.

'And in the cave we tell stories.'
'It has ever been thus.'

Joe picked up the thread.

'Stories are a ways to make sense. To make meaning. To share.'
'The story of infinity is told in many ways,' Jimmy said.
'Call it Socratic dialogue, or physics, or yinyang. Energy that is stored must be expended and then more work undertaken to store it again,' Joe added.

'Even renewable energy needs work to replenish it.'

'Look for the writing on the wall.'

Nick looked. He could barely see the wall. There was no writing. No shadows. No real light.

Nick had a question burning up inside him like fire. He was not yet a stone pig person. He could not reserve the energy within. When he had a question he had to let it out, like a flame.

'I have a question,' he said.

They waited for him to formulate it. Time, if it existed, stood still for a moment.

It was about infinity.

Those are often the hardest questions to frame.

'Can a word be infinite?' Nick asked.

No one laughed. They took him seriously. This was far from the world of Pryce and the Project House and Productive Work. This was 'real' life.

'You have to understand space differently,' Jimmy said.

'Are you ready for some cave art? Joe smiled.

It was his idea of a joke.

Then he drew his story on the wall.

'In 'my' perspective of space we have to allow that $(p)=$ particle and (w) = wave,' he said.

'Then we have (wp) = wavicle – where particles and waves 'reside' together in a dimension. Accepting always that = does not mean equals in any real or meaningful sense.

'So as you want to know it, Words are (p) that can 'fix' – thus name is the thief of identity.

'Each word fixes. A string of words fixes, but the more words you use the less fixed you become. Meaning becomes divergent as you build the sentence. And before long there are so many meanings, options, nuances, readings, that you have lost the fixity and perhaps the identity. Words collapse into waves.'

'Does this matter?' It was a rhetorical question. A question that is not a question. Revealing a deep paradox.

'Only if you live in a fixed world. A fixed mindset. And we cultivate fluidity. That is wu wei.'

'Hang on, that's a Chinese concept.' It was a thought. Maybe Nick's thought. Maybe not.

Jimmy continued: 'It's a story. We all have our stories. Our own myths. Our own ways of connecting and describing. And sometimes it is easier to step outside the known, outside the culture we think we know, the things we have fixed as belief and reality. Sometimes we have to go somewhere else to know where we are. Only then can we see the perspective we seek.

'So let us not worry about who thought it first or who said it first or who discovered or invented, or where it came from – none of that matters. All that matters is how you come to be in that part of the moment. And where you find your home.

"Words are (p) but they can become a portal if you look beyond the fixed dimension. Take them into (wp) wavicle status and through that immerse yourself; because it's not as simple as entering. Entering requires a fixed point to start from and we are trying to get away from points.'

'Immerse yourself in what is behind the word – the 'wave' if you like, but the wave of infinity. If you see it from the perspective of linearity you are caught up in the world of mathematical infinity which will not help you at all. That is maths as language and the language is fixed (and, if I may say so, faintly ridiculous). It is a story but it is not THE story. The way that is named – or enumerated – is not the way. '

'And what about Hilbert Space?' Nick thought he remembered it had seemed important back at the other cave.

'Hilbert space takes you away from Euclid,' Jimmy said.

Euclid. Ah Euclid. Good old Euclidean geometry. A fixed world which made rational sense in the language of mathematics. Hallelujah.

However, not 'true.' Not infinite. No use to us now,' said Joe.

'Hilbert space is a story for scientists. For mathematicians. For those number theorists who like to think of themselves as mathemagicians. Who create evil numbers as part of their narrative - but they are all just storytellers in a cave. And it's not our cave. Never,' said Jimmy.

The answer to Nick's next question came before the question was asked. In the darkness, his grandfather spoke.

'You'll know it when you're there.'

'How?'

'She'll be there too.'

'And you?'

'Yes. But you may not always see me. It depends what part of the moment you're focusing on. But I'm always there. We all are.'

'So, like, you were always there? Watching me?'

'Always there,' Callum nodded in confirmation.

'Always will be?'

'Of course. As long as you live in the moment.'

'Believe in the moment?' Nike was puzzled by the word live. He thought he had a grip on belief⋯ but then⋯

'No. It's bigger than belief. Belief is the doorway but you have to walk through the door to reality.'

'Reality is what you choose to believe, right?'

He spoke the words he remembered hearing somewhere, in another dimension. He couldn't remember who said them. His nan, perhaps. It was the sort of thing she might say.

'Yes and no.'

Silence.

Finally broken.

'I have to go.' Callum spoke.

'It's not safe.'

Nick didn't know why he said it, or how he knew it. The words

204

came unbidden from somewhere deeper and darker.

'Nothing is ever safe. Safety is just a word. It has no power over me,' Callum said.

He was going to fetch Helen. Nothing and no one would stop him.

FORM 37

PRYCE enriches HELEN

Magnolia Walls

'Of all the birthdays in all the world, you send a cake to mine.'

She could do nothing but thank him.

'It wasn't me,' Pryce said.

'Oh, but it was,' Helen replied.

'You just didn't know it.'

They had just moments together, but sometimes a moment is all it takes.

'I wanted to come before,' he said.

'It wasn't your fault,' she replied.

And as he left the room, he remembered his promise and whispered in her ear,

'Your son wants me to tell you he loves you.'

The words were said and accepted.

'Is he alive?' she could hardly get the words out.

'I can't say any more.'

'It's enough.'

Though it wasn't. But it was a start. From a world where her son and her daughter and her husband were all dead, the cake offered something beyond ultimate hopelessness. The words offered something more.

If the cake had been a message from the past, this was a message from an urgent present. Which pointed towards a future choice. A possibility. Beyond hope.

And who sent the cake? Well, that depends on how you relate to the narrative. On how you construct the narrative. Mystery is just clouded perspective. Until you are in the right cave you will not see the writing on the wall.

Helen's mind could not fix perspective by looking at the magnolia wall. 'The Bubble Tree' wall might have held the answer.

But her daughter was dead.

Unable to believe that any of the people who were dead to her in the magnolia cave had baked and sent a 'real' cake, she accepted the more rational view that it must have been a real man, And Pryce was such a man. But Pryce was just the conduit.

It was another version of the story in which he had said he would take care of her daughter. Another version of the story in which her daughter did not die. She was in the wrong narrative cave in 2030. The conclusion came long before an understanding that the end was nigh, yet was infinity staring her in the face.

2005

In 2005 Helen and Nick were out in the biggest field in the world. It was February. Gloves were being worn. Happily.

'Is it really the biggest field in all the world?' he asked, still full of wonder at the enormity of life in all its aspects.

'It is the biggest field in our world,' she replied.

And family names are significant. Despite his avowal that name is the thief of identity, Callum led the way in the naming of things in the family geography. The reason being, it was quicker to find your way around if you created a family map. So 'scone top' and 'the biggest field in the world' and 'badger bottom' and 'bullock brae' each had their own stories attached and the stories aided the memory and helped the family ground itself in place and space if not in time.

The biggest field in the world took an hour to walk round when Nick was four. When he was eight it took only forty minutes and when he was eighteen it would have taken less than thirty or more than all the minutes in a day. Because he was no longer there to walk it, hand in gloved hand with Helen.

On the day they walked the field for his fifth birthday she had been talking to him about his twenty first birthday, which she imagined in the glorious sunshine of a snowy day of sharp flinty blue steel, unlike todays damp earthy brownness whose cold bit with loose, dank jaws not sharp teeth.

'We'll walk round the biggest field in the world and it will only take half an hour. Unless there is snow, then it might take as long as it takes now.'

It was her way of explaining the relativity of time and the phenomenon of growth and the impact of the seasons.

'And will we wear gubbs?' he said.

He laughed because by the age of five he could choose to wear 'real' gloves instead of mittens, and his choice was invariably to wear mittens. Fathers and sons only share so many traits. Or maybe Helen had learned a trick or two in the intervening years. She had knitted Nick's mittens herself. They looked like Beltie cow puppets. He loved them.

On that day, however, he took off his Beltie 'gubbs' and said, 'Nan, please put your hand in mine.'

So formal. So polite

She smiled and took off her glove. She put her hand in his. She felt his warmth and his love as they intertwined her fingers.

'Happy birthday, nan,' he said.

'Happy birthday, Nick,' she replied.

It was the thing they shared, above all else. A birthday.

'Are we twins?' he asked her.

'Why do you ask that?'

'Because my teacher says that only twins have the same birthday,' he said. 'But I told her I have the same birthday as you. And so we must be twins.'

In the rational world, explanation is everything.

'There is a perspective in which we are twins,' she said.

'What's a persp··· perspective?' he asked. 'Is it the kind of glass that grandad uses···?'

She laughed. 'That's perspex.'

'And is it not the same?'

She thought. 'No, perspective is how you see things.'

'If I see through perspex then I see things differently,' he said.

He was right.

She knew it. She just didn't know how to tell him the difference.

And there was no time. The gloves were off. The hands were being held and they reached the gate. They left the biggest field in the world and headed for the family trees. Bleep and Booster, not long out of puppyhood, ran on before them, eager to drink from the hollows at the base of what was then known as the 'drinking' tree. Helen's tree.

'Why are birthdays important?' he asked.

He knew they were. He knew they shared this important day and it gave them a special bond. A bond that allowed them to go out in the February snow and walk through the biggest field in the world and stop at the family trees where he would sit in her lap up the thinking drinking tree and look at the world from a different perspective. So many words in a language that only they could understand because it was only their moment and we can experience such moments only if we live them.

She tried to answer him. In terms a five year old would understand. Terms a fifty five year old struggled with.

'Why are birthdays important? They are the one unique day we have. The one thing worth celebrating. You are only born once. That's the special day. And commemorating that day each year is an appreciation of your uniqueness in a world of homogeneity. That's why it's important.'

She waited for him to pull her up on words like commemorate, and unique and homogeneity. She was never one to indulge in baby talk. The 'gubbie gubbies' were part of the family story.

'Your father hated to wear his gubbies, he said they made his hands like sweating pigs,' she said.

'I know this story,' he replied, solemn. 'You told me last year, when I was a little boy.'

She remembered she had told him some time last year, when they were out on a walk and he had dropped one of his Beltie mittens and been inconsolable at the loss. Even sending the old dog back scenting had failed to find the lost glove. She had knitted him a replacement. He had been lost in love and admiration and promised never to lose a gubb again. He was happy to wear them on strings. Strings helped him keep his promise. And he knew, even at five, that a promise was something to take seriously.

That day, as they sat up the thinking tree, Nick voiced his thought.

'It *is* like sweating pigs,' he said. 'I never thought of that before.'

So serious. So young. So much to learn. So much to unlearn.

He had no need for the difficult words she had used in telling about birthdays. He simply transformed them into words that made sense for him. And that made it simple. We might all learn that lesson.

Birthdays were important because they were a special day. Cake and candles. A walk in the field. Making memories. Just him and her. And the dogs. Of course, always the dogs.

The sun came out. Nick smiled and shifted on Helen's lap. The dogs had finished drinking the tree dry.

'Are you cold?' she asked him. 'Do you want to go home?'

'So many questions, Nan,' he laughed at her. 'You ask too many questions. Questions are for people like me. Not for ones like you.'

'And what is the difference between me and you?' she asked.

'Young and old,' he said, as if he had solved the answer to the universe.

'But we share the same birthday?' she said.

'We are twins of different ages,' he said. 'So I get to ask the questions and you have to give me all the answers.'

'I'll do my best,' she replied. 'But you know I don't know all the answers.'

He smiled at her.

'Never mind, Nan,' he said. 'When you are old as the hills you will.'

She wondered when she would be old as the hills, and whether he was right.

'Tell me about what it was like when you were born?' Nick asked. After all, asking questions had been claimed as his right.

'I don't remember, I was very young at the time,' she replied.

'I mean, tell me a story about it.'

And so she did. As they walked home.

1960

When I was born my world began. Not the world, it was there before and it will be there long after. But 'my' world.

And in my world my dad and mum gave me a present when I was five years old, the same age you are now.

'What was it?'

'A napple tree,' she replied.

'That's a lovely present,' he said. 'And did it grow?'

'It did,' she said.

'As big as the thinking drinking tree?' he asked, looking back.

The tree looked smaller with each step, but he knew it was big. He understood something of perspective.

'Not as big as our tree,' she said. 'Our tree is hundreds of years old.'

2005

He smiled that she said it was 'their' tree. One word with so many happy feelings attached.

'How old was the napple tree?' he asked.

'When?'

'Now.'

'Oh, now, it would be fifty years old,' she said.

'And fifty isn't hundreds, is it Nan?' he said. 'I know that.'

He thought for a moment.

'What happened to the tree?'

'When?'

'In the story.'

'It grew and grew and···'

'And in the end?'

'The end?'

A pause.

'I don't know,' she said. 'I haven't seen it in many years.'

'Where is it?' he asked.

'In the garden I grew up in,' she said.

'Can you take me there?' he asked.

'One day, perhaps.'

She knew she never would.

But the half promise was enough for him.

'And tell me about what it was like when I was born,' Nick said.

'It? Do you mean the tree?'

'I mean the world,' he said, 'Everything.'

'Oh, everything,' she laughed. 'Is that all?'

She took a deep breath. It was easy to remember. The feelings flooded back.

'When you were born I saw the world through different eyes. New eyes. Your eyes, which came from my eyes but moved us forward to a new and different reality. New dreams. New possibilities.'

New pain, she thought but did not say.

'Was I a good birthday present?' he asked.

Still, at five, the world revolved round his own perspective. Everything was framed with him as centre. But the centre would not hold and he was learning to hold hands to stop someone else from falling, not just for the security it gave himself.

'The best,' she said.

'What happens after the best?' he asked.

'I don't know,' she said. 'I hope we never find out.'

'Do you know what my best ever birthday present is?' he asked.

'No.'

He turned round and kissed her.

'You, nan,' he said. 'Just you. And I am lucky because I got my best birthday present before I was even born.

She offered to help him put on his mittens.

He declined.

He took her hand again.

'I will never let you go,' he said.

And he meant it.

But he couldn't see the future, even the near future. And time makes liars, if not cowards, of us all.

Beyond time, however, there is another dimension.

At another part of the moment, the best birthday cake ever was made by a son and a daughter. And also, delivered by a husband and eaten by a grandson - even when he didn't remember those times in the biggest field in the world and the questions and the holding of hands and the promises made.

'Are promises made to be broken?' Nick asked Helen in 2005.

She wondered where he got his questions from.

'Nothing is made to be broken,' she replied. 'It just sometimes happens.'

'Like gubbs?' he said.

'Sorry?'

'If we drop them, like gubbs.'

She laughed. As usual. He was right. It all depended on the perspex of life.

2030

In 2030 these were memories she held close. The Ultimate screen was not a friendly screen to her.   She kept these memories close in her mind. It was a promise she had made herself. Some things are not for sharing.

When Pryce left Helen their stories parted but there were no endings in sight.

Time moves in cycles, not in the linear patterns of beginning, middle and end. No more do narratives have to. The cycle of Helen's sixty years did not start with physical birth in 1960 but with narrative birth in 1984. And so the end, should it come, was due in 2044. In that respect, 2030 just marked a solar eclipse. On Saturday June 1st. Literal and figurative. Narrative fiction and fact combining.

There is always another point in the moment.

The next significant solar eclipse came on Monday November 25th in 2030. By which time many, many worlds would have turned and many, many changes would have occurred.

And Pryce and Helen would come to recognise each other through many different prisms of kaleidoscopic light.

FORM 38

Debts and promises

Did you pass through a transition?
The Cabrach.
Was it death?
Of a kind.
Was it to be feared?
No, because I was shifting from one state to another state
From one way of being to another way of being
Being is constant flux.

And so you woke up and found yourself by the river

With a cave for safety and many caves to explore

And a new understanding of light and darkness

I owe you a debt.

What does this mean?

Something owed. Usually (in Western tradition) money.
But it can be gratitude or appreciation. That is what I owe you.

What does 'owe' mean?
It is an obligation.
A commitment or responsibility

And a commitment is a responsibility.

So you see we can get to promise from debt in five simple steps of
linguistic separation.
A promise is a serious thing to give
And to receive.

A promise is relational. It confers responsibility on both sides.

We cannot use formal syllogistic logic on these statements. At least I cannot.

A debt is paid by a promise.
A debt is a promise monetised.

Nothing of value should be monetised.

Money is not real. It is a metaphor at best.

And, knowing all that, I will make you a promise.

We will make a promise together.

I will give and you will receive this promise.

In all possible worlds. Best and worst.
In all dimension of Qi and for all moments.

And the promise is?

Love.

Beyond word and action and consequence.

Infinity.

And like the way, it cannot be named. It certainly cannot be monetised. Though it often is. But if you sit in the wrong cave for long enough the writing does not appear on the wall. Instead you find yourself throwing mud at the wall to make a picture. That is the monetisation of the caves of narrative and philosophy.

Possible Caves

In a cave. In the darkness.
Where you have to choose your point of focus. Where anything is possible.

Trees, like words, don't stand in isolation (except in forests where no one is listening)

Our family tree was known to our family as the beech. But it was really the beeches. And we all relied on each other.
There were six of us. But one day, long ago, two of the trees got put on the wrong side of the fence. That's because a field boundary was being established and ownership of the land was disputed and no one understood the relationship of the trees. At that point in the stories no one knew about the trees, and even you would wonder why there were six.

Our family, you say, is five. Callum, Helen, Torquil, Catriona and Nick. That's because you are looking into the story at the wrong point.
Who is the sixth tree?
We'll call him Pryce. Or Jason. It doesn't matter which. His name isn't who he was. Jason Pryce will do.
And who ended up on the wrong side of the fence?

Assuming there was a 'wrong' side.

Catriona and Jason Pryce.
Why?
There are many stories that will tell you an answer to that.
But which of them is true?
All of them are true.
At the same time?
Not at the same time, no.
In the same space?

Remember your quantum theory please.

One day in one of the possible worlds of the story a man came and chopped down the trees in the field. To make way for more barley, I suppose. Or just because he could. There was a reason, possibly many reasons. But from our family point of view, none of them were good.

In the best of all possible worlds, Catriona marries Jason Pryce and together they build happy endings. No trees would be cut down. But in the best of all possible worlds would Lauren cease to exist? Without her there would be no Nick. And when a tree is felled in a distant forest, even unobserved, it is said the butterfly effect is felt. An element is lost and without all the parts of the whole there is no whole.

What happens when characters and authors and narrators and readers real and implied sit in the cave together?

'Who is Godot?'
Godot is who or what we are waiting for.
The narrator?
Is the narrator a part of the story?
Is the narrator Godot?
Or Qi.

They can't all be in this cave.
So some things are impossible in the best of all possible worlds?
Impossible is such a difficult concept.

'Let's just say some things aren't. At the same time,' the narrator said.

So what you're telling me is that we can't all be in the same cave at the same time, because someone mucked around with the order of things (or the disorder of things) and chopped them down and displaced them, or changed their being, or trajectory or part in the story...

If that's how you can best understand it, let's go with that.

Okay.

Infinity allows all possibilities but the space-time continuum of the stories we are able to imagine in the space of the thoughts we can convert into words at any time we fix them means, effectively, no.

Once upon a time, when that happens, the easiest thing is to accept that you don't know. That you don't understand. That it's not where you are just now. Which is the equivalency of saying - it's too difficult for you to process or engage with, or deal with. Let go. Just let go. Then you'll be surprised what happens. If you never let go you'll never be surprised and if you're never surprised you always know what's going to happen and so only a very few of the things that could possibly happen ever will, because you are bound by what you expect to be the case. Which is a case but not all the cases in all the dimensions of quantum infinity.

She was lost. Outside and inside.

I used to love the light, because I could see most clearly. But there's something in the darkness, something else that you can see. Like looking up at the stars, pin points in the distance but burning so brightly.

'Always moving,' the narrator said.

Sometimes when you leave the cave it leaves with you. Sometimes the sun and moon are both blotted by clouds.

Sometimes on a clear, starry night, when anything is possible, all connections are there to be made. On such a night, if you take stars into the darkness of the cave, you will find the family trees.

'But I will not be there,' Helen said.

When Particles Collide

'Of all the stories in all the worlds you walk into mine.'

It used to be that we believed that all good stories began 'once upon a time'. We know differently now. We know that narrative is more flexible and mutable than that simple sentence allows. One man in his time plays not just many parts but lives on many stages – each of them a dimension in a multi-verse – and this world is part of an infinitely complex system.

'Tell me the last thing you remember.'

A line from an absurdist play.
A line from an absurdist play?

In that part of the moment when Stoppard shared a cave with Shakespeare, two men shook hands and they both knew that context is everything.

There was a moment, just before all that, when Nick looked into the eyes of a man and didn't know. And then he recognised him. But neither of these moments was once upon a time, though both of these moments marked a beginning.

It began before then. You can go back right to the moment of birth, or even conception, from which time while everything was not certain it was at least possible.

But there were many paths, many roads not taken, until the quantum leap with which the words 'welcome home, son' were spoken and Nick and his dad were together again.

But that time also had passed.

There was darkness all around. He was in transition. Moving but still. No place, no time, no space. Pure thought and pure emotion. Mind and memory in balanced harmony.

He was in a narrative cave. And so are we.

FORM 39

HELEN puts out NICK

Magnolia Walls

Memory plays tricks on you. That can be a good thing. Invented memories can be re-purposed as the stories we want to have told ourselves. The worlds we want to have inhabited exist and are shared simply by using words as tools.

As Zhuangzi said, 'words are not just wind; words have something to say.'

It was Nick's twenty first birthday. Helen's seventy first. Imagine. Just imagine.

'We should have a cake, nan,' he said.

'Of course we should. And a party.'

She wanted so much to have a party.

'Who will be there?' he asked her imagination.

'They will all be here,' she said.

If she wished it hard enough, it would be true. In some possible world, there would be a party. Just not this one.

He listed the people who would be at the party. He gave them their individual names, not their family labels. Helen, Callum, Torquil, Catriona and Lauren,' he said.

He was about to start inviting all the dogs they had ever owned, when she stopped him short.

'Why would you want your mum at your birthday party.'

'Because she is part of my story. Part of my life.'

'Not the best part.'

'But from another perspective.'

The conversation of the imagination was an easier one to have than any reality would allow. But still Helen feared she was putting words in his mouth by bringing them from her mind into being.

Beyond memory. After truth.

She stood back and allowed father and son to talk. Was it in her mind's eye? Or was it in a version of reality she had no real access to? It was as if she was behind a perspex sheet. In a magnolia cave.

There was another cave, in another dimension in which father and son were sharing words and thoughts she felt belonged somehow to her.

'You loved her once,' Nick said.

'And I hated her once,' Torquil replied.

'Can't we get beyond that?'

'She killed my sister. She stole you away.'

'Yes, but.'

'There's no yes but,' Torquil was firm.

'It's my party.'

'I know.'

'So let me have this. Maybe she'll surprise you.'

What father can deny his son even this? Whatever the personal pain. However much he did not want to believe that part of his treasure could never be wholly his.

But how to let go?

'I don't imagine she would even come.'

'Would? Don't you mean will?'

There's a huge gap between those two words and concepts. It's bigger than linguistic form or moral value. It's··· possibility and reality. Wave and particle.

'If you stare at the wall for long enough···'

Lauren and Catriona turned up at the party. They brought presents.

Catriona fell into the arms of her father and Lauren fell into the arms of her son.

'I am so sorry,' she sobbed.

'It's okay mum,' he replied.

'No it's not okay,' she said. 'I should never···'

223

'Forget it,' he said. 'I have.'

'He hasn't,' she said, looking at Torquil.

'You can't forgive what you can't forget, right?'

'We have to be beyond that.'

We don't cover ourselves in glory with every moment we live and we all do things we will regret. Some of us live to regret them. Some of us don't. Does it matter who dropped the glove? Or how or when or even if?

Forgive and forget.

But do you have to forget in order to forgive? Or do you forgive in order not to forget?

The truth of the matter lies deep beneath and beyond the cliched version of living.

Does it matter who made the cake?

You can't have your cake and eat it. This is a more false proposition than its original idiomatic construction: you can't eat your cake and have it. But the thing about cakes is this: Just blow out the candles and make a wish.

The party doesn't matter. It's the people who matter. We forget that. We argue over the detail and lay blame when we should just accept.

If you free the memory from the specific moment of error and shift perspective to all the moments, you will be invited to the party.

The sum of all the moments is bigger than even the biggest single moment. The wave encompasses the particle but we tend to let particles blot out the wave. In doing so we eclipse the sun. We need to open ourselves to the possibilities. Otherwise the loss will shield us from the thing we most desire.

And so, a birthday party in the mind. And in the memory.

Helen told herself: 'It could be like that. In my imagination it is. It's a possibility. And so it's a reality. Of sorts.'

In some time and place Helen spoke to Nick. The future and the past were meaningless in the context.

'Do you have the watch?'

'Which watch?'

'Your grandfather's watch.

'Yes.'

It's a time piece. It tells the time. Or a version of the time. Not a very useful one. While you look at the hands of that watch, you cannot be anywhere but in linear time. You have to stop looking at the passage of time like the hands on a watch before you can really experience time.

And she was hanging on to time.

Time to···

                              Let go.

In the darkness of the Cabrach bunker, out of which he could see even with his eyes closed, Nick told himself, 'It could be like that. In my imagination it is. It's a possibility. And so it's a reality. Of sorts.'

'Can't I at least tell her I'm okay?' Nick asked his father. 'Surely···'

'I mean, you sent the cake··· you're tapping into her memory···'

'I didn't send the cake,' Torquil replied.

'Then who?'' Nick asked.

Torquil decided to go the extra mile. Troy would harness the Immortal Horses one more time. He had got his son back. He did not want his mother to suffer the loss he had felt all those years···

In the magnolia cave Helen's screen lit up.

'Nan, It's Nick.' For the first time Nike didn't mind saying that name out loud. Standing next to Troy, he finally felt a sense of belonging, purpose, identity, family. He wanted to share this with Helen.

'Nick, how··· where are you? Is something wrong?'

Something didn't seem right but Helen couldn't work out what it was.

'I'm with dad,' came the response.

'What?'

'My dad. Your son··· he's here···.'

The connection was lost.

He reached out and felt her hand.
She reached out and felt his hand.
They both wished the perspex gloves were off.
She opened her eyes.
He opened his eyes.
They were alone.
In different caves.

Form 40

NICK softens PRYCE

A Tsilhqot'in Bear Cave

In the cave Joe and Jimmy set up a chant.
And if we sit in the cave long enough···

The ancients used to say that if you stared at the wall for three
years, the writing would appear.
But what is three years?
What is time in relation to space?
And where am I?
Do you need to ask?
Yes.
When you don't need to ask, then you will have found yourself.

In the dark, Nick heard their voices, as if waking from sleep.
'The cave is the place we meet to tell stories.'
'No one looks for a man in a cave.'

Nick looked at the wall. There was no writing on it. There were no
shadows. There was nothing except the noise inside his head.
Nothing except the moments after death.

Transformation.

Nike and Pryce both felt it.
Nick and Jason both felt it.

There was no white light,

There was just word dancing.

There is a time when you are out of place.

227

There is a time when you are out of time.
There is a time when you are out of space.

When everything you are is everything you have.

And you have nothing.

Then you understand.
Perhaps you begin to understand.
But beginning is temporal.

In the beginning was the word. The word is danger.

Before the word was before the beginning.

Before the beginning was the infinite.

The shadows on the walls spoke out:

We have no concept of before so we need no concept of beginning.

We are beyond
Beyond beginning
Beyond word

In the darkness Nick and Pryce were the same and different. They faced the same experience but in different guises. Their paths were the same and different. Nick wanted to reach out to Pryce, to tell him it would be all right. That there was something beyond, after, outside··· but he had no words and the shadows dimmed.

Pryce heard a voice: 'We have to go different ways. I have already gone one way and you have to go another. It's all a question of perspective. And perspective is less about where you stand and what you see and more about who you are.'

Nick reached out beyond the words. He wanted to hold Pryce.

But he knew he could not.

Pryce had his own questions. He must ask them of the shadows.

'By leaving danger will I find safety? Or is this just another kind of danger?'

Words played like shadows on the walls. The drum beat yin and yang.

So why did I have to leave?
You have to move to find stillness.
I don't understand.
Not to find stillness. To become still.
Stillness is infinity.
Immortality is beyond words.
Words bring legacy.
Music is movement but immortality is stillness.

Be careful of words. Use them wisely. They are tools.
Thoughts become words. Words become actions.
Actions have consequences. Consequence brings unexpected change.
Change explained by words is not change.
The vicious cycle. Or the virtuous circle.

You cannot always choose.
But I had to leave my home.
You cannot leave your home.
You are part of the family trees.
Always moving in order to be still.
Blowing with the wind.

Nick closed his eyes. Pryce was in the Cabrach Bunker. He had been there himself. He understood the confusion. The fear.

A people without a place are in danger.
The danger is when you are told 'seek and you shall find.'

229

I tell you, do not seek and you will find.
You are already in the place you want to be.

Desire as craving is dangerous.

The Cabrach was too close to the 100 men. Too close to the world of Ultimate. It was a place where there was something to steal and something to own and people to control and beliefs to requisition.

Nick could not clearly remember leaving the Cabrach Bunker. He knew it had something to do with an eclipse. He remembered the words from somewhere in the dark saying,

You are in more dimensions than you have awareness of. Become aware. Change the perspective.

And then the words in another part of the darkness saying,

When where am I becomes who am I?

And knowing that the words that spoke in the darkness were his own.

The chant continued:
Even in beauty there is pain.
We were rooted in the land.
We were forced to move.
We came back.
To another place that we recognised as home.
Home is where the heart is.
A whole Heart is spirit.
A fractured heart is so full it has burst open and the spirit bleeds into the world.
What is the matter?
What is matter?

When you know who you are
You will be where you are.

I wish. I hope.
In the darkness:

(Nick reached out to Pryce)
These are all dangerous dances to do with words.
(and he was gone)

Better be still.

He was back in the Bear Cave.

'Hilbert space takes you away from Euclid,' Jimmy said.

As if Nick had never been away. As if he knew who or what Euclid was.

'To understand Hilbert Space you have to begin with allowing non Euclidean geometry. Accept infinite dimensions,' Joe said.

Is it even possible? A thought. Not words. In his own head Nick was in the paradox of trying to hold on and let go with each breath. With each beat of the drum. Yin. Yang. Word. Thought. Action. Inaction. Wu wei.

'Wittgenstein, and you, want to hook yourselves onto a dimension, to 'fix' it with your point – your particle point – and yes, that will be the limit. Because that's the one word we let loose. LIMIT. Is that the key word in the sentence?' Joe said.

Nick understood then that philosophers and caves come in many forms and the philosophers in this cave were dimensions away from Plato. And Wittgenstein. And words and equations. And language and reason.

What do we mean by Enlightenment? East and West are never further apart then in this word as concept.

'You see what I'm saying,' Jimmy pressed. 'The more words you use the less certain your meaning becomes.'

So even an aphorism or an epigram are fixed in relativity,' Joe continued.

'The meaning of aphorisms and epigrams goes way beyond the words.'

Nick looked at the wall, he saw writing appearing from the shadows. Symbols, not words, as Jimmy explained:

'Words are trigger points, stepping stones, jump off points, into the Qi[M].'

'First you must understand Qi[ ] and by that I mean you must allow the space to exist in every dimension between the brackets which are our understanding of limit.'

Lying in the half-light with warmth suffusing his back into his body through his spine, Nick was unclear which of the philosophers was speaking. It didn't really matter. The drum beat yin, the drum beat yang. The story was multi-dimensional, coming at him from all angles. He let go, and let the story wash through him. Not over him. Through him. It became a part of him as he became a part of it.

'Welcome to quantum infinity.' Joe said.

And the drum ceased to beat.

'When you inhabit the space and do not see the [ ] as any form of boundary, then you will find [M]

'If you seek to place your own 'm' into the brackets, you are being Wittgensteinian. You place limits when you possess.'

A pause for correction, or effect.

'I said 'find' m and of course you cannot 'find' it. You have to become part of it. One with it.'

'First you will try to view from your perspective. That is natural.'

'You try to find your way into the 'M''

Nick opened his eyes. He saw the writing on the wall
Qi[M].

It was even more elegant than that most lauded equation which had travelled through spacetime even beyond $G\,Rs\,\Omega\,Hist$ or

E=mc2. This equation had more dimensions. Can it be an equation without equivalence, he wondered. Then let go again. But let go with his eyes wide open. Now he would begin to learn.

'You will note that for this notation we capitalise M to mean 'all moments are one moment' and 'm' is the stage before this, think of it as a 'particular' moment.'

Was it Jimmy or was it Joe? Did it even matter? The words came from beyond a particular man, beyond a particular place.

'And this must be beyond wave - But it is also beyond the 'limit' of language and world. Here is how I choose to render it,' the voice said:

$$\text{Qi[ ]} \quad \text{Quantum Infinity}$$
$$\text{Qi[m]} \quad \text{A moment in Quantum Infinity}$$
$$\text{Qi[M]}$$

You might see the first as the 'words' or the language.

Next is your approach –beyond the 'words' into the 'reality' or 'existence'

Then there is understanding that Qi[ ] 'is' all Moments.'

'But even here you have to have moved beyond thinking of the [ ] as bounding or containing. It frames. Multidimensionally. But there is no boundary of [ ] or in [ ]. It is just a way to help you while you still need a place to enter. When you are there you will not need it any more.'

'You have to learn to look at symbols/language/words as simply a conduit.'

'The Way that can be named is not the Way. The Way is Infinity.'

'Does infinity exist? Nick couldn't hold the question in.

The drum beat yin - the breath is out.

233

'What else exists apart from infinity?'

The drum beat yang - the breath is in.

The light flickered. The warmth invaded. Time held no power.
Infinity existed.

Form 41

PRYCE chops TORQUIL

The Cabrach Bunker

'Have we met before?'

Something about the voice seemed familiar to Pryce. He just couldn't place the man.

'Quantum question theory. Nike asked you about it. Do you remember?'

Pryce felt like he remembered everything about Nike, right up till the moment··· he hated to say the words. He hated even to think the thought. He steeled himself: Up to the moment he died.

He noticed he was sweating.

'You remember?' the man pressed.

Pryce was captivated by his eyes. They were so familiar. So··· so like Nike's eyes.

'He was like a son to you, no?'

Pryce wondered if the man could read his thoughts.

'Who are you?' he asked.

'He made you feel like a father.'

It was a statement not a question.

And what is it to be a father? It was a question Pryce had asked himself many, many times. He remembered how Nike had made him feel. Proud. Trusted. Good. And the grief when he died. Nothing had ever felt like that. He had not let it show but it was like it had killed a part of himself. Or maybe it had brought a part of himself alive. The desire to fight back. Even when he knew it was pointless. Even when every part of him wanted to give in. Somehow he knew that he had had to continue. Even when it made no sense.

And now, here he was. Facing the unknown. Waiting for Ultimate.

Pryce had assumed that a father would be prepared to do anything for his son. To die for him if necessary. But Nike had not been his son. He had been a boy who shone bright, and for whom he had taken risks; who had amazed him and confused him and charmed him and aggravated him. In whom he saw much of himself and something far beyond himself. But he was not his father. He knew that. He had not been prepared to sacrifice himself. And Nike was dead.

Out of the darkness the man spoke again.

'Do you remember the tutorial on Quantum Question Theory? "So, what is the purpose of UTheory $\sum$ ®?"'
It was not just Nike's question.
That's when we met.'
'We met?' Pryce was confused.
The aim of Question Theory is to produce data which helps the ULTIMATE® system refine itself.'
The man quoted the definition Pryce remembered working on with Nike, just before···
'You felt like a father then.'
Again, not a question, a statement.
'How did you know?'
'I was there.'
'But how?'
'Cogs in a wheel, right?'
'Why am I here?'
'Our boy.'
'Our boy?'
'Nick'.
'Nike?'
'In one world he is Nike, but in my world he is Nick.'
'He was your son?' Pryce asked.
'Nike is your son.'
'I was never his father,' Pryce said.

It was only when he said the words that he realised how much he had wished it had been true. To be a father. To be Nike's father. That would have been something worth living for. Something beyond the pain and bitterness and emptiness. In a split second he had an idea what being a father meant. The emotion all but overwhelmed him. He added:

'If I had been, I would have sacrificed myself.'

'What?'

'I was not prepared to sacrifice myself for him.'

The admission impacted like a bullet in his chest. Pryce felt sick. And somehow more real.

'It's not about sacrifice,' the man said. 'It's not about whether you would die for him. Whether you would try to trade your life for his. Life isn't a transaction. It's about love. And love is not about sacrifice. You can't trade your way into and out of emotions.'

'But Nike is dead.' Pryce felt that for all the man's sophistry, this was a fact that had to be acknowledged. It was a truth. His truth.

'That is just one part of him. The same part of you has died. Think of it like trees··· death is just part of a larger process.'

Pryce struggled to take it in.

'Oh, come on. You taught the theory: the principle of $UTheory \sum \circledR$ is the acceptance that the theory changes as the system changes. The system has changed. We have changed. The theory, therefore, changes. It's not about life and death. It's all a matter of perspective. Of where you are. Of who you are. Of the choices made and not made.'

There was a silence. An expectation to respond.

And so Pryce looked firmly into the man's eyes, even though he felt a fear.

The man reached out. Pryce braced himself for the hit. This was the man he had let down. The man he had dreamed of being but failed to live up to. How could he be forgiven? Ultimate had stolen this man's son, and he had been responsible···

The father grasped Pryce's hand and shook it hard.

'And now it's my time to thank you.'

'I don't need thanks,' Pryce said, shocked. 'Your son died. You told me. I remember.'

'It was part of the deal. You told my mother. You kept your part. Now I'll keep mine.'

'What is that?' Pryce asked.

'Opening the door to choice.'

'What choice is there?'

'Reality is what you choose to believe,' the man said. 'Do you believe that?'

'Are you going to kill me,' Pryce said.

He had assumed the man was there to kill him. He was ready for that. But that was when he thought he was from Ultimate. Now…

'You're already dead,' Torquil said.

Pryce was stunned.

'Feels good, doesn't it?' Torquil laughed.

So death was not the end. Or even an end. Or this was not death. Nothing made sense. He had no idea where he was, but even more he had no idea who he was any more.

'So what is my name… now?' Pryce asked.

'You want a birth name or a given name?'

'I can pick?'

Torquil smiled. 'We can all pick who we are,' he said. 'It's the one choice they can't take from us, no matter how much they think they can.'

'I don't...' Pryce was overwhelmed.

'To them, now, you have ceased to exist. So now you really live.'

'Without a name?'

'We can call you Jason,' Torquil said, 'because your journey is not yet over. There is unfinished business for you…'

'Jason?' He tried it over in his mind and his mouth.

'Yes, I can live with that.'

It had a familiarity about it.

Jason paused, understanding the ridiculous enormity of what he

238

had just said. Live. A small word, but he felt more alive than he had for decades. Here, in the darkness, with a stranger.

'And now what?' he asked.

'Take yourself back to the world before Angela. To the man you might have been. If you had followed another part of the story. In that world you might have had children. A boy and a girl. There's a boy and a girl who need you. Who have also been uprooted. You need to plant yourselves somewhere new. You have to lead the way for them. They are young.'

'So am I not coming with you?'

'You have another place to be. With them.'

'And Nike?'

Jason, as he now was, knew as soon as he had said the name that he had let go of 'his' boy.

'Nick's safe with me,' Torquil said.

'And who am I to you?'

You are part of our family tree. The words were never said, but whispered like the wind words they were.

In the deep light of the darkness an answer was unnecessary.

They were brothers. They had both been father to a boy.

But their paths were now different. They had come together just briefly, to pursue a greater aim, but now was the time to part.

'Can I see him again?' Struggling to identify as Jason, Pryce felt he could not leave without at least asking this question.

From behind him, out of the darkness, a voice came. A recognisable voice.

'Hey man··· you're here···'

He could feel the boy standing right beside him. He wanted to look, but he knew that if he did, Nike would not be there. He could almost taste and smell his presence. But he dared not look. He tried to stay light.

'You got any questions for me?' Pryce asked.

'Got some answers,' the boy replied.

'You don't need me then,' Pryce said.

'They need you,' the boy said.

'They?'

'Omo and Flora.'

Of course. He knew it.

'We all need each other,' the boy continued. 'Will you..?'

He didn't need to finish the sentence.

'Of course I will.'

'It means you can't see me again,' the boy continued. 'But hey, sight isn't the most important sense now, is it?'

'No? When'd you get so wise?'

'Spend enough time staring at a wall in the dark and you learn some stuff,' the boy replied, laughing.

Pryce wanted so badly to turn round. To see Nike. He had never felt so close.

'Don't do that,' Nick said.

'What?'

'You know.'

Jason looked up. Before, it had been completely dark. Now he was sure he could pick out some lights. Pinpricks in the sky. All the stars in the sky shone down. Every one a possibility.

'Hey, did you know? There's a flaw in their theory of everything.'

Jason laughed, 'I never knew that.'

'Well it's true. Cool, huh?'

Typical Nike. He had so missed the boy.

'But what does it mean?' Jason Pryce asked.

It was more a question to himself, he wasn't even sure if it came out in words or remained in thoughts. But he got an answer, almost before he had asked the question.

'It means that Ultimate does not control the random element. Which means there's a hole in their system of everything. You could call it a worm hole if you like. Actually, it's more like a sieve. There are holes everywhere. You just got to find them. And you don't find them by looking. You find them by understanding. So now you know. Theory only takes you so far. You have to live. Go find Omo and Flora.'

He finally realised he had been offered a choice. A chance. It was still hard not to feel it like a sacrifice. But that might be because he craved love so badly and yet understood it so tentatively. He still wanted to turn and embrace Nike. But Nike was gone. Nick had given him a path to follow. A purpose. Beyond Ultimate. Beyond Pryce. He was Jason.

Form 42

TORQUIL stabilises CALLUM

Transformation

There's a bond between a father and a son which even a mother cannot fathom.

The roots of the family tree spread many ways and nurture comes in many forms.

Even on the darkest of nights, a father and son can feel each other standing shoulder to shoulder. Sometimes they do not need to look each other in the eye. And however much they want to hold each other in their arms, they keep a distance. The embrace is saved for the women. When a father and son are men, especially when they are men who have lost each other along the way, their strength is shown in different ways. Their love is shown in different ways. Just as strong. But different.

Torquil and Callum Christie were a father and a son who could not face each other.

Words had been said. Actions had been taken. The words and the deeds spun through time make the web of existence on every level we cannot even imagine.

'I lost a daughter and you lost a son. Let's not lose each other,' the father said.

And off they went.

Before the sunset. Into other worlds.

Worlds of war as they both raged against the system.

After fifteen years of death on a farm and ten years of trying to deal with the consequences of these deaths, they took actions.

They both needed to learn of the seasons of infinity.

They both had the same question: 'Why must we sacrifice our children?'

But the answer was different.

Now they stood together, side by side, together as long as they did not come face to face. And they talked.

We lost our way.
Our pain isolated us, father and son.

Remember when we functioned as a family?

Torquil smiled at the memory.

'Dad, remember mum's birthday that time. You took her out and we made a cake. Before the decades of death.'

'I remember.'

'We were apart and then we came together again.'

'And will that happen again now?'

Twenty years of death and dying.
Twenty years of life and living.
Twenty years of transformation.

'Just remember, dad.'

'I have so many memories I don't know where to start.'

Callum had nothing left but memories, it seemed. The burden of the years had weighed heavily on his shoulders. The loss piled upon loss had the stench of death he had first smelled in 2001. He had never really recovered from that smell.

Then he lost his daughter. Then his grandson. Then his son. Then his wife. Then himself. Then hope. And so he stood, beyond hope, in the darkness, looking up at the sky. Beside the son he had taken with him. And then lost. Or who had lost him.

A father had to ask his son a question. It was not right. The ways of the world told him that as father he should provide answers, not questions. But he had no answers. He had given his life and the lives of all those around him to find the answers. And answer came there none. So now he had to ask.

'I'm asking you for us to be reunited. As a family. Together again.'

He wondered if his son had that power. He doubted and had faith all at the same time. And he knew that doubt and faith were the wrong language. But he had no words for what he wanted to say. So the son spoke first.

'Dad, if you can only have one person to be with, the rest of your life, who would it be?'

'How can I choose?'

And as he said it, he knew that he had already chosen.

The answer, as always, lay in the question.

There was one more question.

'Did you have to kill me?'

It was a question Callum felt he should have asked man to man, face to face, but he knew that if he turned, his son would be gone and all hope of a future would go with it.

'You came to the Immortal Horses. You wanted me to do something. I did something, dad. I did all that I could.'

'That was then. Now you are still killing people but bringing them back to life in another place. If you've done it for them you can do it for me.'

'Casablanca, dad.'

'What?'

'How did it end?'

'Sacrifice.'

'But we are better than that, right?'

'Are we?'

'Dad, I'm *your* son. I'm better than that.'

'So what can you do? Breathe life into us? Make us all immortal?'

Torquil smiled.

'Dad, it's already done. You just have to go get her. She's waiting for you.'

Could it be that simple?

'Just let go, dad.'

Is it that simple?

'Where are we?' Callum asked.
'You know where we are, dad,' Torquil said.
'I only know where she is,' Callum said. 'And that I cannot reach her.'
'You can, dad, you can.'

We are scattered, like seeds on the ground, but seeds that have died because they were not watered.

'She's the river, dad.'

And he knew he just had to follow the river.

But before he went on his Odyssey, beyond his own understanding of name as the thief of identity, he had thoughts to resolve.
He had to learn to see time differently. Then he would be able to reach her.

And so he learned. His son taught him. And he learned.

A pattern emerged in his being. A pattern which would take him beyond the dimensions he knew of. And when he found himself, he would find her. And when he found her, he would take her and by letting go he would never let her go again. And he would never let go of himself. By letting go. The paradox of infinity cannot be completed. It is not faith or hope or trust or truth. It just is. Enter infinity. Be.

Form 43

CALLUM blocks HELEN'S flow

Letting Go

If stories don't have a beginning then they don't have an end either. But they do have a point where you can be lost.

And Callum became Randall became Odysseus and went on his journey.

He learned as he travelled.

Branches get broken and limbs are chopped off.
Beech trees are not bamboo. They have different root systems.

It may be significant.

He learned as he travelled.

Figure out what kind of tree you are.
How do you move out of the wrong forest?

Find your cave.
Follow the river?
No. Step into the river.
Become the river.

He went to the magnolia cave.
She knew him.
Not by his name but by who he was.

He took her away from there and they went together to places they had been before and places they had only dreamed of.

They sat together at the mouth of the cave. Together in the

moment. In all moments.

'You know I didn't send you the cake,' he said.

'Then who?'

'If it wasn't you, and it wasn't Torquil···'

He smiled.

'Where is she?' she asked.

'I don't know,' he replied. 'But she is somewhere, out there, out on a limb as always.'

And Helen cried. But they were tears of joy not tears of sorrow.

'They are all somewhere but we cannot always see them,' he said. 'It is different now.'

'But it is freedom,' she said.

'Letting go is the price we pay for freedom,' she said. 'I see that now.'

'It doesn't follow the path of logic or rational thought,' he said.

'We are way beyond that,' she agreed.

'But then we always were,' he said. 'We just forgot it for a while.'

'A long while.'

'It's all relative,' he said.

And it was. It is.

Whatever you think about time. It passes.

She held his watch.

'I gave it to Nick,' she said. 'Because I thought it was a way to get back to you. If I let go of it, I would let go of you and if I let go of you, I would let go of myself···'

'And that is when I found you,' he said.

'We found each other,' she said.

He stood on a boulder above the river and threw the watch with all his strength. It glinted in the sun as it spun through the air and crashed into pieces on the rocks in the river. A kaleidoscope of timeless time, flowing as part of the river.

'You loved that watch,' she said.

'It has served its purpose, he said. 'Now time is no more.'

'The watch is just a symbol

To keep time in place

But we know time

We have no need of a watch.
We know how to keep time in our pocket.'
And she knew that he was right.

是不是

We have to find new ways to think about things. New ways to get beyond the naming of things. New paths and new patterns and new ways of engaging with ourselves in all possible worlds.

You might put a date on it. And if you did, it would be the total solar eclipse on August 22nd, 2044. At 18.31, if you are so wedded to time.

All moments came together from the Cabrach to Canada and the darkness fell. It was possible to look at the sun because there was no sun. And in the light of that darkness anything is possible. Day becomes night and dark becomes light to pinpoint a moment in all the moments.

是不是

Helen and Callum were found in that moment outside timeless time, he in the mouth of a cave, looking down at a river. She in the river, looking up at the mouth of the cave. Apart but together in the dog-eared day which usually passes from sunset to sunrise without so much as a whimper.

Of all the sunsets in all the worlds, you walk into mine.

'I never know what day it is,' she said.
'And it doesn't matter,' he said.
She understood.
'Remember the old story?' she asked.
'The fishing line?'
'Yes.'
'The one part of the story we didn't think about was the river.'
And the truth is in the river. The truth is the river. Our truth.
The answer was always in the question.

248

To look for more is futility.

And in the moment when all moments became visible she said
'Do you know my favourite?'
'Favourite what?'
'Time.'
'Time?'
'Moment.'
He drew her closer to him and breathed her in.
'It's when you can see the sun and the moon in the sky at the same time,' he said.
'How did you know?' she asked.
He smiled.
'Because it's my favourite too.'

是不是

We all see the sun in different ways. The beauty found in sunset and sunrise is surely the transformation in front of our eyes. The connectedness through spacetime seen every day but individually unique. You can't truly capture a sunset. You never fully hold onto a sunrise. You can't make sense of them by counting them, any more than by recording them. They just are.

They are and we are.

As a game, they shared a private language, giving Wittgenstein a chance to turn in his grave.

'You came'
'You called'

Lines from another story, and our story, and every story that ends well, especially stories which recognise there is no ending or beginning, only moments which are part of the moment.
Paradox is the path.

是不是

'I want to be with them all again,' she said. 'But I'm afraid of caves. I can't go in.'

She stood in the river and suddenly he felt she was slipping

249

away.

'Why?' he asked though he already knew.

'Sometimes we see most clearly with our eyes closed,' he said.

'Perhaps, but I love the light,' she replied.

'Dusk leads to darkness but twilight leads to early dawn.'

'I know that, but in between is darkness. Real darkness. I hate it. I've lived too long in the darkness.'

'You have just been in the wrong cave,' he replied.

'Some of us are just not cave-dwellers,' she said.

And she was right.

'If I have to go into the cave to see them…'

'You don't,' he said.

'I cannot stand being dead,' she said. 'Even if that's the only way to be with you. I can't do it.'

'You don't have to,' he said.

What frightened her about death was not dying. Not the concept. It was the actuality and the waste and the void.

The sense that it was the final inner darkness. Fear of an endless total soular eclipse. No more sun. No more life.

Philosophers deal in threshold arguments. But this was one threshold he could not carry her over.

'If I step into the cave, I will die,' she said.

'Reality is what you choose to believe,' he replied.

'It's what I believe,' she said. 'I can't follow you there. I can't be with them there. Whatever it costs.'

As the light faded on the mountain, she understood that it is never truly dark in the cave.

He turned and led her away from the river, past the myriad shining pieces of a watch which now was not a watch and for whom time had shattered into more dimensions than could be imagined.

是不是

There is always the river. She was the river. Quantum entanglement in action.

And when they were both dead, or characters, no one would ever know or care that

He loved the twilight.

She loved the dawn.

Or even that they were united in their appreciation of the moments when day and night co-mingled.

It didn't matter

It doesn't matter

What mattered was they had this part of the moment entirely to themselves,

And all the parts of moment come together in the river.

'I love you Helen,' Callum said.

'Don't fight it,' he added gently. 'Just go with it.'

And so she did. She accepted it wasn't about coming and going and waiting and leaving and living and dying. Or dark and light. It was about so much more than that. Beyond caves and boxes were acts of creation experienced in something infinitely more than the best of all possible worlds. He took her by the hand and felt her with him, by his side, at the mouth of the cave. And yet still in the river.

And another voice spoke:

Sitting in the mouth of the cave the warm sun encloses me in a cotton wool daydream. I can hear laughter coming up to me from the river. I can just see her through the trees, running like a hare and he is close behind. She's jumping up onto a big boulder beside the river and has her arms out, turning and turning. Her head looks up towards me at the cave looking and laughing. He stands still. I can't see his face from here but I think he's laughing too. He joins her on the boulder. They embrace. No, more than that, they fall into each other. As they touch, they change form and photons of light replace their humanity with multi-coloured streams - colours such as I've never seen before. I raise my hand to shade my eyes. The light gets brighter and brighter as photons collide with the most amazing bursts of energy as they scatter away into infinity···the river. Beyond their words, in their world, I have found my way.

舞蹈无翼 无耻

We are all together and I have broken out of all the boxes and all the stories in all the worlds. Where everything is relative, everyone and everything is related. And all moments are truly one moment. We just call it here and now because here and now is where we are in our particular part of the moment. We sit in the cave until we understand that being in the river is the quantum leap that allows us to be what and who we are beyond space and time. When we do not need to cast the rod to catch the fish because we are the fish and we are the river.

Letting go is realising that all the worlds are not in the box and caves are not boxes. They are simply places of refuge until we can all dance in the waters of the river. And to suggest that that which cannot be spoken of should be passed over in silence is the prison for those who believe that the limits of language make the limits of their world.

'Nan,hey, Nan, remember life is but a dream.'
'Mum, I'm going to make you a napple pie.'
'Mum, look at the bubble tree.'

She was finally able to thank Catriona for the birthday cake.

The confusion lifted. She held hands with her family. One by one and all together.

They understood, in that part of the moment, that the only escape from dystopia is utopia. And utopia is simply an allusion to guide us beyond equations.

They realised that beyond the Ultimate world is Qi[M].
And that
Life is but a dream whether you are a man or a butterfly.

WUJI
无极

Form 44

Mind the Gap

It's time to open the circle.
It's time to look into the cave of your choice.

Do not fear the gap at the entrance to the cave. Respect it, as you step carefully.

One thing is certain, you will walk this way more than once.

And what you see will determine what you think.
And what you think will determine what you see.

As all good quantum theorists will tell you; the act of observing interferes with and irreversibly changes what is being observed.

Entanglement is the essential property of quantum systems.

And what does this mean for narrative? To get personal, what does this mean for you, hey, yes, that's YOU - reading this book, now! You are part of this as it is part of you. Even if you stop reading. Even if you burn the book. Even if you keep it hidden from your waking mind, now it's part of you. You are part of it.

A lesson from quantum mechanics is that we can't understand the nature of reality. We should learn to live with this realisation and accept we only have partial knowledge of what reality is. We must learn to let go.

Yet this lesson was taught thousands of years ago. It has been repeated in every place and at every time. It is the moment revealed in parts.
Western eyes don't want to hear.
Western ears don't want to see.

They cannot understand or accept the darkness of the Western Enlightenment.

Scientists spend too much time trying to explain, when all you need is to experience.

After all, at the end of the clichéd day when push comes to shove, science is just another grand narrative. Scientists know this. Science is a story, predicated on answers. To measure is to create. But what kind of a creation are they selling us? There are many gaps to mind out for and many people fall into the trap of thinking it is our purpose to fill them all. Some try to fill the gaps with the theoretical language of mathematics.

As the sun should not be looked at with the naked eye, so maths is the language of those who would wear, if not blinkers, then at least sun glasses. Of those who are afraid to be burned by the sun they are obsessed with harnessing. Who want to count and measure and fix. Not content with naming the unnameable, they want to count the infinite. They geld the stallion and call it 'horse'. They put a size on infinity. Their only poor achievement is a fixed 'reality', created hypothetically outside of the system it constrains by measurement. The act of measurement defines what is being measured. At least this is mathematics in the Western tradition.

By putting layers between the unknowable reality and their world, Western culture strives to contain and control and rationalise and fix that which cannot be caught. And so the gap becomes a black hole. A vortex into which we fall headlong, all the while demanding that our box is not a box and our system is not of our making. And that the world should bend to our will and all things bow down before us.

The desire to hypothesise out of the system we created is a will to power. We are just things among things. We are part of nature not the rulers of nature. We have no position of privilege unless we make it so. The world is as we make it And if we create it as a system, we live within that system. How many times and how many ways can one say this.

This is the reality paradox. Be mindful of gaps. Especially the gap between
>language and thought
>Words and ideas
>言 和 思想

If you step over them into the cave which houses the walls of discourse on the nature of linguistic meaning, you may find that the only reality of linguistic science is the word. Its embodiment is its reality.

书不尽 言   shūbùjìnyán
Writing cannot fully express words

言 不尽 以   yánbùjìnyì
Words cannot fully express what is in my heart

This is truth in any version of language.

In this cave you will find angels dancing on the heads of pins, who are also wont to argue/disagree that Chinese does or doesn't have a written alphabet. They are lost in symbols and signs and they try to box up alpha-beta- para-doxia in shiny packages that only the intellectually wealthy can open.

That these angels cannot agree on language and its purpose surely serves as a great example that 'the way that can be named is not the way.'

But the cave of Western linguistics is every bit as dank as the cave of Western philosophy. The walls drip with symbol and sign and signifier and sleazy sentences struggling to survive, all of which are lost in the translation beyond words into the moment beyond meaning.

Which brings us to the gap of truth -or is it a gap of credibility?

Truth might be defined (in a box) as a recognition made in any culture by any generation.

And yet. Over timeless time we discover the same questions. The same needs. Progress is impossible in a timeless environment. So if you must aim, aim for depth not direction. The destination is in the journey. All moments are one moment. Perhaps the same thing is said in many ways because there is only one thing to say and that is everything. And the journey is finding your place in the moment, where everything you feel is everything you are; where you become part of the dao. This is life. Some consider it a burden they carry. Some wear it lightly. Either way, what you are looking for is what you carry with you, mostly afraid that somehow what is behind you will catch you up and crush you, until one day the load is lifted and there is no way back. In that moment you may find you are not tapping yourself on the shoulder or patting yourself on the back.

From small to big, from dark to light, from lies to truth.

When you look behind and come face to face with yourself, there is no more fear.

If you let go.

You just are.

In all dimensions.

This is Qi[M]

Not all questions have answers.
Do all questions have answers?
Is this the question paradox?
And does it matter?
Is this a question?
Quantum entanglement is timeless infinity.
Nothing matters except while you are doing it.

These are not answers.
Nor are they questions.
Or statements.

They are cave writings.

FORM 45

The Cave of Infinity

Breaking free from the constraints of the novel as narrative par excellence, I remember that I was born a philosopher.

'What is beyond infinity?' I asked when I was being taught to count.

'Infinity is the largest thing there is.'

And other voices said, 'The universe is the largest thing there is.'

I used to lie in bed wondering what was outside the universe. I suspect this metaphysical stance is not common in a three year old. It may, of course, be exactly the nature of a three year old. Only the mind of a three year old knows the mind of the three year old, after all.

However long I followed the yellow brick road in childhood, however many mountains I climbed in search of my dreams, I choked on metaphysics when I came back to it in my teens.

I was not the only one.

I first met J.M.Barrie when I was seven, not through *Peter Pan*, but through a back stage pass to the adult world of drama; which hooked me into the sensuality of plush velvet seats and the dangerous comfort they provide, and even more significantly took me to the parts the audience rarely reaches - the dressing room and the stage door. These places held a fascination for me over and far beyond the stage, the bright lights and the applause.

I broke out of the proscenium arch into the empty space possibilities of black boxes and then out of the black boxes towards infinity, and I learned that there is much more in heaven and earth than are dreamed of in a philosophy, either west or east. *The Admirable Crichton* taught me 'what's natural is right' while *Dear Brutus* revealed that 'the fault lies not in the stars but in ourselves', as Shakespeare had noted much earlier. Creative originality is a river without a source.

Barrie was so much more than a dramatist and a novelist, and he shared my youthful reaction to metaphysics. I know because he told us so. Though with Barrie, nothing is ever fixed. He knew the mutability of the human condition more than most and he played with depth in structure in a way that holds me in awe now, even as I was in awe on that first day in that first theatre. Sometimes I wonder if he was a cognitive scientist before it was invented as a concept, never mind a discipline. He was certainly way ahead of his time. We still haven't caught up with him. I believe we still misinterpret just about everything he said.

Which is perhaps how he wanted it.

Whereas I had a burning need to communicate. To share identity through words and beyond the words.

Barrie wrote pencil sketches of his professors. I reflect on mine. The philosophers who shaped my philosophy. Then.

When I was seventeen.
I ran from metaphysics.
Into the arms of fiction.

I told myself it was
Too difficult.
It was not too difficult.
My situation was too difficult.

I recognise now that I was overwhelmed.

261

Not by metaphysics but by education.
By the chance to inhabit my own identity
To be myself, if only I could find who I was.

I went to the beach.
I found myself.
I went to the pub.
I lost myself.

I talked. I listened. I thought. I read.

And when I wasn't talking or listening or thinking or reading,

I became myself.
A human being not a human doing.
Being and not being.
Life as drama. Not narrative.

Somewhere in Beckett, while waiting for Godot, in the absurdity of Stoppard and the rhythm of T.S. Eliot, there was a murder in a cathedral. I moved beyond Tennyson and Ulysses. I believed in the Gods. I became Athene in some small part of my being. Without knowing it.

I left literature behind. Lost words in my pursuit of thoughts. Then the thoughts turned into dramatic actions. Because I was not the first to think that philosophers have only interpreted the world, while the point was to change it.

I would change the world.

I believed it.

Drama takes words and gives them a multidimensional existence. A meaning beyond the private word read off the page. Actors inhabit the worlds and live the meanings. But that was not enough for me.

I thought I wanted to make meaning.
Still a philosopher, I wanted to think meaning into existence. I was trained the western way. The writing on the wall was there. I was not, nor would I ever be, an analytic philosopher. But that was the training manual I was given. The answers and the questions I was allowed. These were not me. I did not recognise myself. I was lost in the wrong cave.

I wanted to create meaning.
I was wrong.
Being is not creating.
I am part of the creation not the creator.
Did I not learn that on the beach?
Looking up at the stars.
Somehow it got lost in the translations.
Of the stories in the songs and the songs in the stories.

But now I return to metaphysics, like Odysseus to Ithaca. To a place I lost somewhere on the journey away from myself [west] selfso/ziran [east] along a path less travelled which nevertheless was not my path. I return to the book of metaphysics called 'The Big Questions', in search of Heraclitus, a philosopher I never knew. A philosopher no one ever knew. A man as elusive as Homer and Lao Tzu.[West] Laozi [East].

They were all brothers in the journey.

The journey goes beyond the blue book and the brown book and that elusive third book of philosophical investigations. Past all the philosophers who talked about 'The best of all possible worlds' and yet none of whom seem to have found what they were looking for, or talking about. They said the path was through logic. The gatekeeper was Wittgenstein. And I was not allowed to meet him. I did not have the right password. My credentials were not measurable in number theory. I was not welcome to play an active part in their best of all possible worlds. I was simply there to make up the numbers. And my numbers just did not add up. I scored 11, repeatedly. In that world this was failure. In my world it was honesty. To be allowed into the inner sanctum I needed a higher score. I had my chance. I sat next to a 96. I could have copied his numbers. But that would have been like stealing someone else's thoughts. Re-writing a story out of cowardice, not honesty. So I threw my dice. I held my 11 fast and firm. And I failed. And in that failing was my success. It simply put me on another path. A path which led through caves of darkness for more than three times eleven. I never accepted the validity of numbers. I never believed in them. I still don't.

Somehow in all the caves I explored I never came across Heraclitus. His fragments were written on a wall, waiting, while I found my way back to the big book of metaphysics. I did not follow as the crow flies. Or even as the rat runs. I was always the random particle. My philosophical spirit was lost in the translation from East to West. A ghost masquerading as a monkey. On a Journey to the West. And my direction of travel was out of the gilded western cage which is still a box by any other name. There are more things in heaven and earth than are dreamed of in any philosophy and any language east or west.

The road less travelled was a shadow on my wall.

The world beyond philosophy, laughingly called the 'real' world, taught me to throw mud at walls, not to sit and look at them. Certainly never to think about the writing that would appear on them if I sat long enough in the right cave.

I was lost in the movie screen wondering if there was *Life on Mars*.

Unlike me, Heraclitus resisted.
Like the Daoist masters he tailored his own cloth.
He did not become part of the cloth.
And so the world turned

264

The drum beats yin
The drum beats yang.
Heraclitus privileged fire.
Analytic philosophy privileges logic.

But in the world of quantum infinity you can't privilege any element.

Metaphysics is bigger and yet, it's just a word. A word with no bigger meaning than many others.

Beyond the word it is something that is learned in the fifty six forms which were first imagined by a three year old self. At least for me it is and has been.

In this text and beyond, I am in a place where metaphysics is no longer something to run from. You can run but you can't hide and I am no longer hiding from my natures. I am indistinguishable from the elements which make me. Mind, body and soul admit of no duality or holy trinity.

Nothing is but what is not.
I have discovered.

Paradoxes should be embraced not resisted. Truth lies in paradox. The ancients knew this. The adepts learn this. Do you understand this?

What you make of this is your part of the truth.

Not our truth, not your truth, not my truth. Not Heraclitus' personal truth, not the anti-realists rejection of truth. Just Qi[M] which is a symbol that represents that which cannot ever be understood through representation.

When you understand that the concept of equation is a problem on a fundamental level, you are free to find

$$\text{Reality} \approx *Qi[M]$$

Equivalency is a flawed concept. Like Metaphor. Metaphor is representational. Things are described 'in terms' of other things. Some say that metaphor is mapping difficult, partly understood concepts onto easier ones. A theory of target and source. I'm not so sure. It seems like the west skirting round yinyang to me.

The symbol = is a symbol for metaphor in a different language.

I don't like looking at my feet and footnotes are not for me, so this is not a footnote, but since I know you wonder: $\approx *$ represents the perspective that nothing is actually equal. Witness, the death of the equation.

If you accept that there is no true equivalency, you come to see that metaphors and equations do not exist $\approx$ in a meaningful way. They are particles (albeit complex particles) in a quantum spacetime.

Things ARE what they are
and all are part of Qi[M]

Feel free to disagree. You have probably been trained in the Western way. You have bought the box labelled 'freedom' which nevertheless constrains.

And so, if you must ask what is on the left hand side of this quantum non-equation, I can give you an answer.

That's you. That's the way. That's what you have to find in order to be.

Let's go mind dancing.

Newton's laws of motion would hold that equations have to resolve to 0

There are so many problems with 0

Can 0 exist?

Is 0 equivalent to nothing in any meaningful way?

Ask Bishop Berkeley. Ask King Lear. Ask yourself.

Trust no one and nothing.

Trust nothing?

And we are in the world of paradoxes again.

That's a good thing.

When a question easily resolves to a paradox, you are in a good place in your being.

In Eastern terms 0 is not a number. It is a concept. It is called Wu Chi. If you use Wade-Giles. If you use Pinyin it is Wuji. Either and both ways, it is an open circle to infinity.

Even simplified as characters, the word as concept has many meanings:

At the click of a button I find three:

舞池 (dance floor)

无耻 (Without any sense of shame)

无持 (wingless)

All depending on your tone.

I was always told I spoke in the wrong tone of voice.

Now I understand.

But finally, it becomes the void, the emptiness, the infinite.

Nothing is ever fixed.

A question you ask me and I ask myself is:
How do you place the void in infinity?
The way that is named is not the way.
Find the answer in the question.

Here in the west, we are lost in a world of words and numbers. Classification and dividing and sortal references.

Words as rules
Words as symbols
Thoughts and ideas.

And if Socratic dialogue was good enough for Socrates (but was it?) and the Greeks, then why is it not good enough for you and I. Or you and me?

Question and answer is just one part of how people arrive by their paradoxes and/or resist the metaphysical world, which is a world of paradox.

Only when you are lost will you be found.

I have read that Socrates may simply have been Plato playing a joke. Reality is what you choose to believe. I believe that. And I don't believe it. Fundamentally what I believe is unimportant and irrelevant to any of the cases.

When I stopped looking for answers, I found that in the space between Heraclitus and Wittgenstein is a dancer. His Wade-Giles name is Lao Tzu. His pinyin name is Laozi. Name is the thief of identity. Also he may never have existed.

This man who perhaps never and always existed says that the western metaphysical tradition (as I understand it, which is not very clearly) seems to be like Western ideas of a garden. Or so I read him. When a garden is something you must create and control, this is not the way. This is not nurturing. Nothing grows honestly unless it is free to roam. Weeds do not exist except in the mind.

One man's weed is another man's medicine.

One man's terrorist is another man's freedom fighter.

And the Ultimate world is not the only possible one. We just got stuck there for a while.

Any way you come to it, it is all part of Qi (because everything is part of Qi)

$$My \ path \ is \ \approx *Qi[M]$$

Let us dance wingless without shame.

If I were to offer a definition of creativity, I could do no better - in any language.

FORM 46

How To Escape

If you start from a false premise, don't be surprised when you reach a false conclusion.

First Find the right cave	Find your cave
Then Sit in the right cave	Sit in your cave
Just Be in the right cave	Be in your cave

It is difficult to ask the right question. Or to frame it correctly. Especially if one comes from the wrong perspective. Or from a perspective where right and wrong are essentially meaningless.

Ask rather: How did we get here?

Ask rather: Where is here?

Brand Loyalty led to the Ultimate World. But the Ultimate World was not the best of all possible worlds. 'Best' is a poor concept and a much worse word. It's a word for a world of hierarchy.

It has no meaning to us.

The Ultimate World of Brand Loyalty might be described as dystopia.

Or reality.
Or not.
Fact or fiction.
Both.

It's a part of 'all' that I don't want to inhabit.

And the only way I know how way to escape from a dystopia is into a utopia.

There are places real and imaginary. There are boxes and caves in all shapes and sizes.

Suspension of disbelief is embracing the narrative.

Science forges its own narratives. From black holes to wormholes, to Hilbert Space. It's all just stories. There are even college courses which teach about evil numbers. Beware of evil numbers; they will check you in to the Hilbert hotel, which is a way to constrain infinity.

Check it out.   Check out.

Pick the flavour of your spin and dance with your mind beyond the words in the text boxes.

Head west, head east, head up/down/in/out/back/forth -

There is no waiting any more

Waiting is a fixed point/particle in the wave

Beyond waiting is being.

You still want to know how to escape?

Even as I learn the fifty six forms
I let go of the fifty six forms

From all the boxes in all the worlds and all the caves in all the minds, when we broke free from the constraints of the hierarchy and of the world of best and real and identity.

We found ourselves.
Yes FOUND ourselves.
And in finding we realised we were already here.

FORM 47

More False Premises

If you start from a false premise, don't be surprised when you reach a false conclusion.

'What if Plato was wrong?'

'What do you mean?'

'Well, the story is about how the people in shackles look at the shadows on the wall and then some of them get out into the light. Then they try to come back and the people refuse to leave the shadows.'

'What if the light was the Ultimate world and the people who went out there got caught up in it. What if the people who stayed and looked at the walls made the best choice?'

'And never see reality?'

'That suggests that outside that particular cave was a reality worth seeing.'

'Sight isn't everything.'

'No, but a sunny day··· who can resist a sunny day?'

'Perhaps learning to accept the dark is a better choice.'

She shuddered.

'I don't think I can ever accept the dark.'

'You do it every time you shut your eyes.'

'Yes, but that's 'my' dark. Not an external darkness. It's my choice. And I can always open my eyes.'

'But you can't control what you see when you open them.'

'That's true.'

They sat for a while.

'What if it's just the wrong cave?'

'Meaning?'

'There's many different caves.'
'So can you take me to the best of all possible caves?'
'Of course I can.'

What is the relationship between actions and consequences?

Watching the waves collapse on the beach. It's a metaphor. But what really is a metaphor?

What is equivalence?

You have to leave metaphor and mathematics behind. Or aside. Or apart.

We will go into many caves where philosophers meet. Where bears sleep.

And we will stare at the wall until the writing becomes clear.

Sometimes you see most clearly with your eyes closed.

And when your eyes are open, sometimes you don't see at all.

It was a beautiful view.
It was.
From that room.
I know that room too.

We shared it. Over time.

It was the best and worst of times.
Somewhere between good and yellow, I thought I understood. As they spoke about game theory, my mind wandered. I didn't realise then that if you learned game theory and played the game and gamed the system you won in the system.

The system only rewards the players who play according to the rules. It's a fact in the factual world which claims to be reality.

I think we shared the same cave for a while. A cave where light and darkness were less important than truth and lies.

> Between belief and knowledge
> Between you and me. Or you and I.

I feel that the logical analytical philosophers are in a dark, dank cave.
> They throw light around in an attempt to reduce the fear
> But I did not need their light.
> Light comes from within.
> Not from rules.

Their rules and reason and logic lead to hierarchy and to brand loyalty and that leads to the Ultimate world. They were as much a part of Ultimate as the paradox of the Glass Bead Game.

There they were, playing that game, every Tuesday at 11am. Thinking they were changing the nature of the world. Thinking they were explaining and understanding but really they were ruling the world by creating themselves in their own image. Gods of philosophy. The cult of analytic philosophy worships at the altar of logic and laughs in the face of those who take their metaphysics in a different direction - who find truth in paradox and whose points of reference are simply points.

Mostly they were clever young men. And one of them was a particularly clever young man. He had the temerity to take on the masters and he spoke their language. But it was only the words of a clever young man who wanted to be accepted by challenging the status quo from within. By adding his light to the sum of their light - by being in their cave. He knew he was not the biggest bear in the cave, not yet. In time he would game the system and rise in the system. But no one beats the system.

They all love Big Brother in the end.

Looking from another perspective I understand that in the hierarchy of the philosophers cave the biggest bears win.

And I was Goldilocks.

I was a quantum being in a world of analytical logic. They failed to teach me the self-referential aspect of failure. They tried. Repeatedly. And when we failed, they shut me out.

I was not welcome in that cave.

It was not my cave.
I learned that.

People who were in that room and people who had never been in that room, but were still in that room because we put them there, they are all the philosophers of the analytic cave. They dance on the heads of pins and think that makes them angels. It does not. It makes them people who dance on the heads of pins.

Dancing on the heads of pins is as pointless an endeavour as naming the Higgs Boson. Which leads, strangely enough, to 'finding' the Higgs Boson and that is the pattern of rational, reasonable science in the Ultimate world.

Some came to tell us that. I think Derek tried to tell me. I was so lost in the light I couldn't see his words or his thoughts. I could see that he scared them. Perhaps that was his appeal for me. To me. His wave rolled from East to West. My wave takes me West to East. Perhaps that is inevitable. Your wave must collapse in a direction away from where it began. If it can be said to begin.

He still scares them. Not wanted. Dead or alive. That much I understand. Though he scares them so much they have to let him into their cave. Sometimes they hold their enemies close. Sometimes not.

It was different for me. I was not a clever young man. I was not a philosopher who could sit in an analytic cave and criticise. I was beyond that. My face did not fit. My identity did not fit. My direction of travel was so much wave interference. How could I not believe in numbers? How could I not believe in money? How could I not believe in hierarchy? How could I not believe? I wanted to sing with Peter. In his cave. I did not know about caves. I thought we had left Plato in his cave and were chasing waves not putting labels on boxes.

They pushed me out of their cave.

From a different place now I see it simply. With no regret or recrimination. No darkness, only light.

I was always in my own cave.
And they are in their cave telling their stories

My story does not fit with theirs.
Until I inhabit a story it is not mine.

I am not interested in the naming of things
Being not naming.

I had no need for naming and necessity.
I was beyond the possibility of altruism even then.

Some enlightened people at one point gave ten percent of what they had. They called it effective altruism. I called it the identity of tithing.
In the caves of identity through economics

276

I gave and I give a hundred per cent of what I am.

Not every cave dweller welcomes that way of being.

Sometimes I wonder whether a cabin in a meadow is just a light-filled cave.

FORM 48

Not Waiting but Being

Am I looking at a version of the Ultimate screen? I don't want to live through a screen. I don't want to look at shadows on the wall.
So shut your eyes
Go beyond memory

Prepositions aren't guides. They are just words that go before.
Staring at the wall...but not waiting.
Time is different for waiting and for reflecting, thinking, acting
(embrace the darkness)
The problem of personal identity over time can be resolved simply by time passing.
(You are part of our family tree)

When we were young we approached it from the wrong perspective. We spent all our energies trying to understand and resolve pi. It was time which was the more relevant part. Not the definite particle. The wave. It took time to understand that!

So what is this thing called meaning?

First we name it, then we find it, then we revere it, then we question it, then we abandon it, then we revile it.

This is capitalism. Aspirationalism. Ultimate world.
It is not the best of all possible worlds.
It is not the cave I dwell in.

I went back to the naming of things.
How can it be that you find something only after you name it?
Do you not find it first, then name it?
Do you have to name it at all?

FORM 49

Personal Identity

When I was young I lived in a world. Call it a real world if you like. A world of philosophers. And I was obsessed with personal identity over time while others were concerned with the best of all possible worlds. Forgive me for repeating myself, it's a hazard when multiple parts of the moment come into focus in the timeless time.

The irony was that I was focussed on the wrong part of the equation (focussing on equations is wrong minded anyway).

And university tried to alienate us from our own culture, indeed our own being, by feeding us the literature of the intellectual; the alienation of modernism in a deliberate attempt to mould us into their characters. But I was always built from radicals.

Free radicals at that.

In looking for something I thought I had not learned or did not know, I discover I have known it since I was a child. More than forty years ago I read the very words but their meaning for this part of the moment was obscure.

Now, with a different perspective I read these words again, as if for the first time, and it is like coming home. All it took was time and space - spacetime to be in a different part of the moment and I am here, fully in the moment.

In order to understand personal identity over time I did not realise that what was needed was time. It was not all that was needed, but it was part of what was needed. As they would have said so proudly (if they had noticed this) it was a necessary but not sufficient condition.

When I was young I held onto my personal identity, close round me like a cloak.

Young people wear hats to frame their identity. Some people never get over that, or past that, or beyond that. Some identities never grow. They become fixed and fused and atrophy. And this is called safety, and security.

But I realised, after many years, that while my focus had been on Personal Identity over time.

It should be
Personal Identity through Time.

And even then⋯

Over is hierarchical.

So - Through. Or should it be across?

The difficulty of words like through, beyond, over, beneath, before is that one gets lost in prepositions and adverbs and classes and grammar and⋯ trying to follow the rules is the quickest way to lose your creativity. If you are me. Which I am. Now. And then

I suspect it has to be personal identity IN time.

Depending, of course, on your interpretation of time. Whether, for example, it does or doesn't exist. A wise man once said 'a text has both entering and departing strokes' and I am not about to argue with that. Whether the statement was made by a man who lived, or an author (dead or alive) or a narrator (real or implied) does not change my relationship to the words.

Open and close. Entry and exit.

Yinyang.

As I have lived through the fifty six forms my grasp on personal identity seems much more flexible. I am more flexible. I am not the person I was who clung onto that identity. That identity is gone, even while parts of it remain. Identity is like skin. You slough it off in your sleep. You change without even knowing it. Till one day you are nothing like your old self, even though you are still your selfso - if you believe in ziran, that is. Otherwise⋯ I don't know.

It's your skin. It's your identity. You choose.

Am I an author or a philosopher?

These are labels. And in so far as they are just words I deny them.

I am all moments.

All the world is caves and all caves are boxes.

I always thought my way out of the cave was through characters.
But here's the irony.
I misread the writing on the wall.
Or at least, I read the writing correctly but I was looking at the wrong wall.

I thought it meant characters in fiction
It meant characters instead of alphabet.
The characters which are the gateway to the open circle.

I misread the writing on the wall.
Because I was afraid of the dark
I stayed in the light too long.
I explored and opened boxes.
I shared what I found.
I gave it away and because I placed no price on it
I was not valued.
It was not valued.

There is no value to lightshadows.

It was in the cave of literary theory that I learned I am not an author - living or dead.

It was in the cave of philosophy that I learned that name is the thief of identity.

I didn't sit in the right cave for long enough for the writing to become truly clear.

The message of short sightedness, the lesson learned by failing eyesight and the flickering of light taught me to shut my eyes in the dark and learn to see the writing clearly at last.

    And the writing said MIND DANCING
    And the writing said ALL MOMENTS ARE ONE MOMENT
    And the writing said LET GO

I've gone so deep into the cave of Western thought that I have to throw out first principles. And with them I throw out the alphabet.
    Start again from the character.
    As you are reading these words.
    They are simply the writing on the wall.
    Sometimes we see most clearly with our eyes closed.

The narrator smiled. And said to an implied reader, 'I want to thank you for reminding me I am a philosopher.'

Now I see that I am a part of all that I have been and all that I have been is simply part of all I am in any particular moment.

I am wave and particle. Collapsing into a wave is a transition which no longer hurts. It is transformation.

    Death holds no fear.

Self is not important.
At least, it holds no primacy.

And as the fifty six forms become clearer and more achievable I begin to see the relationship between individual and society, self and time, self and other, now and then.

And I see that paradox is the way.
At least paradox is my way.
Embracing paradox.
Being paradox.

I do not need to explain it to myself and if I do not need to explain it to you, we are together in the moment.

Explanation is negotiating our relative positions.

Sharing stories is meaningful communication in multiple dimensions.

We share our stories in caves.
And when we open the boxes
we share our stories in the river.
And we are the river.

FORM 50

Best of all Possible Caves

There is no need for God in the best of all possible worlds.

That's quite a revelation.
Quite a shadow to wipe from the wall.

Let's just be clear. Leibnitz was wrong. The best of all possible worlds was not discovered by a Frenchman in a wig in the 18th century. Enlightenment values run so counter to any best of all possible anything, except to those with wigs and money. We can discount his version.

And so God has had his metaphorical chips?
Yes, or his jotters.
Depends on your cultural bias.
No God then.
No need.

As for Voltaire?

Well Candide was comedy, right?

But there are other books.

And some of them were written by men I knew. Clever young men. Philosophers in training.

I read their books. And I lived the writing of them, second hand.

I remember sitting in a room with one clever young man talking about the best of all possible worlds. Before he had written the book. Maybe even while he was writing it. In his head. Before the words came onto paper and became something you had to read.

Passage from oral to written tradition. From wave to particle. No more.

However much he argued against the gods, he was still well trained in the analytical tradition.

If only I knew it then, I was a quantum being in a light filled cave. I watched the waves collapsing on the shoreline and was wondering - what happens to snow where the sand becomes water - just as a philosopher said; 'and if you don't look, it collapses into a wave'. I thought he meant what I was physically looking at. He wasn't. He was talking logic.

And the clever young man was only concerned with the 'strictly philosophical' in his clever young book. He saw personal identity as an abstract thing whereas I always took it personally. Too personally perhaps.

In my cave, personal identity was my only security. It was the light and the fire and I was scared to stare at the wall and I didn't like the darkness if I looked out. When I looked in, I found light. But I always wanted to open the box. Not so much to unwrap it and find out what was inside, but to let what was inside out. I thought the cave was a prison. Of all the caves in all the world, there is nothing good or bad but thinking makes it so. You'll have read your Hamlet? You'll have had your tea?

And so clever men, young and not so young, spoke of identity being strictly numerical. The distinction between numerical and qualitative identity is crucial in the fifty six forms. And I did not believe in numbers. So I was lost. To them and to myself.

The clever young man nearly found the paradox. He understood that twins are not the same, they are two different people. But he thought that this was purely a numerical conclusion. Or, at least, that it was only numerical conclusions that mattered in matters of identity.

But hey, what did he know?

I called him Fardles the Bear. After Hamlet.
After Hamlet?
After Hamlet.

I gave a paper entitled: Who was Fardles the Bear?
It was a joke. We all did it. It was what made philosophy 'fun.'
So I gave a paper, I can't remember what it was about, referencing 'who would fardles bear?'
We all took ourselves so seriously in the world of philosophical jokes.

It's a by-product of thought experiments.

Let's not give the clever young man a name. He doesn't deserve to be part of the naming of things. Or even a number. Do we then deny him his identity? Does he then cease to exist in any meaningful way?

In a different part of the moment I found out that he wasn't who I thought he was, even then. I thought he was a doctoral student when I was an undergraduate. But I discovered that he was just a year 'above' me. The difference was, he knew game theory. He had the Western aura. Confidence. We sat in the same seminars. In light filled rooms where ideas collapsed into waves. He talked. I listened. There was a hierarchy in our philosophical tradition. Not always well earned but always well observed. Except once.

The one time I spoke out of place, the writing was on the wall··· and my 'fate' was sealed. The fate that narrowed my possible worlds and had me standing in Tottenham Court Road in 1984 where we first met. Oh, no, that was not me. That was another version of me. The one I learned to call Helen.

An author in search of a character meets
A character in search of an author.
What is being sought?
What is lost/found?

Perhaps that moment, of speaking when I should have stayed silent, was what made me retreat back into my cave - alone. Into a world of my imagination. My own box.

Perhaps it was that I didn't speak when I should have. That moment happened too.

It was all part of the game. Or a game. The game was tennis. And the player was Smart. A man who had a careless yet significant relationship between name and identity.

He wrote about Time in 1963. He wrote that all moments are one moment, though he didn't say it as simply of course, perhaps because he was a tenured philosopher.

But I never knew. Not at the part of the moment when I knew him.

He came half way across the world to play tennis with me. No. He came half way across the world to do philosophy and in his down time I was detailed to play tennis with him. We played games. But it turns out, not the same game. A tennis court is also a box.

At that time he was in his seventies and I was in my teens. And he beat me hands down every match.

Was it style over substance?

It was simply experience of how to be in the right space at the right time. Made concrete in the practical world.

You can run but you can't hide. And you don't have to run if you know where you are or where you will be at any point in the moment.

I used to say to him, lamely, as a joke: 'I'm better at philosophy than I am at tennis.' I don't know if it was true and I doubt he worried about the truth conditional of my statements. We were just playing tennis after all. He was a philosopher relaxing. I was a student trying not to make an impression - oh, how the clever young man would have dealt with this situation differently - not trying, or just trying not to get my ass whipped. To salvage some shred of what I thought was credibility.

I have since learned, and forgotten and learned again, the danger of cool. Put paradoxically, it is not cool to be cool. Or perhaps it is that it is not cool to try to be cool. The further you go the less you know. The more you try, the less you succeed. Dao has all the answers. If you know where to look. Or more quantumly, if you know not to look.

Back in the story of 1983. A man called Smart was one of the authors of our text book. And that author was made flesh on the tennis court as box. He became real in a different way. I did not understand enough about anyone's personal identity to connect to him in the reality beyond the text book as box.

If I had known then how to do my research I might have found his earlier book (a book deemed too difficult for me by the gods of analytic philosophy and certainly not on my reading list) in which he states that time is tenseless. And then we might have had a really interesting conversation, given that my obsessive preoccupation at that time was not tennis, or making an impact, but the relationship between personal identity and time. Then I might have stopped running and met him at the net. Confluence might have been achieved. And it was. Just not in that moment.

Forty years later, and thirty years after he died, I read his book and converse with him again. I play tennis with him again in my mind, and the experience itself suggests to me that he was right about the tenseless nature of time.

We are together again. He still beats me hands down. But this time we meet outside all the boxes.

And Mr Smart's contribution, in case you have lost the plot, or thread of what is where and where is what, is that time is tenseless.

Thank you Mr Smart. Then and now, and in many parts of the tenseless moment you have come to my rescue, even while you beat me. Good humour, calm spirit and friendship. Then and now. I have brought you into my cave - but you were there all the time after all, weren't you? You didn't need me to invite you. Or to serve.

If just once I had said, 'in the best of all possible worlds I beat you at tennis' my life might have been very different. I would have entered a totally different part of the moment.

And now we are free to leave the cave.
To open all the boxes.
Mind dancing.
Wingless. Without shame.

I thought it was the possibility of altruism that would save me. I thought that clinging to the freedom of anarchism was my way. They were all particles but someone Smart showed me the wave. In the confluence of then and now.

I have been in many caves. I have opened (and closed) many boxes. We have shared. Those others whose names defy their identities. They know who they are.

Nothing else matters. Because nothing matters. Because nothing does not exist in infinity.

I discovered (when I stopped trying to understand) the part of my story that no longer seems to be real. The person I no longer am. The identity that has turned into a shadow of a self. And the paradox is that beyond this shadow - which cannot be soaped back onto a body - is ziran. Self-so. Am-ness, if you will. Deep am-ness.

I discovered that deconstructing boxes can be another way of building boxes. That all the world is in and out of the box at the same time. When Wittgenstein and Schrodinger fight it out, the dim light on the wall is of quantum entanglement.

And the ancients say:
If you stare at the wall for three years···

But you do have to be in the right cave!

First find your cave.
Then,
Go deeper into the cave, without fear.

Then open your eyes to the darkness.
Open your eyes in the darkness.
Accepting the paradox that the darkness leads into the light.

In learning the fifty six forms,
I stepped out of the wrong cave.
I sat in the right cave with my eyes tight shut
Thinking that all I could see was in my box
Making boxes of memory and metaphor.
No wonder I could not see the writing on the wall.

I had pinned all my thoughts on 无为(wu wei) for many a year. It was my brand of choice. But as the fifty six forms deepened I encountered 自然 (ziran).

I understand that everything is lost in the translation
    That even in sharing we have to let go.

    I am learning a new language
    And
    I am learning language in a new way.

There are many translations to be found in many places - in the
words and the symbols and also the places between the words
which are more enlightening even than metaphors.

When I find these words, translated by another, I learn that from
my beginning, from the beginning of my world, from the day of my
birth I was a quantum being. In an atomic, deterministic, logical,
analytic world.

    In simple metaphorical terms: a fish out of water.

    I used to try to be the best little particle I could be.
    But I was never comfortable as a particle.
    I have always been part of the wave.

    The question remained. How was I to be in the river?

When I learn to translate for myself, beyond the language, then I
will be in the river and more than that, I will be the river.

FORM 51

A Quantum Cave

In the cave of quantum hermeneutics, it is written: The world of Philosophical Relations is one of interpretive boxes, literary and philosophical.

Imagine that Laozi and Heraclitus, two men who are not allowed to exist, met in a cave.

What would that conversation be like?

What would they talk about? Certainly not their existence or otherwise.

Grand words like ontological and existential and hermeneutic are just graffiti to their minds. These are words that obscure, as they promise to clarify, but they are not used productively as paradox or analogy, or to shine lights on potential paths home.

Herclitus says: you cannot step in the same river twice.

Laozi says: Am I Zhuangzi dreaming I am a butterfly or a butterfly dreaming I am Zhuangzi?

Heraclitus says: Language is slippery.

Laozi says: The writing is on the wall. Who can see it?

And the crowds nod their heads sagely, thus proving not only that they are not sages, but that they exist even less than these men, who we can never know until we listen to the parts of the moment beyond the words, with our heartmind.

'Is Laozi Zhuangzi?'

You might as well ask

'Is Heraclitus Homer?'

Name is the thief of identity.

A flexible author once said: - or perhaps we should just say 'it is written', which covers the same ground: Language is a tool to hold ideas. Once ideas are conveyed, language is forgotten.

The ancients understood the value of the open circle. Of the flexibility of chapters. They understood that the text is open, not unstable. That the meaning of words is found in their mutual spirit. That behind the author is a person. Many people. That 'behind' is simply a positional word. A perspective. A preposition which is also an adverb. Grammar is not the be all and end all. Language is not just a game. Metaphor fills the gap between language and thought. The roles of speaker and listener are endlessly reversible as the pronouns that depend on them.

A voice in the dark shouts out: How croaks the raven?

And the shadows on the wall ask if hermeneutics is simply an attempt to take the text out of the box.

What do we mean by raven?

The creator. The destroyer. The trickster.

It's culturally relative.

A bear might as well ask, What do we mean by bear?

The bear knows.

And you, if you meet a bear, you too know what it is and who you are in relation to it.

When you meet a bear you understand that the ancients transmute fear to reverence.

We might show such respect for the ancients.

The writing on the wall says:

Reverence is fear let go.

Respect is an acknowledgment of one's own insignificance.

Behind the author is a person. Many people. And sometimes they are editors.

In a light-filled cave once we asked: Did the Pearl Poet write The Pearl? Or not?

That is a question worthy of Laozi and Heraclitus. They applauded us from the cave of non-existence which paradoxically is the cave of daoist literary hermeneutics. If you must put a name to things.

We did not need to name names.

We just laughed.
What if written language is a metaphor?
Is there a quantum raven in the box?
The destination is in the journey
The question is in the answer

So we do not need to know whether Zhuangzi is a fictionalist, or indeed what philosophical fiction is - like a bear - you'll know it when you meet it head on. Reading is an interactive process between reader and text, and reader and author and reader via text. As Shakespeare said and didn't say: 'remember the narrator.'

Questions of authorship are like words blowing in the wind.

Heraclitus and Laozi and Zhuangzi simply lead us back to ourselves in their games of paradox. Only connect.

Laozi said it all, even though he probably never existed and two thousand years later, Li Zhi said much of it again - and people, real and imaginary, have been saying the same words ever since. In every language. And yet the ears are still blind and the eyes are still deaf. Language is a paradox. Heraclitus knew that. He knew the only dao to follow was to search the selfso. All this happened long before Heidegger alerted us to the instability of meaning. People fear paradox as they fear chaos. Even Schrodinger kept his cat firmly alive and dead within a box. In Chasing Waves we opened the box, all the boxes. And flew back to ourselves.

Zhuangzi said the author was dead, long before Barthes had his moment in the sun. Heraclitus knew that there was no way to verify whether the reader's understanding matches the author's intention. And anyway, this is just part of the process. The temporality is not important. The 'order of things' is not important.

Long before? It's just a metaphor for a different part of the moment.

However long you try to gather Bamboo Strips and fragments, you will never read them all. You cannot step in the same river twice. The way that is named is not the way.

The writing on the walls are shadows, when you look with your eyes open.

Sometimes we see most clearly with our eyes closed.

Because all the answers cannot be written,

Nor yet all the questions.

Each culture and age has its own stories and its own ways. Ultimate social media was early identified as soma. And we called this our freedom. Our democratic right. To speak without being heard. To share without giving… to befriend without knowing… to use words as we like, to fight and sell and consume and proclaim and never, never to consider whether all that we really know is our ignorance of where and who we are and what and why. And all the questions in the world are lost in the pictures of cute cats and the process of selling the shiny new brand of loyalty demanded in the ultimate dystopia.

The writing is on the wall and those of open and complete spirits can read that bears and ravens and non-existent philosophers and everyone with hearts to see and eyes to hear will find a way out of dystopia through the cave of utopia.

And this is where we live without fear.

And this is a cave I would happily sit in to hear the stories of all moments.

精神 舞

Meanwhile, in another cave, the literary theorists set up camp. They deal in instability. Their boxes are, as we might say, on shoogly pegs. And in their instability, they are grasping. They grab at the bamboo strips. They grab at any part of a text they can hold. They limit texts and creativity itself by attributing value and structure and reason. They create words and signs and symbols and beat everything to death with their intellectualising of meaning and their fixing of meaning in fetish words like semiotics and signifier. Sneakily small sounding substance soaked symbols.

Intertexuality is the battleground of meaning. The Postmodernists are our own Terracotta Warriors made flesh. By championing radically plural texts and liberating the disruptive force, that which they seek to disrupt becomes its own code.

In this sense literary theory is a metaphor for capitalism, the giant which consumes itself.
   Is that analogous enough for you?
   A simile stands between is and becomes.
   A metaphor leads to the paradox path.

Barthes tried to recreate the box - changing reader from consumer to writer. Barthes was dancing round paradox but his eyes were not fully open. He was trying to create a new language. He railed against the predictable cultural codes of readerly texts while creating his own version of Schrodinger's box. All the while breaking paradox into para and doxia and thinking he was doing something more than missing the point.

Still, the paradoxical text admits that culture is a contested term. But the radicalism of what may be called the 'post-perfect' world is not the same as speaking truth to power. Not even analogous.

The privileging of intellectualism is the act of creating power in one's own image.

And we should know that humans are simply things among things.

Literary criticism is so much stumbling around in a dark, dank, slightly musty cave.

Analytic philosophy is no more than making boxes to sit in and on and throw at other people.

Quantum physics is a desire to write on the walls while sitting inside boxes made by analytic philosophers.

If you happen to find yourself in these caves, I suggest you don't sit on the box or open the box. Look at the shadows for the writing on the wall left by Laozi and Heraclitus, beyond fiction and/or fact:

> You can't find Dao in the words
> The way is not in the words
> Not even in the pattern of the words

In the world of the empirical author, a literary text is ontologically an empty structure which derives its meanings from the omnipresent Dao.

Which simply stated says:

You can't get there from here.

We do not need to lose ourselves in the words.

To find ourselves, we need to lose the words.

FORM 52

Paradox and Meaning

No longer worried by what paradox means

a seemingly absurd or contradictory statement or proposition which when investigated may prove to be well founded or true.

the uncertainty principle leads to all sorts of paradoxes, like the particles being in two places at once

    Is paradox 'true'
    Is truth true?
    Is truth paradoxical?

What is the form in which you express, communicate, be.

    Some call it poetry. We call it word dancing.
    But word dancing is only thought dancing fixed

    The Ancients did not need to fix their words or thoughts
    That is the oral tradition.

    It is like the river.
    It can be dammed and it can be damned
    And in both ways it stops flowing for a time

    But rivers move.
    Rivers and trees understand quantum states of being
    We have to 'fix' this into something we call 'life'
    Which is only a part of the whole
    A staging post in the journey.
    The journey is Qi.

FORM 53

Space and Time

You can be in another place. Just not at the same time as you are here. But of course that depends on your understanding of time.

Lost a thought
Lost a memory
Got it back

Can you see the shadows on the wall?
What are they doing?
Shadow dancing

Why?
It's what they do.

There is a cave for all time and all people. You just have to find it. Its name is Legion because there are many.

It was to a cave up in the mountains Laozi went, because he realised that people would venerate the likes of Confucius as a philosopher. Because they love order and hierarchy and don't understand that it isn't the answer. Or the reality. The theory of everything might be staring you in the face every day but people only see what they want to see.

The only limits are my imagination.
Imagination is limitless.

For me the only limit is my creative communicative competence.

Meaning?
That others have to find their own way. Coming together is a rare thing. And it's not equivalency. Or metaphor. But we live in those

worlds because most of the time we can't reach beyond those dimensions of fixity. We can't let go. First accept. Then let go. Then find.

You control yourself by letting go.

The quantum paradox of entanglement is as old as Chinese philosophy.

If you are counting time and space.
There are no numbers to count beyond infinity.
Quantum is the language, the alphabet, the story of the way.
Shouldn't that be ways?

When one can resolve the way with the ways, that's Qi[M].

The implied reader might ask the unreliable narrator the following question:

I wish you would explain to me what the symbol means.
What it means to me isn't what it means to you.
Are you sure about that?

We can only experience it how we express it.
We are stuck with metaphor and meaning and myth.

What is a 'real' character?

Beyond the death of the author, still the author exists as part of the narrative web. The paradox of authorship is part of the way of intentionality. Which is entangled with agency. Do you see?

The text escapes from the box and the author, reader and characters (both those in search of an author and those happy to be fictional) go along for the ride. Pandora opened a box.

I kicked my way out of every box I found by redefining it and in doing so, became a person, real and fictional, in and out of stories whose reality is in my mind. Is my mind.

There are multiple worlds inside my head. Boxes in the box from which I have been trying so hard to escape at the same time as yearning to be a brain in a vat. To be lost in the story of my own existence and non-existence.

Why have I felt the need to share these worlds - these thoughts? They seem to make up my identity - to validate myself in space and time.

And what I've learned is that externalising the interior landscapes is a dangerous path. In trying to validate myself through sharing I somehow lost the wholeness of my own identity.

The whole person is in the cave. The cave is all moments. The reality of identity lives in the worlds in the head which are a box without shape or form.

So what is this sharing thing all about?

Is it better simply to 'be' in one's own reality? How does one step outside of the worlds in one's head?

And is it really worth doing?

I had a friend. I called him a friend.
He didn't need to step outside of his head.
His communication needs were minimal.
He was happy where he was.

He would share on his own terms
But he was complete in himself and
Uncompromising as such.

301

Is this the lesson I need to learn?
Is this the person I need to become?

You lose something of yourself when you externalise your thoughts.

Finding the balance is the art of life.

And plot can get right in the way of the story. This happened. That happened. You said that happened before so this can't have happened. Open your eyes. It's all possible. All paths lead not to Rome but to ⋯ balance. If you let them.

Balance is not about teetering, it's about relaxation. It's not about being on the edge it's about being in the centre of reality.

And reality is what you choose to believe.

So when Wittgenstein says 'The limits of my language form the limits of my world,' he issues a paradox about the fixity of meaning.

An obsession with meaning will not help you to attain balance.

Form 54

Butterfly Dreaming

The relation of things.
A caterpillar cannot understand a butterfly.
Am I a butterfly dreaming I am a man or a man dreaming I am a butterfly?
I am both and neither, until I flap, or do not flap, my wings.
    Waiting, not being.
I am now only slightly connected to that person I was. And that does not scare me. Person is quantum.
    I am like water that flows.
    But I am also the definite particle
    This is selfhood

I used to fear non-consistency. Thinking that constancy somehow it meant permanency.

And death - the ultimate non-existence was a thing to be feared.

Now I begin to appreciate the relationship between part and whole

    First find your whole.
    Then be in it.

Form 55

Beyond Language

All verbs are one verb
That verb is 'be'
For 'beings' (human or otherwise) this holds to be the case.

All words are one word.
Word is a symbol
Word is a concept/idea
Word is particle and wave

Written words can only take you so far
They can only reach in so far
And sometimes it is not far enough

You need to get beyond the marks and the symbols
and reach into the mind of the word
Dance with them.
And in the dance you find yourself.

You find who you are
But you cannot write this down
It defies written language

You cannot tell who you are
It defies spoken language
You can define ways but not something beyond 'the' way.
Each word becomes a particle in the wave.

The wave is.
This is Qi

Form 56

Caves of Enlightenment

Sitting in a cave, we come to understand that there is more than one enlightenment.

What shall we say of them?

All the worlds are in the caves and all the caves are all the world. And all exist between possibility and probability.

Is it a question of West meets East?

Western views of Enlightenment are tied up with economics. Adam Smith. THE Enlightenment.

The definite article.

That should provide a clue to the error straight away.

It was an historical period in which science and reason were constructed as the pinnacle of human achievement. Skepticism and liberty were principles but founded on ideas of progress. The hierarchy shifted but it was still a hierarchy. From Enlightenment came Intellectualism.

There was some good in the thoughts of the Enlightenment. But they threw the baby out with the bathwater.

It led to individualism which leads to selfishness and unequal power.

Eastern enlightenment is much more fluid. Much less fixed. It is a journey, a path. It is unknowable except to the inner spirit. It does not manifest in architecture or profit and it dances to the tune of a different drumbeat.

There is relativity beyond culture.

God is an answer for a question that has no answer. In religion people strive for enlightenment as in reason they strive for it. However, true enlightenment is no more and no less than awakening to the natural state of being.

You do not need to seek to find.
You just have to let go.
Open. Accept.

To talk of enlightenment is to talk like a child. I want to be a farmer. I want to be an astronaut. If you talk of enlightenment you do not have it.

And where is enlightenment to be found?

Ultimate will feed you forever.

Ultimate has all the answers to the questions it is pointless to ask.

But you will never find enlightenment however hard you look for it. Seek and you shall NOT find.

Be and you are.

All we have is all we are.
All we are is nothing.

We are all we have.
If you have many possessions
this is your identity.
Nothing is everything.

Caves are crowded places. The walls are covered in writing.
  Inside the boxes are the stories.
  Open the boxes and the stories fly out.
  And you become the story and the story becomes you.

  If you let go.

The symbol for the river $\approx$ is also part of the non equation
$$\text{Reality} \approx *\text{Qi [M]}$$
  It is not the answer, or even an answer.

It is just a way to understand boxes and moments and caves and people and places and facts and fictions and beginnings and endings and⋯ infinity⋯

If you are looking for an ending at the end you are looking in the wrong place. And in the wrong way.

  We are beyond endings and beginnings.
  We are mind dancers.
  We are.

  Just let go.

Or how to read this book differently···

This creative narrative allows you to explore a text (particle) and narrative (wave) from a number of perspectives, encouraging you to engage with it personally and in doing so to create your own waves/particles/creative narrative experience.

I have selected some entry/exit points from all the moments. There is method in what may seem like random madness. But it's a choice. Feel free to experience the forms your own way. Your narrative purpose may not match mine, and that is fine. My choices were made with intentionality and agency and a desire to 'dance wingless without shame'.

If you have not read *Brand Loyalty* first, you may well want to read it after you have finished this book. Or not. If you have read *Brand Loyalty* and your main interest is the *Brand Loyalty* inspired/connected narrative, you might choose to read the WuXing section first, before returning to Open Circle, directly or via WuJi.

Through 2020 an online project 'RAM' will explore more aspects of this work. It will be available through the PROJECTS tab at www.aytonpublishing.co.uk – just follow the links. You won't necessarily find answers there, but there will be explorations and some explanation of the themes, devices, linguistic and stylistic choices and other points of entry/exit into some moments.

It's a bit late for a warning, but let me say I appreciate this is not a beach read. It's a book for mind-dancers. And in the quantum leaps between fact and fiction, no real or implied readers, authors or narrators were truly harmed during the creative process. And some were healed.

Cally Phillips
02/02/2020